The **Parisian**
PRODIGAL

The Parisian
PRODIGAL

A FOOLS' GUILD MYSTERY

Alan Gordon

Minotaur Books ⚏ *New York*

THE PARISIAN PRODIGAL. Copyright © 2010 by Alan Gordon. All rights reserved. Printed in the United States of America. For information, address St. Martin's Press, 175 Fifth Avenue, New York, N.Y. 10010.

www.minotaurbooks.com

Library of Congress Cataloging-in-Publication Data

Gordon, Allan (Alan R.)
  The Parisian prodigal : A Fools' Guild mystery / Alan Gordon.—1st ed.
    p. cm.
  ISBN 978-0-312-38414-2
  1. Feste (Fictitious character)—Fiction. 2. Fools and jesters—Societies, etc.—Fiction. 3. Murder—Investigation—Fiction. 4. City and town life—France—History—13th century—Fiction. 5. Toulouse (France)—Fiction. I. Title.
  PS3557.O649P37   2010
  813'.54—dc22

                                        2009034745

First Edition: January 2010

10 9 8 7 6 5 4 3 2 1

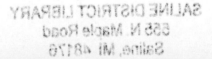

To my artful and slightly wicked aunt,

Hildy York

In translating the accounts of the jesters Theophilos and Claudia, I have occasionally been forced to place sections either out of chronological order, or to append later sections for the sake of completing the narrative. In my last translation, published under the title *The Moneylender of Toulouse*, I dealt with those of Theophilos's reports to the Fools' Guild that covered events that took place from December of 1204 to the following month. However, I included an addendum from October of 1205 to bring closure to that particular story.

The present translation brings together reports by both jesters, and takes place during May 1205.

The **Parisian**
PRODIGAL

CHAPTER 1

Locks make you careless. You close the door, you turn the key, you hear the iron slide into place and think, There! I am safe. There is a closed, locked door protecting me from all danger.

But the truth is, I can pick most of the locks that I encounter in the world, and I am far from being the best lock-picker in the Fools' Guild. That honor, by the way, may eventually go to Helga, my apprentice, who has taken to my lessons on this particular subject with an enthusiasm far beyond that which she has demonstrated for juggling, music, knife-throwing, or even boys. I sometimes fear that I am teaching her too well, and the Guild will lose a promising jester to the world of burglary.

My point about the locks is that even though I don't trust them, and even though I will follow the ritual locking of our door and barring of the shutters on the lower floor of our home by then rigging an elaborate system of trip lines that will ring bells and cause clanging pans to tumble to the ground, with the added surprise of a bucket of water poised to topple onto any would-be invader coming through the front door despite its lockedness (a proud innovation of mine that Claudia, my wife, would prefer stayed unimplemented, given the increasing mobility of Portia, our fifteen-month-old daughter), I am much less likely to spring into action—fully alert, dagger in hand, poised and ready to throw—now that we live in a house in the city with locked doors, as opposed to sleeping unprotected outside in, say, a forest clearing. Then again, I've never had good luck with forest clearings.

Of course, it could also be because I am getting older.

So, when the banging on our front door commenced while we were all sound asleep on the second floor, the first to wake was Portia, who, finding herself in the dark with what was no doubt some kind of monster trying to devour her, did the sensible thing and screamed at the tops of her lungs. This in turn woke Helga, with whom she now shared a room to the dismay of both. The twelve-year-old scooped up the toddler in an unsuccessful attempt to comfort her, then gave up and marched into our bedroom and unceremoniously dumped her into our bed. Portia scooted onto her mother in an effort to restore recently revoked nursing privileges. Claudia yelped and dislodged her, which set off a new round of screaming for different reasons. This no doubt would have roused me, had not the repeated kicking of my beloved in the general vicinity of my rib cage already done the trick.

"What's the matter?" I asked.

"There's someone banging on the front door," said Helga.

"Then go answer it," I said.

"I can't," she said. "It's dark."

"That explains why I can't see anything," I said. "I'm relieved. I thought that I had gone blind, and the way I was drinking last night, that would have been no surprise. Go answer the door."

"The rule is that I don't answer the door when it's dark," said Helga. "And it's dark."

"Who made that rule?" I asked.

"You did," she said.

"Then I'm changing it. Go answer the door."

"You can't change rules at night," said Helga. "That's another rule."

"Who made that rule?" I asked.

"I did," said Claudia. "Now, get downstairs and answer the damn door before we wake the entire neighborhood."

"I'm going back to sleep," announced Helga, leaving us to our doom.

"New rules in the morning," I called after her as I groped around for my boots. "Lots of new rules. And there will be a test afterward."

I staggered downstairs to the lower room and promptly managed to stumble over most of the trip lines. By the time I got to the front door, my ears were ringing, I had a pounding headache, and I was drenched with a bucket's worth of water.

"This had better be worth money up front," I growled as I unlocked the door and flung it open.

Sancho, one of the count's guard, was standing there, a torch in his hand. He looked at me quizzically. "Hallo, Pierre," he said. "What was all that ruckus? Are you rehearsing a new routine?"

"Yes, Sancho, that is exactly what I was doing," I said.

"You're all wet," he pointed out helpfully.

"I know this," I said. "Was there anything else you wished to tell me? If not, I am going back to bed."

"Oh, yes, now that you mention it, there was," he said. "The count wants to see you. Nowish, or thereabouts. Sooner, if possible."

"What's wrong?"

"He's in one of his fouler moods and wants cheering up by his fool," said Sancho. "Can you be funny at this hour?"

"No one can be funny at this hour," I said.

"Well, I suggest that you put the lie to that," said Sancho. "See if you've got any dry motley, and come along."

"Fine," I grumbled. "Care to come in?"

"I am thinking not," he said, peering cautiously into the dark interior at the tangle of ropes now littering the floor. "I will stay out here in the Godforsaken city night, where it is safe."

I thought I had accounted for all my trip lines on my first pass through the room, but one I had previously missed caught me just before the stairs, sending me headlong into the wall. Fortunately, I already had a headache, so it only made it worse.

"Who is it?" asked Claudia sleepily as I came into the room in search of my good motley.

"Sancho," I said. "The count wants me."

"Just you?"

"Just me."

"Good," she mumbled as Portia nestled contentedly against her bosom.

Dammit, that was my spot.

I changed hurriedly, then leaned over and kissed my daughter and my wife.

"You're wet," Claudia murmured.

"So I've been told," I replied. "However, a dry fool . . ."

A snore floated up from the bed. I didn't know if it was real, or her way of stopping me before I completed a joke she had heard too many times before. Either way, it was my cue to leave. I slung my lute and my gearbag over my shoulder and went back downstairs.

"How's the family?" asked Sancho as I locked the door behind me.

"Well, thank you, and asleep, thank you again," I said. "When are you going to get one?"

"When the dice roll more favorably for me," he sighed. "Just when I think I've made my nest egg, along comes the snake with its beady little eyes to suck it dry. Aren't you going to put on your makeup?"

"When my face is dry," I said.

"You don't need a glass to do it?"

"You can get your armor on in the dark, can't you?"

"In less time than it takes to sing a psalm," he said. "Long as I'm sober, and unencumbered by the soft white arms of a willing maid."

"It was not the arms of my willing maid, but her feet that drove me out of bed," I said.

"They smell that bad, do they?" he said sympathetically.

I reached over and rapped him gently on his iron cap.

There was a pause.

"Ow," he said finally.

"Why is the count in such a foul mood this early?" I asked.

"This late, rather," he replied. "Been up all night, far as I can tell."

"He hasn't been to bed?"

"I didn't say that."

"He has been to bed, but he has not slept well," I surmised. "He's been doing that more and more lately, hasn't he?"

"Not for me to say."

"Of course it is, good Sancho. If I go into his chambers unprepared, then chances are that I will not lighten his mood, and we will all suffer."

"You've convinced me," he said. "Well, not that I am one to gossip, but as one who stands outside his door, ever alert as one is required to be, one occasionally hears things."

"And what did one hear tonight?"

"He's coming up along fifty years, he has a new hot-blooded wife of eighteen, and although numbers have never been my strength, I would say that they do not favor him."

"The eyes of the snake have struck again?"

"A man sorely needs a laugh at a time like this," said Sancho. "As long as he is the one laughing, not being laughed at by his new hot-blooded wife of eighteen."

"That is all I need to know, friend Sancho," I said. "And I thank you for it."

Usually when I see a city at this time of morning, I am coming home from an unusually lengthy and debauched party, my safe-passage pass clutched openly in my hand for immediate presentation to the nightwatch, my senses somewhat dulled by wine and exhaustion yet on the alert for any danger lurking in the alleys. Now, on the other hand, I was on my way to work with a friendly and heavily armed companion, which allowed me to take in the sleeping city of Toulouse with only the distant torchlight of the watchtowers and the thin sliver of moon to illuminate it. No colors now in the Pink City, just silhouettes and shadows, the rats and the wraiths flitting about while the unperturbed populace dreamed peacefully in their beds, their own locked doors protecting them. As far as they knew.

It was a warm month of May in the Year of Our Lord 1205. We had come to Toulouse the previous December, sent by the Fools' Guild on a complex mission that we had completed with difficulty, ingenuity, and not a small amount of personal risk. By the time the Twelve Days were over, we had made our mark as the new jesters in town, and were very much in demand through the long winter nights. Then, when the days were beginning to loosen up, along came the New Year's celebrations in the beginning of April, which meant we made a tidy amount to tide us over until the wedding season.

And that was just our legitimate work.

But now I had a morose count on my hands. He had

been more than generous to us, so I did not begrudge him this early start to my day. Much. More important, it was my principal job as Chief Fool of the city to keep him in power, given the turbulence that surrounded him. The Toulousain occupied a middle territory in the world, which people needed to cross to get from one place to another, whether for profit or pilgrimage, and in either case, Toulouse took its share. Count Raimon VI and his father before him had maintained a tenuous peace, sometimes by waging war, 'tis true, but more through diplomacy than had most of their blood-thirsty neighbors.

So the Fools' Guild wanted Raimon to stay in control of his domain, and to be a merciful and wise ruler.

It is difficult to be merciful and wise while trying to please an eighteen-year-old bride.

The count, when he was in Toulouse, was still not quite in Toulouse. The Château Narbonnais, the walled governmental complex where he stayed when not making the grand tour of his other holdings, sat south of the city walls, its three towers guarding the Toulousans from attack from without while protecting the count from attack from within. The Round Tower and the Tower of the Eagle flanked Sancho and me as we walked through the gates unchallenged. Deeper into the courtyard, the Grand Tower shot up into the night, capped by the torches of the watchmen on its summit.

"Which room?" I asked Sancho as we entered it.

"Oh, he's in the Grande Chambre," said Sancho. "In a tiny part of that great big room all by himself."

"Then I shall occupy the rest of it," I said. "Stop a moment."

I pulled out my makeup bag from my kit. I slapped on the whiteface hastily, then took more time with the rouge and the malachite. When I was done, I turned and grinned at Sancho. He chuckled.

"Cheers me up, anyway," he said.

"Then I have accomplished my mission," I said, turning to leave.

He clapped his hand on my shoulder and dragged me to the Grande Chambre, where two guards stood, alert and irritable. They looked at Sancho and me, then pulled open the double oak doors.

"Brought what you asked for, Dominus," called Sancho; then he whispered to me, "Funny as your life is worth, Pierre," and threw me into the Grande Chambre. The other guards closed the doors behind me.

Strange how a room already large can become cavernous in the dark. No, not entirely dark. One small candle flickered at the far end. I started walking toward it.

"I am assuming that you are adjacent to yonder candle, Dominus," I called. "I pray that this not be a trick of some sort. I tend to be jumpy in the dark, and will not hold myself accountable for my reactions."

"Want some wine?" asked the count, leaning into the light.

"The answer to that question is always yes," I said. "Pour away, my noble tapster."

He produced a silver goblet and upended a wineskin. His aim was uncertain, but most of it got in.

"Thank you kindly," I said, taking the goblet and raising it. "Long life to you."

"Thanks, good Fool," he said, raising his own goblet in response. "I thought you might make some pithy comment about it being too early in the day, or late in the night, or some such thing."

"Am I awake and alive?" I asked.

"You appear to be both," observed the count.

"Then no words that might jeopardize a free drink will

ever come out of my mouth," I said. "I value your wine too highly. Oh, and your company, of course."

He raised his goblet in ironic salute. "That pretty fool you're married to," he said, slurring his words slightly. "She your first wife?"

"As far as she knows," I said.

"Hah!" he barked, and downed his wine in a single gulp. "I was betrothed for the first time when I was nine, did you know that?"

"I did, Dominus," I said. "It must have been a very strange experience."

"Nine," he repeated. "Boy of nine should be out chasing hounds with his friends, or whispering rude comments about the bishop in church. Instead, there I was in the chapel, kneeling before the priest in all my finery, wishing to Christ I was anywhere else. It was a travesty of a ceremony, like when they used to have the boy bishop at the Feast of Fools before that was banned, do you remember?"

"It wasn't that long ago," I said.

"Whole point was so my father could get hold of Provence and Mauguio and a couple of other places. Her name was Douce. Nice enough girl, older than me, but she didn't bemoan her fate overmuch. But then her father dies, so my father decides to bypass me and marry her mother. And a few years later, just when I'm getting used to the idea of marrying, Douce's aunt Ermessend becomes a widow, so Father drops Douce like a hot ember and marries me off to Ermessend instead. I'm all of fifteen, mind you, and here's this older woman occupying my bed, and I was supposed to call her wife."

"A lusty widow doesn't seem the worst thing to have in bed when you're fifteen."

"You think so?" he said, shuddering suddenly. "Not when

you're the fifteen-year-old being compared to the real man she was married to before. Four years of listening to that song over and over. Fortunately, she dropped dead during the fourth year. I guess she missed her first husband so badly, she wanted to join him."

"Or all the complaining wore her out," I suggested.

"God knows it wore me out," he said. "Put me off marriage, I can tell you that. Yet when Father needed another alliance nailed down, whom did he volunteer for that dangerous marital mission?"

"I'm guessing you, but I shouldn't be the one telling this story," I said.

"I'm nineteen now, and there's another widow in my bed, twice my age and with children to boot."

"Lusty this time? Please tell me there was at long last lust."

"Oh, lusty enough. Of course, it was like sleeping with someone's mother, and not the good-looking one you were secretly yearning for."

"Poor little you. I hope that you at least had a decent mistress stashed somewhere."

"Did my best, but Father was busy picking off all the best ones," he sighed. "Finally, finally, I was able to shed myself of this widow. And then came Bourguigne."

"She was your wife when I first met you, was she not?"

"She was," he said, refilling his goblet. He stared into it without drinking, swirling it gently as if hoping to conjure her up from its depths. "That was the first time I ever loved a woman. Truly loved—mind, body, and soul. Is that how you love your wife?"

"In truth, she owes me money," I said. "The moment I collect—but I'm interrupting."

"I've seen how you look at each other when you are performing together," he said. "Unfeigned passion and joy. I envy you."

The count envies the fool, I thought. Lord knows I would not want to be a count. I have seen my share, a few kings and emperors, too. Those who lasted did so either through brute force or raw cunning, both of which took their toll. Those who lasted were never happy. Those who were happy were fools, and soon shoved out of their ignorant lives.

I knew the answer to my next question, but I asked it because he wanted me to.

"Why did you abandon Bourguigne when you loved her so?"

"Because Richard the Lionheart laid claim to Toulouse," he said. "I was the count at last, heir to my father's years of playing all sides from the middle. I could cling to the woman I loved and condemn my subjects to war, or I could repudiate Bourguigne and marry Richard's sister. I am my father's son. I married Richard's sister."

"Another widow."

"His favorite chess piece," he said bitterly. "Dragged her everywhere, ready to marry anyone useful to him. Almost matched her with one of Saladin's cousins if rumor was true, only the bastard turned her down. I married an infidel's leavings."

"I understand that she was a lovely woman, for all that."

"There was nothing of her that displeased the eye," he conceded. "And she did give me a son, died doing it, and I honor her for that. We had quite a few troubadours write songs in her memory. But I never loved her, Fool."

"Yet there was peace between Toulouse and England. Still is."

He nodded. I shrugged.

"You like the new wife well enough," I said.

"My last chance," he said. "They started dangling her in front of me when she was twelve. Damn those Aragonese for being better looking than the rest of us. At twelve, she was already a paragon among women. They insisted upon my waiting until she was of age, periodically allowing me visits to see how she was blossoming, like I was having a prize heifer raised on a farm. Agonizing, the wait. Every time I saw her, her beauty had increased. Thought 'of age' meant sixteen; turned out they meant eighteen. Six years! Craving her more and more until the merest thought of her drove me mad."

I refilled my goblet to cover my discomfort. "You kept celibate during your wait, of course," I said.

"I dipped my staff into anything that moved," he said. "Wanting her every moment, and no mistress could satisfy me as much as the thought of this girl. We finally wed—by proxy, no less, so I had to wait even more for her to be in my bed. Finally, she had her first taste of lovemaking—dear God, Fool, I felt like Zeus incarnate. I wished I had the gift of poetry, to compose an erotic epic account of that first night."

He sighed.

"And it never was that good again," he said.

"How could it possibly be?" I asked. "You have achieved such lofty heights of love that just the idea of scaling them again would exhaust most mortals. I'm exhausted listening to it."

"I set the bar too high," he said ruefully. "She expects it to be like that every time. She doesn't know any better."

"You've ruined her for life, this paragon from Aragon."

"Oh, God, what have I done?" he moaned, and I started to laugh. He looked at me outraged, then started to chuckle. In moments we were roaring with laughter. It eventually subsided, with him wiping the tears from his cheeks with his sleeve.

"So, I didn't hear any advice," he said.

"I didn't hear you ask for any," I replied. "Is that what you need? Advice from a fool? I cannot prescribe the cure until I have diagnosed the illness. Is it lovesickness that plagues you, or intimations of mortality?"

"Some of each, I imagine."

"Then the remedy is simple," I said. "I advise you to grow younger."

His expression turned dark, then thoughtful. "I dye my hair," he confessed. "Do you think that unmanly?"

"You are speaking to a man wearing makeup and powder, Dominus. Who am I to judge?"

"How old are you, forty?"

"As far as my wife knows, Dominus."

"Hmph. I will not pry any more. And thank you for cheering me up."

"All I did was listen, Dominus."

"Which is why I value you, Fool."

The first rays of sunlight were angling through the high windows.

"Soon, my friends will be coming in from their nocturnal adventures," he said. "Boasting of their conquests and their prowess. How shall I respond to them?"

"By saying nothing," I said. "The man who shows no need to brag is the one who has done the most."

"That's good," he said. "That's very good. Start playing something gentle. I hear my cousin approaching."

The doors swung open and Bernard, Count of Comminges, strolled in. About Raimon's age, with a lazy charm that concealed a quick ruthlessness that I had seen already on one memorable occasion.

"Heard you were up already, cousin," he said. "What is happening to us in the middle of our lives? We should be sleeping until noon, then trying to figure out who the lovely maid next to us is."

"We have responsibilities now," said Raimon. "I do, anyhow."

"And I do, as well," said Comminges.

"What are yours again?" asked Raimon.

"To be your friend in all matters," pronounced Comminges grandly. "For a start, I am going to keep you from drinking all of that wine. Pour me a cup, would you?"

"Seems to me I have servants to do this sort of thing somewhere," grumbled Raimon as he filled another goblet and passed it to his cousin.

"Ho, Anselm!" I called. "Your master's arm grows weary!"

Anselm, one of the count's servants, dashed in. "Dominus?" he inquired.

"Food," said Raimon. "And someone to wash me. Time to start the day."

"So, let me tell you about the tapster's daughter at the Blue Wheel," began Comminges.

And he was off. Raimon nodded, smiled, and guffawed at all the right places, while a team of servants ran in and out, placing trays of food in front of him, peeling off his tunic, scrubbing him down and shaving him, and throwing a fresh tunic back on. Anselm was busy combing out and replaiting his hair when another pair from the entourage showed up.

"Food!" bellowed Raimon Roger, the Count of Foix, heaving his bulk through the doors. "But you've started without me. How very churlish of you."

"Yet we shall forgive you," said Rostaing, Baron of Sabran. "Bernard has no doubt already regaled you with the tale of the tapster's daughter?"

"He has," said Raimon.

"As if that were anything to boast about," said Sabran. "That bloom was plucked long ago. Why, I doubt that I had more than the fifth petal or so, and that was ages since. Does she still make those mewing noises, Bernard?"

"Well, yes," said Comminges, looking slightly crestfallen. "But a worthy ride, nonetheless."

"If you like them cheap," said Foix. "Now, I have an exquisite little tale to relate, a conquest long sought after and finally come to fruition: the widow de la Turre."

"No!" exclaimed Comminges. "She actually succumbed to your charms? Must have been desperate."

"Or destitute," I suggested.

Raimon smirked in my direction.

"Anyhow," said Foix, ignoring us. "There we were in her bedchamber . . ."

It continued on in that vein. Finally, Peire Roger, the count's viguier, came in to begin the day proper. Various officials arrived to insist on the importance of their bailiwicks at the expense of the other officials in the room, leading to arguments and accusations that were settled with tact and skill by the count, hangover and all. In between, I offered snide commentary, while Comminges, Foix, and Sabran ogled the maidservants as they passed through. Then came merchants with offers and complaints, members of the clergy with requests and complaints, and commoners with petitions and complaints. In the midst of the latter, one of Peire Roger's underlings came up and whispered something to him. The viguier's eyebrows rose slightly, and he left the Grande Chambre with the underling. A few minutes later, he came back and cleared his throat. The count looked at him.

"Dominus, there is a man here from Paris," said the viguier.

"What sort of man?" asked Raimon.

"A nobleman, from his dress and manner," said the viguier. "More than that, I would not venture to guess on such short acquaintance."

"Is he here on the king's business?"

"No, Dominus."

"Do we know anything about him at all?"

"No, Dominus. He says he traveled all this way to see you."

"Well, in that case, did you have him searched thoroughly?"

"Of course, Dominus," said the viguier, looking slightly offended. "He has no more weapons than befit his appearance."

"Fine, let's see what he wants," said Raimon. He glanced at his guards. "Keep an eye on him."

"Right," said Sancho.

The underling left, and came back with the Parisian, who had a man of his own. The visitor appeared to be my age, maybe younger, and was shorter than me by a head. His clothes were travel-stained, but he wore a magnificent red cloak lined with black miniver, which he twirled about him as he swept in front of the count and bowed low. He had clearly practiced the cape-twirling.

"Your Gracious Sovereign of Toulouse," said his man, stepping forward and offering a bow equal to that of his master. "May I present my lord and master, Baudoin. I am his humble companion, Huc."

"Pleased to meet you," said Raimon, nodding and gesturing to them to straighten up. "Welcome to Toulouse."

The Parisian's man muttered something to him, and Baudoin held out his arms as if he expected to be embraced.

"Thank you," he said with a thick accent, and he continued to stand in that position as the count looked on, amused.

"Well?" said Raimon finally. "What is your business here?"

"But this is Baudoin," explained Huc, pointing to his master.

"Yes, I understand that part," said Raimon. "But I assume he came here from Paris because he wants something. What is it?"

"This is Baudoin," insisted Huc. "This is your brother."

CHAPTER 2

There was silence in the room, the expressions ranging from shock to dismay to a bemused smile on the face of the count.

I cannot abide silence.

"No, no, no, no, no!" I cried, stepping forward and shaking my marotte menacingly at them. "I will not have this! Not after I have worked so hard for so long!"

"What on earth are you going on about?" demanded the count.

"Why, the threat to my employment," I said, turning to him. "Tell them, Dominus, that the position of Court Fool has already been taken."

"You have my permission to tell them yourself," he said, nodding toward them.

"What are they saying?" asked the putative brother in langue d'oïl.

"I am saying that you are a shabby excuse for a fool," I answered him in the same language.

"What did you call me?" he screamed, reaching for his sword. He stopped as the shiny but scary ends of four halberds surrounded him.

"I haven't called you anything yet," I said, standing safely behind the guards. "I am still trying to figure out what you are. A fool would have more wit than to draw steel in a strange castle. A pretender would have enough ambition to learn the language of the realm to which he pretends. An adventurer would have more style. I have it at last! You, senhor, are a puppet."

"I wonder who holds your strings," commented the count in fluent langue d'oïl. "Who are you, truly?"

"I am Baudoin," said the man angrily. "Your brother."

"Now, as to that," said the count. "The number of bastards propagated by my illustrious sire could make up a legion. There may be a few in this room, for all I know. I care not whose parentage you claim. It will bring you nothing in this house."

"I am no bastard," said Baudoin haughtily. "I am your father's son. And your mother's as well."

The count stood, his face turning a deep crimson. "Peire Roger, come here!" he shouted.

"Yes, Dominus," answered the viguier, stepping to his side.

"Take whoever currently occupies our deepest dungeon and move him to the most luxurious accommodations that we have," said the count. "Then take this arrogant filth and shove him into that dungeon. And while he ponders his sins, I want you to have an even deeper one dug. When it is done, alert me, and I will personally throw him in to rot."

"As you command, Dominus," said the viguier calmly.

"What?" whispered Baudoin to his man. "What is he saying?"

But Huc stood there, gaping in bewilderment.

"And since you haven't had enough assistance from this fine translator, I will have him join you to explain," finished the count.

"But Dominus, I protest!" squeaked Huc, finding his voice at last. "We protest! We come in honor. We have all the necessary bona fides. Look, I can show you—"

He reached into a leather pouch at his waist, then paused as another pair of halberds stopped just shy of his sleeve.

"Why are they still here?" shouted the count.

The viguier snapped his fingers, and the two were dragged off. The count collapsed back into his seat.

"If you kill him, could I have his cloak?" asked Foix.

"On you, it would be useful only as a napkin," said Sabran.

"Shut up, the pair of you," said the count. "It's been a long day, and it isn't even noon yet. I need some sleep."

"We should talk about this," said Bernard quietly.

"There's nothing to discuss," said the count.

"Raimon," said Bernard.

"It's done," snapped the count. "Do not question me on this subject."

One of the guards who had transported the two Parisians to the dungeons returned with Huc's pouch and handed it to the viguier, who shuffled through the documents inside it, then cleared his throat.

"Dominus," he said. "May I suggest that you take your cousin's counsel?"

The count turned to him, concern creeping into his face. The viguier was his oldest counselor, one of the few remaining from his father's reign. He was a tall, gaunt man with skin like parchment that had been written on extensively and scraped clean again several times. His expression at the moment was calculatedly blank.

"Peire Roger and Bernard stay," said the count. "Everyone else leave."

The room cleared quickly. Foix and Sabran were somewhat peeved, the former no doubt because the noon meal was approaching. I stood my ground, playing a little marching song on my lute as they left. The doors closed. The viguier and Bernard looked at me with annoyance.

"The fool, Dominus?" began the viguier.

"He stays," said the count.

"But you told everyone else to leave," said Bernard irritably.

"I am not everyone," I said. "I am no one, in fact. Barely even here."

"The fool stays," said the count. "I might need to be amused on short notice depending on what you are about to tell me."

"I have the Parisian's bona fides," said the viguier, handing them to the count. "They appear to be genuine."

The count riffled through them, his cousin leaning over his shoulder.

"Sworn to by the Bishop of Paris himself," observed Bernard. "Impressive. And one from the court."

"Forgeries," pronounced the count. "Why, I know two men here in town who could produce the like. Isn't that right, Fool?"

"I know three," I said. "But I've been here only a few months."

"And the bona fides are besides the point," continued the count. "He claims to be my full brother, not some bastard of my father's. That's impossible."

"Actually, Dominus," said Peire Roger hesitantly, "it isn't."

"There is space in that dungeon for one more person," said the count. "Especially if we tamp you in with something."

"There was a rumor at the time your mother left Toulouse," said the viguier, "that she was with child."

"Ridiculous," said the count. "I would have known."

"You were still a young boy at the time."

"I remember who I was when my mother abandoned us," said the count.

"You were shielded from much," continued the viguier. "And much that was known about your mother was—suppressed."

"Do you know for certain that she bore one last son after leaving for Paris?" asked the count.

"For certain? I do not," said the viguier.

"Then it's settled," said the count.

"But I do not know for certain that she did not," said the viguier.

"And therein lies your problem," said Bernard. "It isn't settled, and burying the problem in the deepest dungeon won't settle it. I'm speaking as your advisor, your cousin, your friend, and for all I know as your half brother—thanks for mentioning that, by the way."

"I didn't mean you," said the count. "What exactly is the problem?"

"Your overreaction, if I may describe it as such," said Bernard.

"I didn't take his head off on the spot," said the count. "I consider that remarkable restraint under the circumstances."

"It showed fear," said Bernard.

"Fear—" The count laughed. "—of that pathetic little cloak-twirler?"

"Yet you treated him as if Satan had forced his way up from the depths of the earth to claim you," said Bernard.

"If Satan had walked into my tower, I would have invited him to dinner," said the count. "We could have traded stories over who had the worse upbringing. Fool, you are being far too quiet. It worries me."

"I find myself agreeing with your cousin, Dominus," I said.

"That's a first," said Bernard. "Maybe I should change my opinion."

"It worries me, too," I confessed.

"Your reasons for this unusual convergence of opinions, Fool?" asked the count.

"Well, either Baudoin is an impostor, or he isn't," I said. "Either way, I wonder why he is showing up now, what he really wants, and most important, whom he knows in town. You can't find out any of that if he's dancing on Hell's rooftop."

"We could have him followed every minute of the day, Dominus," said the viguier. "And in the interim, we could dispatch a messenger to our ambassador in Paris and learn if there is any truth behind these bona fides."

"I wonder how many capable forgers there are in Paris," sighed the count.

"I know of seven," I said. "They are thinking of starting their own guild."

"I need to think about this," said the count. "I'm going to my chamber. Fool, I could use some music by my bedside."

"Certainly, Dominus," I said, rising and bowing to the other two men.

If they had resented my presence before, I was certain that they truly despised me now. Served them right for not learning how to play a lute properly.

I followed the count up a flight of steps to his rooms above the Grande Chambre. A servant materialized, bowing low.

"No one is to disturb us," said the count.

"Including your wife?" asked the servant.

"Especially my wife," said the count. "Where is she, anyway?"

"Riding with the ladies," said the servant.

"Then don't tell her what I just said. I'll be down in a while."

"Yes, Dominus," said the servant, backing out of the room and closing the doors behind him.

The count looked dolefully at his marriage bed, which had been made up since its last use.

"Best to dive right back in," I advised, strumming my lute in fanfare.

He flopped onto the bed, kicking his boots off. "Play me something," he said.

"Anything in particular?"

"A song in langue d'oïl for a change," he said. "Something tells me you know a few in that tongue."

I summoned up a trouvère song that poked fun at the vanity of the Parisians. He chuckled at the punch lines.

"Your langue d'oïl must be quite good," I said. "They say a man is truly fluent in another language when he gets the jokes."

"The biggest joke I've heard today is that false sibling of mine," he said. "Idiot doesn't even speak our language."

"What are you going to do with him?" I asked.

"Let him out, I suppose," he said. "Bernard and Peire Roger were right. I can't panic over every little ambitious fraud who struts into my court."

"Good," I said.

"It will take six weeks to send a rider to Paris and back," he calculated. "Especially if he has to make inquiries. I don't suppose you know someone in Paris who would be close to the best gossip, do you?"

"In truth, Dominus, I have not been to Paris in many years."

"But there must be another jester there you could contact."

"Why a jester, Dominus?" I asked.

"Because jesters always know what's really going on, don't they?" he said.

"Quite the contrary, Dominus," I said. "They call us fools for good reason. Perhaps you should contact one of those forgers, although they generally don't write letters. Too much like work for them. And you never know whose hand it truly is."

He stared at the canopy overhead, a damask drape with gold threads running through it, embroidered with a brace of saints looking down from Heaven. No wonder he was having troubles in bed. I would be certainly intimidated with them watching me.

"I remember about thirty or so years ago, there was a great assembly of crowned heads and lords at Limoges," he said. "My father went to render homage to Henry the Second. He took me with him, introduced me around, pointed out who was likely to help us, who would betray us, and who would out and out attack us the moment Henry died."

"Quite the lesson in diplomacy," I said, stopping my playing to tune my low string, which had developed an annoying tendency to go flat on me.

"We took a large contingent with us, of course," he said. "Including our fool, Balthazar."

I played a chord. The string was back in line with its fellows.

"One day, I was walking down a hallway, and I saw him duck into a room," continued the count. "I don't know what impulse made me do it, but I waited outside the door, listening. All I could hear was murmuring. My curiosity got the better of me, and I peeked in."

"What did you discover?" I asked, picking up the melody where I had left off.

"There was Balthazar, along with Henry's fool, the fool to King Louis, and two dozen others. They looked at me for a moment in silence, then Balthazar jumped up and said, 'Behold! The lost prince, come from an arduous journey through untold perils to bring us his tale. Young Raimon, divert us with your adventures.' I must have looked like a complete simpleton, standing there with my mouth hanging open. He came to my rescue and regaled them with an improvised account of my fantastical pilgrimage that had us all laughing within seconds."

"He was a funny man," I said. "I remember that from my visit here."

"You weren't in Limoges, were you?" he asked abruptly.

"Thirty years ago, I was waiting for my voice to break and discovering some wonderful new uses for my hands," I said. "I take it you saw no such children in that fool-filled room."

"No," he said. "But it made me curious about fools. They all seemed to know each other. And to get together secretly like that at a counsel of the great—"

"Nothing strange about that," I said. "Probably exchanging stories, jokes, songs. Maybe a little friendly competition, who knows?"

"There was none of that happening while I listened at the door," he said. "And how is it that they were so well acquainted?"

"Why, most of us have received training at the Fools' Guild," I said. "It wouldn't be surprising if some of them—"

"How long do you intend to maintain this charade to my face?" he asked softly. "I know that you are all connected somehow, and that you are more than mere entertainers. Your own conduct since you've come to Toulouse, along with that of your remarkable wife, would tell me as much."

"Just because we stumbled on some useful information—"

"Which is all I want from you now," he said. "Useful information from Paris, from any source you have. I believe that you enjoy my patronage—"

"Of course, Dominus."

"And that you wish to see me continue as count."

"For a long and healthy reign, Dominus."

"Then do me this favor," he said. "Please."

A request. Not an order. A count was asking for my help.

And, damn it all, I was curious about it myself, and it would take much longer to learn anything through Guild channels.

"I might know a jester in Paris, Dominus," I said. "If he still lives, he would be a man who knows much."

"Thank you, Fool," he said. "My man leaves in the morning. Be here at daybreak."

"Up at dawn two days in a row?" I protested. "You are mistaking me for a working man."

"You may go have a nap now," said the count. "Thank you for your advice. On everything."

I bowed and left.

As I walked into the courtyard, Bernard fell into step by me. "How is he?" he asked.

"Calming down," I said.

"Well done," said Bernard. "You're good for him."

"It's what a fool does, senhor."

"He trusts you an awful lot for such a short acquaintance," observed Bernard.

"Well . . ."

"I don't," he said.

"I hope that I may become worthy of your trust in time, senhor."

"Trust with me must be earned, Fool," he said. "Once earned, it must be constantly renewed."

"Sounds like hard work for low pay," I said. "I am averse to working hard. It's why I became a fool in the first place."

"I look out for him," said Bernard. "More than anyone. You cannot betray my trust, because you haven't earned it yet. But if I find that you have betrayed his, you will not draw another breath on this earth."

"I understand, senhor."

We passed through the gate into the city proper.

"Good day to you, Fool," he said.

I bowed low, and we continued our separate ways.

It was midafternoon. I decided that it was time for ale. I am capable of deciding that any time of day. I turned toward the Porte Montgalhart, which was the next gate up from the château, and walked until I saw a sign showing a tiny man who shone like the sun.

The Yellow Dwarf served good ale, and the tapster, Hugo, was pleasant toward all and particularly tolerant to fools in that he didn't have us perform as part of the price of our long sessions at his table. Balthazar had kept a room in the inn above the tavern when he lived, and though he had been dead nearly a year, we honored him by making this the center of the Fools' Guild for Toulouse. Any visiting fool or troubadour would know to turn up here first, so I made a point of checking in several times a week.

Oh, and the ale was good. Did I mention that?

Hugo, who was a hale man in his mid-fifties, was serving a group of soldiers when I came in, but he waved and pointed me toward a table in the corner. Pelardit was already there, a pitcher and several cups in front of him.

"Are those all for you?" I asked him as I sat down.

He looked at them, appeared to think for a moment, then reluctantly slid one over to me.

He was a fool, of course, one who had been in Toulouse

for years, but he had accepted the appointment of an outsider like me as Chief Fool with grace. He was an unusual man, even for one of the Fools' Guild, for he was a silent man. His humor came from the exquisite precision of his gestures and a malleable face whose features could instantly resemble anyone's. He wore motley of the red-and-blue mesclat cloth that the city was famous for, and could produce from its sleeves and pockets a stunning variety of props without ever letting you see where they came from.

He made a small ring with his right thumb and forefinger, then slid it over the fourth finger of his left hand and looked at me questioningly.

"She and Helga should be joining us shortly," I said.

Right on cue, there was a cheer from the soldiers, and I turned to see my wife enter, now in full makeup and motley, Helga right behind her carrying Portia.

"Look, Mama! Soldiers!" cried Helga. "May I go play with them?"

"Behave, child," scolded Claudia. "You are much too young. I, on the other hand, am the perfect age to entertain— Oh, damn, my husband's here!"

There was a good-natured groan of disappointment from the soldiers as my wife sashayed past them, a lewd grin on her face. Helga did an exaggerated imitation of the walk as she followed her, prompting hoots of laughter. Claudia came to our table, leaned over, and kissed me hard, bringing on more hooting. I didn't care. It was the part of the act that I enjoyed the most.

"Oh, look," said Claudia, sitting by me. "The saddest sight in the entire world."

"What is that, my love?"

"An empty cup," she said. "How very tragic."

Pelardit dolefully separated another of the cups from his

pile and filled it, then passed it to her. Another one went to Helga.

"To Balthazar," I said, and we knocked cups and drank.

"Well, is it true?" asked Claudia. "Did a long-lost brother descend from an angel's chariot to claim his inheritance from the Count of Toulouse?"

"Not exactly, and nobody knows for sure," I said.

I recounted the events of the morning.

Pelardit looked thoughtful.

"Know any of this story?" I asked him.

He shrugged, pointed to himself, and mimed holding a babe in arms, then shrank the imaginary child until it was no more.

"Of course," I said. "You weren't born then. But did you ever hear of this unheard-of heir? Gossip, rumors, anything?"

He shook his head.

"It sounds wonderfully romantic," sighed Helga. "Was he handsome?"

"He had a magnificent cloak," I said.

"Just the thing for concealment," said Claudia.

"I wonder if he's married," said Helga.

"I will ask him, first chance I get," I promised.

"Really?" exclaimed the girl.

"Any chance to have you taken off our hands, no matter how small, must be pursued."

She pouted.

"I don't know his mother's story," said Claudia. "Do either of you?"

"Her name was Constance, she was the sister to King Louis, and was married to Raimon the Fifth for the usual reasons."

"Peace between France and Toulouse," said Claudia.

"Not love?" asked Helga.

"The great cannot afford such frivolous emotions," I said.

"I hope I never become great," said Helga.

"Another step toward wisdom," said Claudia, patting the girl's head. "How did the marriage end?"

"Apparently not well, but I don't know that part of the story," I said.

"None of this was in our briefing at the Guild," she said.

"I suppose they considered it not worth considering," I said. "It was ancient history. But you can understand the count's reaction. After all, his mother abandoned him when he was just a child, and—"

Claudia was on her feet in an instant, her ale spilling across the table, the rage forcing its way through her white-face.

"And what?" she shouted. "What happens to children when their mother abandons them at such a tender and impressionable age? Tell me that, husband!"

The soldiers, brave men all, carefully looked down at their trenchers. Hugo watched us from the safety of his place behind the counter.

"Even for me, that was a remarkably stupid thing to say," I said. "Forgive me."

Tears started streaking her makeup. She picked up Portia and stormed out of the tavern. Helga turned toward me with a stricken expression.

"Stay with her," I said. "She'll calm down eventually, but stay with her."

Helga fled. Pelardit looked at me with concern.

"She left two children behind when she joined the Guild and came with me to Constantinople," I explained. "They had already been placed under the control of a regent, so she would not have been— Anyhow, she hasn't seen her son in over a year, and her daughter in three. Sometimes, she— It doesn't matter. I shouldn't have said that."

Hugo came over with a cloth to mop the ale from the tabletop.

"You'll be wanting some food, I think," he said. "I'm guessing you'll not be having dinner cooked tonight."

"Thank you, friend Hugo," I said.

He came back with a tray holding two slabs of brown bread and ladled some wonderfully aromatic lamb stew over them. Pelardit and I tasted it.

"Delicious," I said. "For a man who did not eat meat for so long, you certainly know how to bring forth its magic."

"Ah, all those years wasted as a Cathar," he sighed. "If the Church would just open some taverns and serve good food, there would be no heresy. I heard a little of what you were talking about. The count's long-lost brother showed up, did he?"

"You know about him?"

"Has to be a fraud," said Hugo. "The countess would have been showing when she left town."

"You were around then?"

"Helping my mother run this place," he said. "Don't know if Constance left the old count, or if he threw her out, but she didn't go right away. Took the marriage part seriously, I suppose. And she didn't have any money, was what I heard. Finally got some help from her brother and went back to Paris, and that's the last anyone heard of her around here. But I knew someone who saw her leaving, and they said nothing about her being with child."

"Might have been early in the pregnancy," I said.

"Then how come no one knew anything back here?" he argued. "She whelps one more of the old count's pups, you'd think he'd be galloping off to Paris to lay claim, especially if it was another boy."

"Maybe King Louis thought it would be like keeping a hostage," I said.

"Well, the maneuverings of the high and mighty are beyond me," he said. "I still think he's a fraud."

"Most likely," I said. "All will be revealed in time."

"Or not," he said.

"Or not," I agreed. "What do you think, Pelardit?"

The fool shrugged without breaking the rhythm of his dining.

I finished and trudged home. When I turned the key in the lock, Helga opened the door and beckoned me in.

My wife was standing by the table, holding Portia. A kettle simmered over the fire.

"I made dinner," she said. "I hope you're hungry."

"Starving," I lied.

After, when Helga had cleared the table, I fetched parchment, ink, and quill and laid them out. Then I sat, thinking.

"What are you going to say to him?" asked Claudia.

"It's awkward," I confessed. "I haven't seen him for so long, nor written. I hear about him only occasionally, when the gossip drifts my way. I suppose it's the same for him."

"If it makes it any easier, keep it to Guild business," she said. "No point in letting personal feelings get in the way."

Something in her voice stung me, although her face was impassive. Helga sat on the stairs, watching us, Portia asleep in her arms.

"What would you have me do?" I asked. "I told you that we could go back to Orsino once Mark comes of age."

"Could go?"

"Will go. We will go."

"Unless there is some crisis that demands our services," she said.

"Well . . ."

"And there always is a crisis, isn't there?"

"There have been some quiet stretches here and there," I said.

"Things are quiet only when you don't listen," she said. "My children are being raised by my greedy, venal sister-in-law and my weak-willed brother. For all I know, they are being turned into monsters. All because I became a jester."

"They were placed under Olivia's thumb before you decided to change lives," I said. "That's the way I remember it."

"I ran," she said. "I fled from my responsibilities."

"You say it as if it were an act of cowardice," I said. "You ran toward danger and war. You've fought bravely and well when many lives were at stake. Including yours."

"I should have stayed and fought for my children," she said. "Would you let me go back?"

"Now?"

"Now. And speak as my husband, not as the Chief Fool of Toulouse."

"Go back without me?"

"Yes. And don't you dare mention anything about the dangers of the journey. Right now, I am the most dangerous thing you have ever seen."

"I believe you," I said. "What about Portia?"

"She's not dangerous yet."

"You asked me to speak as your husband. I am also Portia's father. I wouldn't let her make that journey with you."

"You wouldn't."

"No," I said. "And speaking as one who was a motherless child, I would not have her raised by only me."

"Who said anything about—?"

"If you go without us, who knows if you make it back?" I asked her. "Who knows if you even get to Orsino safely on your own? If anything happened to you, then not only would your older children still be without you, but so would your baby."

"And you, husband?" she asked. "What of you?"

"I think," I said, "that having waited so long and having been through so much to win your love, that I would die if you left me."

She sat down at the table across from me, resting her chin on her hands while she looked at me. I could not read her expression.

"Well," she said finally. "We can't have that, can we?"

There was a knock on the door. I have never been so grateful for an interruption in my life. Helga, who seemed to have been holding her breath for the entire conversation, exhaled loudly.

"Who is it?" called Claudia, her hand at her knife.

"Sancho," came the response.

She opened the door a crack, peered outside, then swung it open.

"Come in, good soldier," she said. "Would you like a bit of chicken stew? It's still warm."

"I wouldn't say no, and thanks, Domina," said Sancho as he came in, eyeing the floor for any trip lines I might have left lying about.

"What brings you here, friend Sancho?" I asked as he sat at the table and my wife placed a bowl in front of him.

"My commission is in three parts," he said, producing a

small square of parchment and handing it to me. "The first is to give you this."

I took it, noting the count's seal and shooting a glance at my wife, who stood behind me to look at it over my shoulder.

"The second is to watch you read it," continued Sancho, rapidly shoveling stew into his mouth.

I broke the seal and unfolded it.

The message inside read, *Play the scene with the letter.* It was unsigned.

"The third is to watch you burn it," said Sancho, upending the rest of the bowl down his gullet.

I touched one corner to the candle flame, then held it as the edges glowed, before turning to ash. When the flames neared my fingertips, I held it up for inspection.

"Very good," pronounced Sancho, wiping his mouth on his sleeve. "I will be here at sunrise to fetch you."

"And I thought you were my friend," I grumbled.

"Only on my own time," said Sancho.

"When is that, exactly?" asked Claudia.

"A good question," replied Sancho. "Thank you for the stew, Domina."

He nodded to Helga and left. Helga came down the steps and locked the door behind him.

"I like him," she said.

"A good man," I agreed. "He knows only what he needs to know, and nothing more. I wish I were like that sometimes."

"What scene are you to play?" asked Claudia.

"An impulsive request, I suppose, so that no one thinks my letter is at the behest of the count. He doesn't want to be seen as relying upon me."

"Then you had better write it," she said. "You have to get up early. Come upstairs, Helga. Let's get this child to sleep."

Helga brought Portia over for me to kiss; then all my

foolish women abandoned me to my epistolary efforts. Sighing, I dipped the quill in the inkpot.

"My dear Horace," I wrote.

I am in Toulouse. Imagine that! This stone that you set rolling all those years ago has finally come to rest, complete with wife and family. When I think of our wild youth together in Paris—well, some things should not be put in writing, lest the stories come back to bite us in the ass.

Anyhow, a most amusing situation has come up locally. A fellow arrived claiming to be Baudoin, long-lost full brother to the Count of Toulouse. What makes his story possible, if not plausible, is that he says his mother was Constance, sister to the last King Louis. She was discarded by the old count long ago. Did she bear another heir and bring him home to Uncle? I thought that if anyone knew the gossip in a backwater town like Paris, it would be you. Is he the real article, or merely a poseur with ambition? It would make my fortune to know either way, and I would be sure to send a share back to you.

Regards to our mutual friend.

Yours in Christ, Tan Pierre.

I read it over a couple of times, then folded the note in a particular way. I tilted the candle to let some wax drip onto the overlapping edges. Both the fold and the unsealed wax would let Horace know that the letter was not coming by a secure route.

A fool writes one way when going through Guild channels, another when he isn't. I had faith in Horace's ability to understand my words, both the ones I used and the ones I left out.

After all, he was the one who had recruited me to the Fools' Guild in the first place.

I slept in my motley, knowing that I would be rising early again. When Sancho knocked on our door, I was up in a trice. I opened the shutters and whispered to Sancho to cease, then flew into the girls' bedchamber to pick up Portia and comfort her before she woke the others. Reassured that the monster had been chased away by her heroic papa, she nestled into my arms and fell back asleep. Reluctantly, I put her back in her bed and kissed her on the nose. Then I grabbed my kit and tiptoed downstairs. This time, I avoided the trip lines.

Sancho greeted me as if we did this sort of thing every day, and we walked through the city as the first rays of the sun began to bring out the rosiness of the brick towers.

"How is your lord and master this morning?" I asked.

"Better, I think," said Sancho. "A successful night, and a well-earned sleep after."

"Must be frustrating to hear all that while you're just standing there," I said.

"I'd rather hear that than arguments, shouting, and tears," said Sancho. "Heard enough of that from my parents growing up. And I have my own rewards in town. Tell you all about them after a few drinks sometime."

"Never tell a married man about your romantic conquests, my friend. It can only arouse envy."

Anselm, the chief servant, showed me into the Grande Chambre.

"He'll be down shortly," he informed me. "He said to grab some food while you can."

"Sounds like he means to keep me busy," I said, but I

wasted no further breath on conversation, concentrating my efforts on the feast laid out on the sideboard.

I had a muffin studded with currants jammed into my mouth when the count came in with Bernard. I strummed away, trying to chew and swallow without using my hands or choking. The remainder fell from my mouth. I caught it, tossed it into the air, played a chord, caught the muffin in my mouth, played a chord, bit down, caught the smaller remainder, tossed it in the air, and repeated the process until the muffin was devoured and my hands were free to play uninterrupted.

"Impressive," commented the count.

"Although disgusting," added Comminges.

"Two words that neatly sum up my career," I said. "Good morning, noble folks."

"Good morning, Fool," said the count. "Some music without muffins, if you would."

"Easily done, but where's the challenge?" I asked.

I played through the arrival of the rest of his coterie. Then came the viguier, a man following him respectfully.

"Dominus, this is the man I have chosen for your Parisian mission," he said.

"Arval Marti, is it not?" asked the count.

"It is, Dominus," said the man, bowing.

"He is fluent in langue d'oïl and is well acquainted with Paris," said the viguier. "I have full confidence in his ability to learn what we need to know."

"Very well, then," said the count. "You have our commission and our love. God keep you safe on your journey, and fare you well."

"Excuse me, Dominus," I called. "I beg that you grant me a small favor."

"Yes, Fool?"

"I thought, since you were sending a man to Paris, that he might do me the favor of delivering a letter to an old friend of mine who resides there."

The count glanced at the viguier, who shrugged.

"I see no reason why not," said the count.

"Good Senhor Marti, he is a fellow jester named Horace," I said, handing him the letter. "I believe that he lives near Les Halles, but anyone who is anyone in Paris should be able to direct you to him."

"I have seen him perform," said Marti. "I should be able to find him with no difficulty."

"My thanks, senhor," I said.

Marti turned back to the count, bowed once more, and left.

"Now, to our Parisian guests," said the count. "Bring them to me."

Shortly thereafter, the two were dragged in, their hands manacled. They looked at the count fearfully.

He smiled. "My friends, I trust your accommodations were to your liking," he said in langue d'oïl.

Baudoin stood mute. Huc simply whimpered.

"I have been prevailed upon to release you," continued the count. "You will be placed in quarters more to your liking until I have made up my mind what to do with you. You may not leave Toulouse."

"I did not come to Toulouse only to leave it," declared Baudoin.

"Well said," the count applauded. "Now, you may have free range of the city, but I have one requirement."

"Anything my brother commands shall be done," said Baudoin.

The count bristled at the word *brother*, but held back from lashing out.

"My requirement is that you immediately begin learning our language," he said. "It ill befits an heir to Toulouse to be so ignorant of its tongue."

"I shall do as you say," said Baudoin. "My man Huc shall—"

"I do not have confidence in your man Huc," said the count. "I want to be sure you have a teacher whose abilities I can trust."

"Very well," said Baudoin. "Who is your scholar?"

"Tan Pierre, my fool," said the count.

"What?" I exclaimed.

CHAPTER 3

Baudoin and Huc stood in a small anteroom, watching as I paced back and forth, spewing curses. Huc was not translating. I don't think he needed to.

"Why me?" I fumed. "A waste of my time, playing pedagogue to a Parisian pretender. What was he thinking?"

I turned to look at them.

"What were you thinking?" I yelled at them.

Huc backed up a step, but Baudoin stood his ground.

"What did you ask me?" he replied in langue d'oïl.

I took a deep breath.

"I am a fool," I said in the same language.

"I know," he said.

"No, you don't. Repeat it. 'I am a fool.'"

"What?"

"Lesson the first. We start with the basics."

"But I assure you, I am not a fool."

"Your assurances are noted and hereby ignored. Say it!"

He shrugged. "I am a fool."

"That is the beginning of wisdom," I said. "Here is the same phrase in langue d'oc. 'I am a fool.'"

"I am a fool," he said in langue d'oc with a pronounced Parisian accent.

"You are a fool," I said.

"You are a fool," he repeated.

"He is a fool," I said, pointing to Huc.

"He is a fool," he said, more enthusiastically.

"She is a fool," I said, pointing to a serving wench who was sweeping the corridor outside our door.

"She is a fool."

The woman shot him a dirty look.

"We are fools," I said, my arms sweeping around to indicate all of us.

"We are fools."

"You are fools," I said, pointing to both of them.

"You are fools."

"They are fools!" I shouted out the door so that everyone in the tower could hear me.

"They are fools!" he shouted with me.

"Truer words were never spoken," said Sancho, appearing at the doorway. He bowed to Baudoin and nodded amiably at Huc. "Good morning, senhors. Your belongings have been assembled. Excuse the disorder, but we had to search them first."

Huc translated to Baudoin.

"What did he just say?" asked Sancho.

"He just said what you just said," I said. "That's what translators do."

"Makes sense," said Sancho. "I might have figured that one out for myself, had I any sleep the past few days."

"Do you speak any langue d'oïl?" I asked.

"I picked up a little bit from some of the French lads in my squad," he said proudly. "Let me try it out."

He turned to the two Parisians and uttered a phrase with extreme confidence. Huc's face became a mask of horror, while Baudoin stared for a moment, then began to roar with laughter. Sancho looked back at me in consternation.

"What did I just say?" he asked me.

"'Roll over, whore, so that I can take you from behind,'" I said.

"Oh," he said, crestfallen. "Not at all what those French boys told me it meant."

"Apparently not."

"Still," he said brightening. "A useful phrase should I find myself in that part of the world."

Huc translated his comment to Baudoin, who laughed again and said something.

"What did he just say?" asked Sancho.

"That if you ever go to Paris, he knows just the place where it will come in handy."

"Tell him much obliged," said Sancho. "And, if he will be so good as to follow me, I shall take him to his lodgings."

The count maintained a couple of houses within the city walls: one for visiting dignitaries, one for mistresses and gatherings too debauched to be held in the château. Sancho took us to the first one, which was not far from the count's mills on the river Garonne. A pair of servants carried the bags. It made for a very small parade. The Toulousan children bounced around me, begging for a performance, but I had to decline, regretfully. I tossed them some candies I kept in my pouch to console them for my failure, and they vanished, satisfied. If only adult annoyances could be shooed away so easily. I knew of no candy that could get me out my current predicament.

The house had an arched opening in the center, leading to an interior courtyard. A pair of soldiers opened the iron gates, nodding at Sancho and looking at Baudoin and Huc with mild curiosity. The room was located directly over the stables, and the two Parisians sniffed the air disdainfully when Sancho showed us in. It was bare of decoration, holding only a pair of beds, a small table on which rested a tin basin and a ewer, and a pair of stools. It looked like it had been recently vacated by a pair of servants.

"Your horses have already been brought here," Sancho informed them. "The count thought you would want to be close to them, having traveled so far together. You are to continue with your lessons each morning. In the afternoons, I will be here to show you around town, starting tomorrow. Your man may go to the stalls at the square to buy food."

"Are we captives, then?" asked Baudoin once Huc had translated the soldier's speech.

"Yesterday, you were in a hole deeper than a grave," I replied. "Today, you have sunlight and air. Count your blessings, and bless your count. And what are you?"

"I am a fool," he said in langue d'oc.

"Well done," I said. "I will see you in the morning."

Sancho and I walked out together.

"I didn't know you gave language lessons," he said.

"I didn't know you gave tours," I replied. "We have both come down in the world."

"Oh, I don't know," he said. "At least I'll be out in the fresh air and sunshine. Do me more good than standing outside someone's chambers all night."

"I take it the count wants me to report."

"Right. I was going to tell you that part next."

"Was it his idea to house them over the stables?"

"Actually, that was mine," said Sancho. "Thought I might take a little initiative."

"You'll go far," I said.

The count and his coterie were still having their luncheon when I walked in. My irritation must have been written across my whiteface, for he took one look at my expression and started to chuckle.

"I am supposed to be supplying jokes, not becoming one myself," I said.

"Forgive me, Fool," he said. "If it's any consolation, it amuses me terribly."

"You chose me as his instructor as a deliberate insult to him," I said.

"Of course," said the count. "I am not going to waste the talents of one of my men on such as he. It would show that I am taking him too seriously. What better way to show my contempt than to send him my fool to teach him our tongue?"

"What does it say about Toulouse when its best teacher is a fool?" I replied.

"When you have calmed down, you will find I have put some thought into this," he said. "Use your talents for observation and conversation to pierce that cloak and find out what lies underneath."

"He lies underneath, so I must go underneath the lies," I said. "I may have to tunnel deep."

"Use something sharp," said Bernard.

"A language instructor," snickered Claudia. "You poor thing!"

"I am tempted to teach him a completely different language and let him try to survive," I said. "Dalmatian would do nicely."

"You should let Pelardit teach him," said Claudia. "He speaks more eloquently than any of us without saying a word."

Pelardit made an elaborate gesture of thanks.

"And Baudoin is still a prisoner, despite the luxury of the prison," she said. "The count did not plan this well. I would leave them unhindered, and have them followed wherever he goes."

"It may come to that," I said. "But until then, I shall be conjugating verbs with a middle-aged simpleton."

"I have always enjoyed it when you conjugate," she whispered in my ear. "Tonight, we should have a conjugal visit."

"I heard that," said Helga. "I know what she means by it, too."

"Then you know enough to keep your sharp ears behind a closed door and not bother us," I said.

"Don't I always?"

"You are the best pretend daughter in the world," said Claudia.

The next morning, I walked to the lodgings of my new student with a renewed vigor. The conjugation of the night before had been sweet and loving. I hoped that meant I had returned to her good graces, at least for the near future.

It was the not-so-distant future that concerned me. Mark, her oldest child, would be turning fifteen in August. Although titular Duke of Orsino, his powers were currently vested in the regent, his aunt Olivia. I tried to remember at what age Orsinians reached the age of majority. I hoped it was eighteen. I needed time to figure out some way to get my wife back there once Mark had the power to keep her safe from retribution.

And me, for that matter. She at least had the protection of being the duke's mother. I, on the other hand, was the lowly jester who stole her away from him and gave him a lowborn half sister in the process. Mark and I had gotten along fine during our last visit, but that was while passing through in the dead of night, with no subjects to see us, and no Olivia to oversee him. But with a few more years under her tutelage, he might see me as a monster, and she might see me as a threat.

Hell, they could both be right.

I picked up some freshly baked rolls as a peace offering to Baudoin. I was being paid a little extra by the count for my shift to pedagogy, and a little more to appease my indignation. It was the indignation that paid for the rolls.

Baudoin and Huc were in the inner courtyard when I walked through the gates, running through some basic exercises with their swords. I watched from the shadow of the archway. Baudoin's sword had a magnificently detailed hilt, studded with jewels and a hammered design that looked Saracen in origin. I noticed a matching dagger at his belt. Huc's sword was plain, but he wielded it like he knew what he was about.

They faced each other and ran slowly through some practice drills. My arm twitched in sympathy, and I thought back to the fencing lessons of my childhood. I had been fairly proficient once upon a time, but I had not kept up with my swordsmanship over the years. It is not the weapon of choice in the Fools' Guild. In the amount of time it takes a man to draw one from its scabbard, I can put two daggers in his throat. One from each hand. Claudia, on the other hand, was more than adequate with a sword, having trained with her husband's fencing master for years.

Her old husband. Back when she was a duchess.

The two Parisians picked up the pace, the blades coming dangerously close to actually striking each other. I had the sense that Huc was the better swordsman but was holding back in deference to his master. Made sense to me—you don't want to slice off the hand that feeds you. Yet Baudoin certainly would be a formidable opponent in a match. I wondered how he would do in a tavern brawl.

Then he whipped off his cloak with his free hand and whirled it in a blur of red and black. From its midst came his sword thrust, stopping with the point touching Huc's chest. The servant fell back, holding his hands up in defeat.

"Well done," I said, applauding from the archway.

"Thank you," said Baudoin. "I did not hear you arrive."

"I did not want to distract you when sharp objects were about," I said. "It's very important to keep your concentration. When I'm juggling knives, you could have an elephant come up with a naked slave-girl riding it, and I would never take my eye off the knives. Of course, they don't have elephants here, so it's rarely an issue."

"Do they have naked slave-girls?" asked Baudoin with interest.

"Not my department," I said, hauling Huc to his feet and handing him the rolls. "Consult with friend Sancho later. Now, let us proceed with our course of instruction. Repeat everything you learned yesterday."

"I am a fool," he began, and he ran through the rest of it fairly well.

"Good," I said. "Let us name people and professions."

Huc left during this, and returned with some cheese and wine to go with my contribution to the repast. Baudoin proved to be an eager student, although his accent remained. It wasn't easy to learn a new tongue this late in life. I thought of Helga, our apprentice, who was already fluent and accent-free in five languages and learning Arabic with ease. But she was a fool and a child. I could hardly expect Baudoin to be up to that standard.

We ended the lessons around noon. Huc had the food and wine set up on a bench on the side of the courtyard farthest from the stables. The three of us sat and ate, enjoying the warmth of the sun overhead.

"Have you been to Paris?" asked Baudoin.

"More than once, but not in years," I said.

"I think I would have remembered you," he said.

"There are many fools there," I said. "I don't know that I would have stood out. And I never performed at the court, so you wouldn't have seen me there, would you?"

"I suppose not," he replied.

There was no hesitation in that response, so the idea of being a regular at the French court did not strike him as anything out of the ordinary. Or he had that part of the lie ready.

"What fools were popular in Paris when you left?" I asked.

"There was one called Horace," he said. "Very funny fellow."

Huc nodded in agreement, a smile on his face for the first time since I had met him.

"I have heard of him," I said. "Never saw him perform."

"Wonderful juggler, and quite a flirtatious fellow," he said. "The ladies adore him. Do you juggle?"

I took three rolls and did a quick routine. One-handed.

"A fool who does not juggle is like a soldier without a sword," I said. "It is one of the fundamental skills of our trade."

"Is it a trade?" asked Baudoin. "I would have thought you would describe it as an art."

"Art doesn't pay," I said. "I'll stick to trade, thank you very much."

Sancho ambled into the courtyard, squinting in the sunlight like a man who had just gotten up. He saw us and gave us a wave.

"Good morning, good soldier," called Baudoin in langue d'oc.

"Well, good morning to you, senhor, and well done," returned Sancho. "Although I think it is afternoon now. Unless that was meant to be a sarcastic joke at my expense, in which case, well done again. Sarcasm is very much the coin of the realm around here."

Baudoin looked blankly at most of this while Huc murmured the translation in his ear, then nodded.

"This fellow is a wise one," he observed in langue d'oïl.

"What did he say?" asked Sancho.

"That you have wisdom," I said.

"Most perceptive," said Sancho. "I am to show you the city today. You fancy churches or the houses of the rich?"

Baudoin made a sour face at the mention of churches.

"Right, I should have expected that," said Sancho. "Let's go look at some towers."

I tagged along, just in case there were any pertinent comments in Baudoin's native tongue. Sancho took him to some of the wealthier neighborhoods in the old city first, where the buildings were so crammed together that the wealthy were squeezed upward in brick towers that competed mostly in height rather than in beauty. Sancho had limited commentary outside of naming who the owners were, and Baudoin had few questions.

At one point, as we walked through the old wealth near Montardy Square, I saw Huc nudge Baudoin, and the other man nod slightly. We were passing by a house that stood out among the surrounding affluence. Not because it surpassed them—just the opposite, in fact. It must have been grand once upon a time, but the time had long since vanished. Brick rose two stories from the street, with a third floor that had partially collapsed, making a home for a flock of rooks that flew in and out, screeching. The front gate was old with rust, and the padlock securing it looked like it would shatter at the insertion of a key, if key there still existed. Grass had taken root in the cracked and broken stones of the courtyard visible from the street, and the wooden shutters had rotted away, stripped of whatever colors had once protected them from weather's onslaughts.

Baudoin whispered something to Huc, who tapped Sancho on the shoulder.

"Why does this horrible eyesore stand amidst such beauty?" asked Huc.

"Don't know," said Sancho. "I suppose whoever owned it left no heir. Or maybe he went off on Crusade and hasn't come back yet. Not my business, so I pay it no mind. Now, if you want to see some real fancy houses, we have to go into the bourg."

"What is that?" asked Huc.

"That's the north part of town built past the old walls," said Sancho. "New money, new families with the new money, and bigger towers for all of them. I've picked out one for myself if God ever sees fit to let the dice roll in my favor about a thousand times in a row."

"That would truly be a miracle," I said. "One that would have the baile taking both you and your dice to jail."

"Oh, I expect the Dicemakers' Guild would be on me long before the baile," laughed Sancho. "They guard their own."

"There is a Dicemakers' Guild?" asked Huc in amazement.

"Well, you wouldn't want dice made by just anyone, would you?" asked Sancho. "For all my complaints about the dice around here, I can't say for sure that they have ever rolled untrue. The dice are my vice and my punishment, so I accept how they come up as God's will."

"If that is your only vice, then that is not such a great stain on your character," commented Baudoin once Huc had translated Sancho's remarks.

"Oh, would that were the only one," sighed Sancho when he had Baudoin's response.

"Ah, now I am beginning to be fascinated," said Baudoin. "What are the others? Wine? Women? Cockfighting?"

"Can't say I've ever gone in for cockfighting," said Sancho. "And I prefer beer to wine. But women, there you have me. I've got years to go before I can leave service and settle down, you see. And we're on the march half the year, escorting the count through his holdings, which means I really have no time for a regular sweetheart. So, I spread my love about."

"And the women of the Toulousain are grateful for it," I added.

"I do my best," said Sancho modestly.

"The best possible motto for a soldier," I said. "Speaking of which—Sancho, tell them the story of why you became a foot soldier."

"Because I didn't have a horse," said Sancho.

There was a momentary delay as Huc translated. Then Baudoin broke into laughter and slapped him on the back.

"I like you, friend Sancho," he said. "My brother is a fortunate soul to have men like you about him. I had thought at first that he chose you as another means of insulting me, as he did this fool here, but I see now that he could not have made a better choice."

"My thanks, I think," said Sancho.

"None from me," I said.

"Now, show us to an establishment that serves some of that Toulousan beer that you like so much," said Baudoin.

"What do you think?" Sancho asked me.

"It's afternoon, so the decision is all yours," I replied.

"In that case, where should we take them?"

"In the bourg? I would go for the Tanners' Pit."

"That sounds disgusting," said Huc, wrinkling his nose.

"They get their beer from a brewery that's upriver a ways," I said in langue d'oïl. "The water is much cleaner than what's used by the breweries inside the walls, so the beer is better."

"You have convinced me," said Baudoin. "Take us to this blessed spot."

I preferred the brew at the Yellow Dwarf to anything in miles, but that was the jesters' special place. I didn't want to share it with outsiders.

Sancho took us the long way, through the gaudy clump of houses near the abbey of Saint Sernin. This had the added benefit of skirting the cluster of actual tanners' pits that stank up the area north of Saint Pierre des Cuisines. We came to the group of taverns and inns that crowded around the Bazacle Gate at the north end of the bourg by the river.

It was late afternoon, which meant that the tanners, never shy about cutting their work short, were well into the drinking portion of their day. As we came up to the doorway of the tavern, two of them came flying out, their hands on each other's necks, and began rolling about in the mud as several of their fellows followed from inside and began cheering them on. No one favored either party as far as I could tell—it was for the spectacle of the fight itself that they offered their support.

"Looks promising," commented Baudoin, stepping around the combatants.

Once inside, we commandeered a table that had been up-ended by the recent fracas and ordered a pitcher of beer and a bowl of eel stew. We all dug in to both the meal and more conversation. Huc and I alternated as translators, depending upon which of us had his mouth full at any given moment. Considering that someone else was paying for the meal, it was more often me who was prevented from speaking.

"Not bad at all," pronounced Baudoin, dipping some bread into the stew. "And the beer is more than satisfactory."

"I suppose you're used to much finer fare than this at the King's court," said Sancho.

"I have had epic meals on tables longer than battlefields, where the servants outnumbered any army I have ever seen," declared Baudoin. "And I have picked through the leavings of the worst taverns after the diners had collapsed into a drunken stupor."

"Quite the range," I commented. "Which was the more satisfying meal?"

"The one you get when you need it the most," he replied.

"Food always tastes better when you are hungry," I agreed. "Drink, too."

The tavern maid came by, replacing our empty pitcher with a full one while planting a quick kiss on the top of Sancho's head. She scampered away, smiling over her shoulder.

"I would have enjoyed that more if I wasn't wearing my cap," grumbled the soldier.

"One of your irregular sweethearts?" I asked.

"A gentleman does not tell," he said.

"Gentlemen always tell," I said. "Gentlemen brag about their conquests at length."

"But a soldier doesn't need to brag," Sancho said, winking at Baudoin.

Huc was watching her wistfully as she glided about the room.

"Do you fancy her?" Baudoin teased Huc. "I could find out her price."

"She's not that pretty," said Huc. "It would be a waste of money."

"Food tastes better when you're hungry," said Baudoin, nudging him. "It has been a while since we've eaten properly."

"What are they going on about now?" asked Sancho.

"I think he's about to ask you where the nearest bordel is," I muttered.

"Friend Sancho," slurred Baudoin, the beer starting to take effect. "In exchange for the location of that house of wondrous women I will send you to in Paris, what say you take us to an equivalent establishment here? I need to find my friend Huc someone prettier than this tavern wench."

"What do you think?" Sancho asked me.

"It's evening, which is an extension of the afternoon and therefore still in your bailiwick," I said. "I am responsible only for the mornings."

"In that case, where to go, where to go?" he pondered. "The Comminges quarter is too public, but there aren't any good places in the bourg—wait, yes, there is one, right outside. You know the house up past the Villeneuve Gate? With the red shutters?"

"That's a leper house."

"Right," he said.

"You want to take them to a leper house? That's carrying the initiative a little too far."

"The leper house is in front of the bordel," he said. "You've never gone there? In your performing capacity, of course."

"Of course, and no, I haven't."

"Then you ought to come along. Might be a useful connection for your line of work. And you might see a lady you like."

"Got one I like already," I said. "A regular sweetheart."

"Lucky you," he said. "Good thing you're not a soldier."

Oh, but I am, I thought.

"Fine, let us go see this house of shame behind the house of woe," I said.

Baudoin paid for the meal, and we resumed our tour of the bourg. I casually sidled up to Sancho.

"We are being followed," I muttered so that the Parisians could not hear.

"Damn well better be," he said.

"They're yours?"

"Think I would be taking these two around alone?" he asked. "I'm just the visible watchman."

"Got it," I said. "Carry on."

The Villeneuve Gate was on the eastern wall of the bourg, not far from where it met up with the original city wall. The leper house was on the outside of the wall, of course. The sun was setting, which meant that the gates were closing, but Sancho had no difficulty talking the guards into letting us through. I imagine that they had a steady secondary income in bribes from wayward patrons returning in the dark.

There was a small cluster of shops and taverns outside the gate, taking advantage of the lower rents to undercut their city competitors. The road into the gate was not one of the major routes, so the traffic was light, mostly farmers returning home with whatever goods they had been unable to unload at the markets.

The leper house sat in isolation beyond the shops. At least it must have, but all one could see was the high brick wall surrounding it, keeping the gawkers out and the contagion within. The upper story was visible, as were the red shutters that marked it, but they were all closed. There were five such houses scattered around the outside of the walls of Toulouse. I did not know what charity ran this one.

Sancho walked past the far corner of the house, then turned left like a man who had done this before. A narrow path ran between the brick wall and the fence of the adjoining farm, leading to the rear of the house.

The brick wall was lower in back, and the shutters were not so well maintained, but that did not matter. What drew us on was another two-story house, hung with many lanterns that glowed with a welcoming promise even as the sun was setting on the other side of the bourg. There were bursts of laughter, mostly women's, escaping into the evening, and someone was sawing away passably at a viol.

"This is the place," said Sancho.

"If the women here are as good as the beer in the Tanners' Pit, then we are in for a rare treat," said Baudoin.

"No woman is as good as that beer," said Sancho. "But they'll do."

He walked up to the door, nodding at the large man who sat by it with a serious-looking club resting against his thigh.

"I vouch for them," said Sancho, and the guard looked us over, then opened the door and beckoned us through.

There was a copper lamp suspended from the center of the room, its leaves hammered and punched into a delicate filigree that cast undulating webs of shadow on the walls. Red cushioned chairs rested against the walls, and in front of them was a low table covered with a cloth embroidered with scenes of Greek maidens in varying states of undress fleeing from satyrs who were not dressed at all. The maidens did not appear to be trying that hard to flee. The viol player must have been playing outside one of the ladies' workrooms, for the music floated down from somewhere farther into the interior of the place.

"Is that Sancho?" asked a low, mocking alto of a voice. "Could the dice have given him enough to grace our house with a visit?"

She appeared from the shadows of the hall opposite the entrance, wearing a dark green damask gown cut so low in front that the missing fabric could have made for a large tablecloth. She glided across the thick rug that I had just noticed contained more scenes of mythological debauchery. I also noticed that her feet were bare. I found myself thinking about what nice feet they were, and what it would be like to—

"No dice for me tonight, I'm sorry to say," said Sancho, Lord High Interrupter of Erotic Reveries. "But I've brought you some customers, all the way from Paris."

"You are most welcome, gentlemen," she said in perfect langue d'oïl.

"Does everyone in Toulouse speak our tongue?" wondered Baudoin.

"Only those of importance," she said. "And in this house, you'll find that our tongues are quite talented."

"What shall we call you, Domina?" asked Baudoin, bowing.

"I am the Abbess, senhor," she replied, returning the courtesy.

"An abbess? Is this a convent, then?"

"It is a place of retreat from the harshness of the world," said the Abbess. "As for its holiness—well, I can only say that we often hear God's name invoked. Are you on a pilgrimage?"

"I am hoping to have a religious experience," said Baudoin.

"Excellent," she said. "Then—"

We were interrupted by a thumping of footsteps, and suddenly, Raimon Roger filled the doorway, blinking in surprise.

"Well, if it isn't the prodigal brother," he said. "Domina Abbess, is there a fatted calf anywhere in the house? Slay it immediately."

"Ah, my dear count," purred the Abbess. "Was everything to your satisfaction?"

"To mine and, I am happy to say, to hers," he replied. "I see that you have attracted a pair of wandering Parisians."

"Good evening, senhor," said Baudoin in langue d'oc, bowing as he did.

"Will you listen to that?" praised Raimon Roger in langue d'oïl. "Fool, you have made excellent progress."

"He is an apt and willing student," I said.

"I must get you to teach me something," he said. "I have already hired someone here to instruct me in something new. I do so enjoy broadening my mind." He turned his attentions back to Baudoin. "Now, senhor, since you are a visitor, you must permit me to make you a recommendation."

"I am guided by you in all things, senhor," said Baudoin.

"You are a man whose liberty to enjoy the pleasures of life depends on a count who, although I love him like a brother, is unpredictable in his whims," said Raimon Roger. "If you should find yourself back in a dungeon tomorrow, it should be with the best possible memory of our fair city. You must have La Rossa."

"If she is as remarkable as you say, then you have my gratitude in advance," said Baudoin.

"Not at all," said Raimon Roger. "After all, you're family now. Almost family, anyway. Well, my sainted Abbess, I must bid you a lucrative evening and be off."

He bowed to her, nodded to the rest of us, and heaved his bulk out of the house.

"It seems that I must have La Rossa," said Baudoin.

"Then have her you will," said the Abbess. "I shall return with her."

She glided out.

A dancer, I thought. She must have been a dancer. I remembered a sultry Egyptian dancer who had enticed me when I was a young fool in Alexandria. I knew she was untrustworthy from the start, having been warned about her by colleagues I did trust and by my own observations, all of which I promptly ignored when I saw her dance, which ultimately led to a disastrous outcome in that particular mission, but not before it led to—

"I've heard about La Rossa," commented Sancho. "Never had the chance to have her."

The dancer disappeared in a puff of smoke, a taunting smile on her lips.

"You did it again," I muttered, snapping back to the present.

"Did what?" he asked.

"Never mind."

"Senhors," said the Abbess. "May I present—La Rossa!"

The color red overwhelmed us. A bright red gown, clinging to a body that wanted nothing more than to be rid of it. Red stockings peeped out from the bottom, red talons stabbed menacingly from each finger, glistening red coated a pair of lips curved into a smile that welcomed anything and everything, and a curly torrent of red hair cascaded from her head, floating about a pale white neck that invited, no, demanded to be bitten.

Baudoin looked at her appraisingly while Huc gawked. Her smile subtly shifted to a smirk as she returned their gazes.

"Have you come all the way from Paris just for me?" she said, her voice a rippling brook in summer.

"Had I known what glories awaited me here, I would have made the journey long ago," said Baudoin, bowing.

"A gallant," she said. "You put our local courtesy to shame. But perhaps this is merely a veneer. Are you this gallant all the time?"

"All the time," he assured her.

She glanced at Huc, who was still standing with his jaw somewhere around his navel, then turned back to Baudoin. She reached toward his face and trailed her long sharp nails along his cheek. He winced slightly.

"I must put your gallantry to trial," she said. "I find that even the most courteous of men will reveal his coarser, truer nature as the night goes on." She leaned forward and murmured into his ear, "And that's what I like the most."

"Then we must have the entire night," he responded. "So that a proper assay may be made."

A quick muttered negotiation took place. Money changed hands; then she hooked one nail under the clasp of cloak just below his throat and led him away.

"All night," sighed Sancho. "Same job, different place. They must be brothers."

He plopped himself onto a chair and made himself comfortable.

"But what about you, senhor?" the Abbess asked Huc. "Will you not partake?"

"I—I, no," he stammered. "I must wait upon my master. This is all too rich for my blood."

"Then sit by me, and we'll pass the night with stories, friend Huc," said Sancho, patting the cushions next to him. "I know this particular duty all too well."

The Abbess was looking at me.

"And you, Senhor Pierre?" she asked, walking slowly toward where I was sitting.

"You know my name," I said.

"I have seen you perform," she said. "You made me laugh." She lifted one exquisite foot and rested it on my knee. "I like a man who can make me laugh." The foot began to inch forward.

"Alas, I am a married man," I said, watching its progress like it wasn't part of anything.

"We serve many such," she said, her foot more than halfway up my thigh.

I reach down and stopped it. I thought that was what I was doing.

I was holding her foot.

"I am a happily married man," I said, trying to get my breathing under control.

Still with her foot on my thigh, she bent at the waist until her face was just in front of mine.

"I can make you a happier married man," she murmured.

"You are kind to ask," I said. "But no."

There were giggles from the doorway, and I looked past her to see several other residents of the house watching. The Abbess straightened up and turned to them.

"Behold, my sisters," she cried. "That rarest of mythical beasts, the happily married man."

I nodded amiably at them, and they giggled some more. The Abbess turned back to me.

"You are a challenge, Senhor Fool," she said. "I like a challenge."

"I must decline," I said. "Respectfully. Regretfully."

"Then leave here in shame," she replied. "Oh, and I will need my foot back."

I relinquished it reluctantly, and got to my feet.

"I guess I'll meet you back here in the morning," I said to Sancho and Huc.

"If I'm asleep, wake me," said Sancho. "If I'm asleep next to a beautiful woman, do not wake me. Ever."

"But what if you are only dreaming of a beautiful woman?"

"Then Brother Huc had better not sit too close," said Sancho.

"Sounds like good advice to me," said Huc.

"I will leave you to your duties, my friends," I said. "I must to my wife."

"Give her one from me," called Sancho as I walked outside.

I nodded at Sancho's fellow watchmen as I passed by what they thought was protective cover.

"Going to be there all night," I informed them.

"Oh, great," muttered one.

I showed my pass at the gate and was allowed back into the bourg. From there, it was a brief walk home.

I unlocked the door and went in. Claudia was standing there, pointing a crossbow in my direction.

"If I told you it was me, would you still be pointing it?" I asked her.

"Can't be too careful," she said, lowering it. "How was your day, Senhor Tutor?"

"Long," I said. "Yours?"

"Helga and I worked the flower market," she said. "We did all right. Oh, and one of the flower-sellers sold us these at a discount."

She showed me some slightly wilted geraniums sitting on the table.

We went upstairs, and I peeked into the girls' room. Both were asleep. When I came into ours, Claudia was sprawled on the bed. I sat by her feet and pulled off her boots.

"Thank you, lackey," she said.

I placed her feet in my lap. Good solid jester feet, suitable for acrobatics and kicking husbands in the posterior. I started massaging them.

"That feels wonderful," she sighed. "You're a good husband."

"I try my best," I said.

CHAPTER 4

Red. The color red overwhelmed us.

Red drapes hung by the window, which gave a good view of the leper house. Not that we were looking at the leper house.

Red damask canopies surrounded the bed, pulled asunder to frame the sleepers.

The red gown, removed in haste, lay in a puddle of silk near the bed. A red coverlet partially concealed the bed's occupants, one of whom was snoring away. The other was not.

Red hair, spilled in wanton profusion across the red pillows.

A red spray of roses in a vase on a stand by the bed.

A red spray of blood on the wall.

Red glistened on a white body, the remnants of a stream trickling down a savaged breast that must once have been as perfect as its unstained companion, both exposed to view. The stream ended in a shallow pool in the slight hollow of her stomach. More coated the underside of the coverlet. The dagger—Baudoin's dagger—was nestled in the folds.

"Hell," muttered Sancho, surveying the scene.

"I agree," I said.

Huc stood in the doorway behind us, his jaw in that all-too-familiar gape.

"You pulled the cover back?" I asked him.

"Yes," he whispered. "I wanted to—I wanted to see if she—"

"Was the dagger still in her?"

"No," he managed to gasp, then he made a choking noise, clapped his hands to his mouth, and fled downstairs.

I held up the coverlet, then pointed out the holes to Sancho.

"He stabbed her twice through the covers," I said. "The blood on the wall must have come when he pulled it out the first time."

"And he sleeps on!" roared Sancho. He rushed the bed and grabbed Baudoin by the shoulders.

"Bastard!" he shouted.

Baudoin snapped awake in confusion as the soldier threw him against the wall. The Parisian reacted quickly, grabbing for his scabbard from the pile of his clothes on the floor, but Sancho's sword was already out, its point stopping just short of Baudoin's Adam's apple, which bobbed rapidly up and down.

"Give me your sword," directed Sancho, trying hard to control his breathing.

"What did he say?" Baudoin asked me in panic.

"He said—," I began.

"I said, 'Give me your goddamned sword!'" shouted Sancho in langue d'oïl.

"What is this all about?" squealed the Parisian as he handed it over.

"What is this all about?" echoed Sancho. "What is this all about?"

He grabbed the Parisian's chin and angled his head toward the bed. Baudoin took in the gore with deepening shock.

"How did this—?" He gasped.

"How did this happen?" said Sancho, driving the man's head against the wall. "Is that what you were about to ask me? How did your dagger end up piercing one of the most beautiful women this city has ever seen?"

"My dagger?" gasped Baudoin.

Sancho grabbed it from the bed. "Your dagger," he said. "The match of this same sword which you have surrendered to me. La Rossa's blood still on the blade. Your dagger."

"I never did this!" protested Baudoin.

"I should kill you right here," said Sancho. "But I'm not sure my initiative would be appreciated. Pierre, go get my men from wherever they're hiding, and tell one of them to get a squad here. Then track down that useless Huc, and when he's finished heaving his guts out, bring him back."

"Right," I said, slipping into the hallway.

"And close the door," he said.

I did.

It was Sunday, just after dawn. I had come with the general idea of getting my pupil out of the bordel before too many people were aware that he was in one. Maybe invite him to attend Mass with us. New sins to confess, and all that. Turned out there were more than I thought possible.

Sancho and Huc were side by side on a couch, a near-empty wineskin on the table before them. Sancho was awake when I came in, and nudged Huc, who had his head back and his open mouth to the ceiling. The Parisian sat bolt upright and dabbed at a stream of drool with his sleeve. We made the usual lewd, stupid jokes that one makes under such circumstances; then Huc went upstairs to rouse his master.

And came flying back, choking in terror.

Sancho's companions had moved from their post of the night before, no doubt thanks to my ease in finding them.

I had no time to play hide-and-seek. I stood in front of the bordel and said, "Sancho needs you. Now!"

I thought I saw a movement from an upper window at the rear of the leper house, but then the two soldiers emerged from behind a woodpile.

"What's going on?" asked one of them.

"Can't talk about it," I said softly. "But one of you has to get a squad back here immediately. The other come with me to Sancho."

"Why isn't he telling us this himself?" asked the other one.

"You'll see when you get back. Now, hurry!"

Despite my whiteface, they took me seriously. The first ran off, while the second drew his sword and followed me back inside.

"A rare treat for me, coming in here," he said, looking around appreciatively.

"I'm about to spoil it," I said, leading him upstairs.

I knocked softly at the door. Sancho opened it. His fellow took one step in and stared.

"Him?" he asked, looking at Baudoin, who was dressed now and sitting in a chair.

"Oc, him," said Sancho. "We have to keep this quiet until the others get here."

"Right," said the other soldier. "Nothing like a whore-house for quiet and secrecy."

He looked at La Rossa with an expression that somehow combined pity and lust.

"Wouldn't have minded spending my last night on earth doing her," he said.

"Did you find Huc?" asked Sancho.

"Sorry," I said.

I ran downstairs and did a quick look around. There was

a kitchen in the rear, with a door leading to the gardens in back. It was barred from the inside, I noticed. There was a large table in the middle. Huc sat by it, resting his face on his folded arms. From the smell, he had been violently ill in the last few minutes. I couldn't blame him.

"You're wanted upstairs," I said softly.

"They're going to put us back in that dungeon, aren't they?" he said without looking up.

"Just your master, I would think," I replied.

"But I am his man," he said. "I will have to go with him to serve him."

"You may have to do that from without," I said.

He sat up and shook his head. "I must go with him," he said with determination.

"Then come upstairs."

As we reached the red room, the Abbess suddenly appeared, her hair loose, a blue silk robe wrapped around her.

"Senhors, why are you all up here?" she asked. "Does your Parisian still sleep on?"

Sancho stepped into the hallway.

"Domina, I regret to inform you that La Rossa has been murdered," he said.

She clapped her hands to her face, her eyes wide in horror; then she shoved him aside with surprising strength and rushed into the room.

"Holy Mother save us," she whispered, looking down at the dead woman.

She turned to see Baudoin flinching in his seat, and a low, guttural sound escaped her.

"You!" she shouted, and she flew at him, her nails aiming for his eyes.

Sancho grabbed her and pinioned her against the wall.

"Give him to us," she cried.

"He's ours," said Sancho.

"I will make it worth your while," she said. "Sancho need never worry how the dice roll in this house again."

"No, Domina Abbess," he said.

"If you take him, will he come to justice?" she asked.

"I take him now, but after that, higher forces take over," he said. "I cannot say if justice will be one of them."

"Then send for the baile," she said. "I will not have mere mercenaries tell me what to do. I want the count's man here."

"The baile's jurisdiction ends at the town walls, Abbess," said Sancho. "Outside the walls, I am the count."

He released her. The other soldier was still staring at the dead woman.

The Abbess strode angrily to the bed and flung the coverlet back over her. La Rossa now looked as if she slept. The Abbess gently caressed her hair, then turned back to us. "I will have justice for her," she said defiantly. "Even a whore is entitled to that."

"You get what you pay for," said Sancho. "You, of all people, should know that. And we will start by paying for your silence."

"What?" she said, her color rising.

Sancho removed a purse from his waist. It was heavier than I expected. He removed several silver coins and held them up.

"This would be a year's earnings for her," he said. "Allowing for Sundays off. You do go to church on Sundays, do you not?"

"You think that you can buy me?" she asked coldly.

He sighed, tossed the coins onto the bed, then suddenly rushed at her, his sword in his hand. He shoved her against the wall, his forearm at her throat, and held the blade against her cheek. "Listen to me, Domina Abbess," he said softly.

"This stays quiet, and you play along. If you can't play nicely, then I will take you out of this particular game for good. I will have regrets, but I have a large pile of them already. Do I make myself understood?"

She was still for a moment, then nodded. He released her, then picked the coins up from the deathbed. He placed them in her unwilling hand and closed it around them.

"The squad's here," said the other soldier, glancing out the window.

"Good," said Sancho. "Take him to the count's dungeon. Same one he was in before. Not a word gets out."

"What about her?" asked the other soldier, nodding at La Rossa.

"We bury her," said the Abbess in a small voice. "We bury our own."

Sancho pulled one more coin out of his pouch and flipped it to her. "For the funeral," he said. "I can't get her to Heaven. Just make sure she gets to the church." He grabbed Baudoin and hauled him to his feet. "Hands behind your back," he ordered in langue d'oïl.

The Parisian complied, and Sancho bound his wrists.

"Let's go," said Sancho, and we followed him as he guided Baudoin down the steps.

"Wait," he commanded.

He took a large cloth from his pack, threw it over Baudoin's head, and secured it.

"Rather not have people know who our prisoner is," he said.

"Thank you for that courtesy," said Baudoin.

"I'm not doing it for you," said Sancho. "And shut up."

He took him outside, where the squad was waiting.

"Half of you with me," said Sancho. "We escort the prisoner to the dungeon, and not a peep out of you. Take him by the outside route. The fewer people see us, the better. The rest of you stay here. No one goes in or out of that bordel."

The soldiers assigned to the bordel looked at it like ravenous dogs at a pile of steaks.

"And none of you goes inside," added Sancho.

The men gave a collective groan.

"I have caused thee to see it with thine eyes, but thou shalt not go over thither," I muttered.

"What's that?" asked Sancho

"Deuteronomy, chapter thirty-four, verse four," I said. "Moses saw the promised land, but was not allowed to enter it."

"Poor Moses," said Sancho. "You better come, too. We'll have some explaining to do."

"I'm just a humble tutor of languages," I said as the squad began marching Baudoin along the walls. "Something you apparently don't need, my humble soldier."

"You noticed that, did you?" he asked, falling back to my side.

"And your purse magically swelled to accommodate this emergency," I continued. "Was it a gift from some grateful magical creature you once rescued?"

"The purse is not technically mine," he said. "I was merely given the use of it."

"I see," I said.

"You can stop seeing any time, by the way," he said.

"One last comment," I said.

"What is it?"

"I think I may have underestimated you all this while."

He snorted.

"Underestimated by a fool," he said. "That will cheer me up enormously when the count kicks my ass all the way back to Castile. Which he will do personally."

"You are more than just one of his guards, in other words."

"In case you haven't noticed, I am his personal guard," he said. "Do you think he'd send any old idiot on this assignment? He chose me for a reason, just like he chose you."

"And you pretended you couldn't speak langue d'oïl in the hope that they would let down their defenses around you."

"You finally caught up," he said. "I take on special assignments for the count. I was the one he sent to tail you when you first showed up in town, as you may recall."

"I recall spotting you pretty easily."

"But not many would," he said. "The fact that you did spot me so easily told me something about you back then, so I allowed you to continue to think I was good, old, inept Sancho. You think you're the only one who plays dumb around here, you have another think coming."

"It came," I said. "My apologies. You're not just another soldier, and I'm not just another fool. I shall adjust our relationship accordingly."

"Which is not to say that we still can't have a drink together," he said. "I'm going to need one after this."

"You buy," I said. "You can afford it."

"This purse is to be used only for emergencies," he reminded me.

"It will be an emergency drink," I said.

We rounded the curve by the Jewish cemetery. The Château Narbonnais was just ahead of us. The squad picked up the pace, two of them dragging the prisoner between them. Huc trotted behind them.

"Why do you suppose he did it?" I asked Sancho.

"How the hell should I know?" he replied. "Maybe he was not the man he thought he was, or the gentleman he pretended to be. Maybe she pointed that out to him. He wouldn't be the first drunken idiot to stab a whore in a bordel."

"True enough," I said. "But I wonder why he would travel so far and aim so high, only to betray himself so easily."

"Maybe this is what he does," said Sancho. "Maybe that's why he left Paris. There might be a whole string of dead women in his wake. It will be interesting to hear what the viguier's man learns."

"Will they wait that long before hanging Baudoin?"

"Not my decision, and thank Christ for that," said Sancho. "I don't know if the count will make a quick public example of him or hush the whole thing up. That might depend on whether or not he's really the count's brother."

"Will that help him or hurt him?" I wondered.

We entered the grounds of the château. The squad took the prisoner to the Palace of Justice, where the dungeons were. Huc paused outside the door, looked up at the blue sky as if he was memorizing the shape of every cloud in it, then took a deep breath and followed his master inside.

"Loyal man," I observed.

"How can you be loyal to a murderous, whoring bastard?" asked Sancho.

"Which reminds me," I said. "The count will be expecting us."

We entered the Grand Tower and walked up the stairs to the count's rooms. Two of the inner guards smirked at Sancho, no doubt thinking his strained looks were a product of trailing a night of debauchery by Baudoin. Which they were, come to think of it. Sancho took a deep breath and went in. The guards closed the doors behind him.

The doors muffled most of what followed, but a few choice words escaped into the hall, as did the occasional crash of things being flung. The guards' expressions shifted from smirking curiosity to concern.

"Did something happen last night?" one of them asked me.

"Well, since you asked me so specifically, I will tell you," I replied. "Yes. Something happened last night."

"Thought so," he said.

"You were handpicked by the count, too, weren't you?" I asked.

"Certainly was," he said, puffing up proudly.

"Thought so," I said.

After one more particularly loud crash, there was a tap on the door. The guards opened it, and Sancho emerged, a fresh bruise below his left eye.

"How's the ass?" I asked him.

"Soundly kicked, but still here," he said. "He would like to speak with you now."

"I will be blaming you for everything," I informed him as I passed by.

"You won't be the first," he said, and the doors closed behind me.

The count sat behind his desk, looking at me moodily. The remnants of a vase and an assortment of flowers littered the floor, as did a steel helm that I had last seen hanging on the wall behind him.

"I must warn you that anything you throw at me will be caught," I said.

"That certainly takes all the fun out of it," he said. "What if I commanded you not to catch it?"

"Then where would the challenge be?"

He picked up a small bronze horse that had been made with great artistry and was now acting to weigh down a stack of documents. He hefted it experimentally, then heaved at me.

I caught it easily and put it back on the stack.

"You're the worst language tutor ever," he said.

"I resign my position," I replied. "Will you give me a reference?"

"Not a chance in hell."

"Then I must go back to my old job. Your fool awaits your bidding, Dominus."

"Good. Tell me what you know."

"Nothing, really. I left him at the bordel, romping with a redhead. When I returned in the morning, the redhead was dead in bed."

"Providing you with an excuse for morbid extemporaneous doggerel."

"I didn't have time to compose anything more formal," I apologized. "I will have a sestina ready by lunch, if you like."

"Don't strain yourself. Did you learn anything about my putative brother before he turned butcher?"

"He sounded like he was familiar with the Parisian courts," I said. "He's decent with a sword, likes to drink, and is a bit of a bawd. None of these exclude him as a relative of yours, in my opinion."

"I should have kept him in the dungeon," he sighed. "Every instinct screamed lock him away. But I chose to be reasonable and listened to more sensible people. And now, a woman is dead."

Having been one of those who provided that ill-fated advice, I decided to not say anything in rejoinder.

"No one could have expected this," he continued. "That he might be a spy from France, or an impostor, or an adventurer, none of these would have surprised me. A common lecher and killer—I'm disappointed, I have to say. There is no style in that."

"What will you do with him now?" I asked.

"Hang him, I suppose," he replied. "What else is there to do? I hear La Rossa was a force of nature in the bedchamber. I would value such over a dozen bastard brothers."

"He did say full, not bastard."

"Say he is. Would you let him go free?" asked the count.

"I? No, I would want justice done," I said. "If you would hang a beggar for stealing a candlestick, then you should hang a nobleman for stealing a whore's life."

"Right," he said, drumming his fingers on the desk. "Right. Only—"

"Only what?"

"I would like to know for certain who he is before we execute him," he said. "I would like to sit down across a table and have one meal where we could talk about my mother."

"Then you must await the viguier's messenger," I said.

"Toulouse will wonder at the delay," he said.

"Remind them that he if he is indeed your brother, he is also then the cousin to the King of France," I said. "That brings diplomacy into the matter. The delay will be understandable."

"That would work," he said. "Of course, he's the King's kin. Good. I'll send another courier to Paris. Thank you."

"Glad to be of service," I said.

"Now, I want you to go out there like I've given you a drubbing," he said. "Do you mind?"

In response, I thumped my fist on the table, yelped in pain, then smacked my fist against my palm several times, grunting with each one. Raimon watched the performance with interest.

"If only I had a puppet theater," he mused. "We could make some money."

"You do have a puppet theater," I said. "Only the strings are invisible."

My body jerked out of the chair as if yanked from above, and I danced like a marionette to the door and banged on it.

The two guards opened it, and I trudged out, rubbing my jaw.

"He went rough on you, did he?" asked one sympathetically.

"No more than I deserved," I said. "Where did Sancho go?"

"He said he'd find you at your usual place," he replied.

"I guess he would know," I said.

As I came out of the Grand Tower, I saw Huc watching me by the Palace of Justice. He nodded toward the stables. I followed him inside.

"My master is despondent," he said.

"La Rossa is dead," I said. "That makes her day worse."

He flinched as if I had slapped him, then looked around to make certain we were not being overheard.

"He wants to talk to you," he said.

"Me? Why me?"

"He wants your help," he said.

"Forget it. I don't arrange escapes."

"He will not flee his predicament," Huc said, swelling with pride. "He will face it like the noble man that he is. Please, will you speak with him?"

My curiosity got the better of me. "All right," I agreed. "Take me to him."

I had been to the dungeons before, but not to the lowest level. Much of it was taken up by storage rooms, but there were a handfull of cells that were shut off from the corridors by thick wooden doors with only a minuscule square opening hacked out at eye level. The guards nodded at Huc and looked at me in surprise, but I had the run of the château, thanks to my patron, so I passed by without challenge.

Huc led me to Baudoin's cell, knocked twice on the door, then three more times. There was a rustling inside; then a pair of eyes peered out through the opening.

"Well?" I said.

"I am a fool," he said in langue d'oc.

"Language lessons are suspended for the duration of the term," I said. "At the end of the term, you may find yourself suspended. By the neck."

"And if I had killed her, I would accept that fate," he said.

"If you had killed her?"

"You sound as if you had no doubts in the matter," he said.

"Not my call if I did," I said. "But I don't, so there's an end to it."

"What reason would I have?" he asked.

"Reason had nothing to do with it," I said. "I have seen acts of depravity in my life, the very description of which would frighten reason right out of the room. To make love to a woman, then kill her, then sleep soundly the rest of the night next to her bleeding corpse—that takes a special kind of man, Senhor Baudoin. I don't know what you were thinking, and I don't care to know."

"Do you really believe that I would do that?" he asked. "That I am that wicked?"

"I've known you for less than two days," I said. "I cannot tell what manner of man you are, except by what I have seen."

"You did not see me kill her," he said.

"No, but . . ."

"And, putting aside the depravity of the act, do I strike you as a man so stupid as to stay with the woman he killed so that he could be captured so easily?"

"You haven't struck me as a smart man," I said.

"But you are one," he said.

"I am a fool," I said.

"But fools, they know things," he insisted. "They know people. They see through pretense and lies."

"You overrate us," I said. "I haven't seen through you yet."

"I am transparent," he said. "I have been stripped of all rank, all hope, all dignity. There is nothing left but the truth. I did not kill her."

"That is not for me to decide," I said.

"Someone is trying to set me up," he said. "I arrive, I announce myself, and somehow become a threat. Or a pawn, a way of embarrassing my brother."

"Oh, you've become much more than an embarrassment," I said.

"Please, Senhor Pierre," he whispered. "I have no other recourse."

"What about him?" I asked, nodding at Huc.

"I know no one here," said Huc. "Nor will anyone speak with the companion of Baudoin while Baudoin is here."

"I will pay you, if that would help," said Baudoin.

"Get stuffed," I said. "I am the count's fool. Do you think my loyalty is so worthless?"

"I am prepared to be as loyal to him as any man alive," he said. "Can a brother do more?"

"I've seen brothers gouge each other's eyes out, and their blood was even more noble than yours pretends to be," I said. "I'm not impressed."

"Then I am doomed," he whispered.

"That's about the size of it," I agreed. "I will come by for another visit, though. This is on my rounds." I walked back toward the stairs.

"Fool," he called after me.

"What?" I said without turning.

"If they hang me for this, an innocent man dies, and a murderer goes free," he said. "Is that the justice you seek?"

"What I seek is a roof over my head," I said. "I seek a full belly, a warm fire, a loving wife, and happy children. Most of all, I seek laughter that I have brought into existence. I am not in the justice game, senhor. But I certainly hope it finds you."

I climbed back to daylight and sought out the gates. As I passed through them, Sancho fell into step beside me.

"What did he have to say?" he asked.

"I thought you were going to find me at my usual place," I said.

"I was, but then I thought since I left you that message, you would probably go somewhere else, just out of spite."

"You could have followed me."

"In which case, you would have spotted me with your customary skill and lost me within two streets. So, I have dispensed with all my cleverness and cunning and have approached you directly."

"Good plan."

"What did he have to say?" he repeated.

"Who wants to know?"

"Me," he said.

"But are you only you, or are you someone else right now? We are inside the walls, so you are no longer the count."

"I am the man who is about to buy you a drink if you tell me what Baudoin said."

"Why didn't you say that in the first place? I've been looking for you."

It was late morning, so the tavern he chose was relatively empty. He paid for a pitcher and a loaf of bread from his emergency purse, then poured two cups and slid one to me.

"Spill it," he said.

"I wouldn't dream of wasting wine like that," I replied.

"I mean, tell me what he said."

"He said he didn't kill her."

"Right," he snorted. "Well, there's a load off my mind. I

was worried sick about that poor bastard being guilty. What else?"

"He wanted me to find who did it."

Sancho stared at me. "That's taking a bad joke too far, if you ask me," he said slowly.

"I told him to leave the bad jokes to professionals like myself, but you know how those murderers are. No sense of proportion."

"The gall of him," said Sancho. "And what else did you tell him?"

"What else?"

"You're not planning on investigating this, are you?"

It was my turn to stare. "Is that what you wanted to ask me?"

"It is now."

"Good God, Sancho. I work for the count, for one thing. And for another, as the baby fox said to its mother when she told him to kill the tortoise, what's in it for me?"

"Then why did you go talk to him in the first place?"

"Curiosity, my dear Sancho. Which has now been satisfied."

"Fine," he sighed. "I suggest you keep it suppressed. I have a hunch it will only lead you into trouble. Sorry. Not working on much sleep at the moment. I had to go back there and make sure everything was quiet."

"Was it?"

"There were no other customers," he said. "The Abbess has the girls in line. They're going to bury La Rossa tomorrow, and that will be an end to it until the count hangs Baudoin."

"Thus ends our mutual assignment."

"Until the next pretender shows up," he said. He knocked his cup against mine. "To bastards everywhere."

"On their behalf, I thank you," I said, returning the toast.

"What are you doing back already?" asked Claudia as I came through the door.

"Put the crossbow down and I will tell you," I said.

By the time I was done, she and Helga were at the table, the girl with her chin resting on her folded hands.

"Poor woman," said Claudia.

"No one ever dies of old age in a bordel," said Helga softly.

We looked at her. She was expressionless, but tears were trickling down her cheeks.

"Something my mother used to tell me," she said, running her sleeve across her face. "Excuse me, I'm going to go check on Portia." She got up and ran upstairs.

"Damn," I said. "Thoughtless of me. It's getting to the point where I can't even open my mouth without upsetting one of the women in my life."

"She'll be all right," said Claudia. "She can't live her life without hearing about things that remind her of the past. Nobody can. What happens now?"

"I expect Baudoin will hang. The count believes in making examples of people."

"Good," she said. "Justice for La Rossa."

"There's only one problem," I said.

"What's that?"

"I think he may be innocent."

She could have questioned me, or given a cry of astonishment or outrage, or merely picked up the crossbow and put a bolt through my stupid head. But she knew me, knew me better than anyone, save perhaps one blind old man in the Black Forest, so she just looked at me thoughtfully and asked, "Have you gone completely insane?"

"Years ago. Thought you would have noticed by now."

"What makes you think he didn't do it?"

"Nothing tangible. Just my gut telling me he was telling the truth."

"So that's where you do all your thinking."

"You thought it was my brain all this time?"

"No. Considerably lower, considering you're a man."

"Speaking of which, if he was set up, someone in the bordel probably knows about it."

"Could someone have come in from the outside?"

"Maybe. But Sancho was in the front parlor the whole evening, and two of his men were watching from the outside."

"Is there a back door?"

"To the kitchen. It was barred from the inside. I noticed that when I fetched the retching, wretched Huc."

"But someone inside could have barred it afterwards," she mused. "Oh, hell, you've got me thinking it's possible. Did you tell Sancho you were going to investigate this?"

"No."

"Why not?"

"Because he wanted to make sure that I wasn't going to. And that bothered me."

She gnawed absently on her lower lip. "This could be coming from somewhere high up, in other words," she said.

"Baudoin stirred things up. Someone could have panicked."

"You said the Count of Foix was there."

"Yes, he was just leaving. He . . ." I stopped, trying to remember. "He specifically recommended La Rossa to Baudoin."

"Interesting. And he's part of Raimon's inner circle."

"I should return to the scene of the crime."

"No. You shouldn't."

"Why not?"

"Because it's a bordel," she said. "That makes it a bad idea."

"Because I am a married man."

"More to the point, because you are a married man whose wife happens to be me," she said. "Therefore, you going into a bordel is a bad idea."

"Then how do I find out what happened there?"

"Simple," she said. "I'll go."

CHAPTER 5

You live with a man for years, perform together the bawdiest of acts with the raunchiest language in the seediest of taverns, romp with him in bed with abandon, and still, he thinks you know nothing.

My husband looked at me in astonishment, then began to splutter. "You can't go there," protested Theo. "No matter what people may think, you still have some semblance of decency."

"Abandoned long ago," I assured him.

"And what makes you think those women will talk to you?"

"Because I am a woman," I said.

"And that gives you an advantage in a bordel?"

"Well, for one thing, I am less likely to succumb to their charms than you are."

"I did not succumb to anything," he said indignantly. "You must think me a complete and utter—"

"Which one had the talented feet?" I interrupted.

"Feet?"

"Come now," I said. "You come home from a bordel and immediately give me a footrub. If you think that I haven't seen the connection there—"

"I thought you liked the footrub," he said, looking wounded.

"I loved the footrub," I said. "If you gave me a footrub like that every night, I would be the happiest woman in Christendom. But you don't give me a footrub every night. In fact, I cannot even recall the last time you gave me a footrub. So tell me the truth, husband. Which of them had the talented feet?"

"The Abbess was barefoot," he said guiltily. "But I didn't—"

"Were they pretty feet?" I sneered.

"They were all right," he muttered.

"Prettier than mine?"

"I have never really compared women's feet before," he said. "Yours are very nice."

"Mine are worn and rough from dancing and tumbling and walking for hundreds of miles on Guild business," I said. "They have calluses and cracked nails, and they are usually swollen by the end of the day. Tell me again how they compare to those of one whose living depends on the roundness of her heels."

"I did not sleep with her, or anyone else there, or any other woman since I have been with you!" he shouted.

"Not even Thalia when we were in Constantinople?"

"For the last time, I declined all opportunities on that front."

"It was a very tempting front," I said. "Not all saggy from nursing your one and only child, or—"

"All right, if I have to prove it to you," he said, and he swooped forward and kissed me hard.

"I'm not that easy," I said after we caught our breath.

"No, you're not," he agreed, and he kissed me again.

"I haven't forgiven you yet," I said at the next interval.

"Then I shall continue doing this until you do," he said.

Helga came down the steps in the middle of it and picked up Portia.

"I'm taking her for a walk," she announced.

"Really? Why?" I gasped.

"Because I know what's going to happen next," she said.

The door opened and closed behind them. My husband and I looked at each other.

"Upstairs?" he suggested.

"I'd rather not wait that long," I said.

The room was in shambles, and Theo was sprawled across our table while I searched for my sewing kit.

"Found it," I said, and I began working on the splinter that had lodged itself in his buttock. "I can't believe you didn't feel this."

"I was distracted," he said. "There was a—Ouch!"

"Hold still," I admonished him. "Almost done. There was a what?"

"A voracious woodland nymph attacking me," he continued. "She—damn you, woman! Did you have no training in surgery when you were young?"

"I had people do that for me back then," I said. "Before I was reduced to this life of squalor and debauchery. Really, you are being such a baby. No, worse. Portia would just watch the operation with unholy fascination."

"I would watch as well," he said, trying to look over his shoulder at my handiwork. "But I have no clear view of the—Ow! Please tell me you got it this time."

I held it in front of his nose.

"I thought you said it was a splinter, not a plank," he grumbled.

"You squawk so much about a splinter, yet you once took a crossbow bolt through your leg with equanimity."

"I thought I was going to die then. This time, I thought you were going to kill me."

"Still might," I said, wiping off the blood. "There. Get your motley back on, Fool, and let's discuss this calmly."

He pulled it on quickly, then looked at me and grinned. "You're like this table," he said. "Rougher than you look."

"But, like the table, sturdy," I replied.

"We proved that well enough," he said, slapping me playfully on the rump.

"Do that again, and I will respond in kind," I warned him. "And you wouldn't like that in your present condition."

"Right," he agreed, hastily backing away. "So, what were we talking about before the distraction?"

"Me going to the bordel."

"Right. And I was against it, so you used your powers of seduction to change my mind."

"Crafty of me, wasn't it?"

"You caught me in a weak moment. My defenses were down."

"It was all too easy. You see why I fear for your virtue going back to a place like that?"

"But do you see why I fear for yours? Why, with skills like those that you have just demonstrated so ably, you would be recruited in an instant."

"What, and leave jesting? Never."

"The money's better," he said.

"How much better?" I asked.

"Depends on how many years you keep at it," he said.

"Longevity is an issue in both professions," I said. "Especially given your penchant for getting us into life-threatening situations."

"Me?"

"You. Although poor La Rossa might not agree with us at the moment."

"True enough," he conceded. "All right, see what you can

find out. I'll start poking around the Count of Foix's faith-lessness."

"Seems like a place to start. How much do we know about him, besides that he's one of Raimon's inner circle?"

"Not enough," he said. "But I think Balthazar had one or two mentions of him in his notes. Helga, stop listening at the door and come back inside."

The door opened, and the two girls came in, hand in hand.

"How did you know?" asked Helga.

"The base of the door doesn't fit tight," said Theo, pointing. "I saw the shadow."

"Have to remember that," said Helga.

"How long were you there?" I asked her suspiciously.

"We came back a minute ago. You were talking about the Count of Foix." Her face was devoid of guile, but I saw her eyes dart toward the table, then at my husband, and the faintest trace of a smile lurked at the corners of her mouth.

"May I come with you to the bordel?" she asked.

"Why?"

"I want to see how you play it," she said.

"I was thinking of wounded wife," I said.

"I am the one with the wound," said Theo plaintively.

"Shut up, husband," I said consolingly.

"Wounded wife would work better with children in tow," said Helga. "Makes it all the more pathetic." She let her eyes grow wide and suddenly looked ten and frightened.

"Take her," pleaded Theo. "Take them both. I can get some reading done in quiet."

"Fine," I said, taking Portia from her. "Come, girls, let's go visit a whorehouse."

"Hooray!" said Helga.

"Where is it, exactly?" I asked Theo.

"It's the one behind the leper house outside the Villenueve Gate, right?" said Helga.

"How do you know about that?" asked Theo in surprise.

"I know all kinds of things I shouldn't know," said Helga. "Isn't that what an apprentice fool is supposed to be learning?"

"I suppose," he said, sighing. "Have a good time."

We left him and started to walk.

"Seriously, why do you know about that?" I asked her.

She was suddenly quiet and subdued. "You know about my mother," she said. "About where she raised me."

"Yes. I do."

"Once a bordel brat, always a bordel brat," she said. "That's what they used to tell me. They were only waiting for me to get old enough. Some of them didn't want to wait."

"But you got out," I reminded her.

"I got out," she said. "I joined the Guild. But they're still waiting for me somewhere. I'm always aware of it. So, I need to know where they are. I always know where they are."

"You know where all the bordels are in Toulouse?"

"Three in the Comminges quarter, two in Saint Cyprien, one in the bourg near the Bazacle Gate, a small one near Saint Sernin that is supposed to be a secret because the monks go there, and this one."

"There's a third one in Comminges?"

"Near the bridge," she said. "Last stop for the pilgrims before they head off to Compostela and absolution."

"Good location," I commented. "What else do you know about that you're not supposed to know about?"

"I don't know," she said. "I mean, I know what I know, but I don't know what I'm not supposed to know, you know?"

I impulsively wrapped my arm around her head and drew her into my body as we walked. "I miss my children," I whispered, kissing the top of her head. "But I'm glad I have you with us, Apprentice."

"Me, too," she said, her voice muffled with her face pressed against my side.

I released her, and she looked up at me, her face more sorrowful than any child or any jester should ever be. "My mother is dead, isn't she?" she asked.

I knew that she would ask one day. I knew that when it came, I would tell her the truth. That foreknowledge didn't make it any easier.

"Yes, Helga," I said.

"When did you find out?" she asked.

"Before we left Swabia," I said. "Father Gerald informed us. He suggested that we wait for you to ask us."

"I knew it, somehow," she said. "Konrad, the jester who recruited me, would send me news once in a while. But then I heard nothing. I just looked up one day in the middle of tumbling class and knew she was gone. How did she die?"

"A fever took her," I said. "It happened quickly."

"She got out," she said. "She finally got out."

"I am so sorry, Helga."

She looked straight ahead. "She saved me," she said. "I was going to get her out someday. When I became jester in full. I was going to go back and save her. But I can't now, can I?"

"You saved her when you got out," I said. "No matter what happened to her after that, she knew she was able to do that much for you. And now you save other lives."

"Whose life are we saving right now?" she asked.

"I don't know yet," I said. "Here's the gate. Let's get into character."

I handed Portia to her, then thought of every woman who has ever been betrayed by a man, and stormed through the gate, barking at the guards to get out of my way.

I recognized the leper house immediately by its high walls, and took the sharp turn at an angry trot, Helga hurrying to keep pace.

"Maman, I'm scared," she whined as the bordel came into view. "I don't want to go in there."

"Shut up, girl!" I snapped as a large man with a club looked at us in weary concern.

"Go away, lady," he said. "This is no place for you."

"If it's good enough for my husband, then it's good enough for me," I said. "Out of my way."

"Now, Domina, do not be overhasty," he said, reaching out to grab me.

I grabbed him first, my hands gripping his coat at the collar. Then I jumped high, still holding on, and swung forward, my legs in front of my body. My feet landed solidly in his stomach, and he pitched forward with a surprised grunt.

Which meant that he was falling on top of me, but I bent my knees and kept my back curved. As my body hit the ground, I rolled back and kicked up as hard as I could, still keeping my grip on his collar. I let go once his body had cleared mine. He landed with a thud behind me.

I got to my feet and stood over him, bending so that my face was over his, albeit upside down. "Never put your hands on me again," I said. "I don't like it."

He mumbled something incoherent.

"I accept your apology," I said as I straightened up.

The girls were looking at me in awe.

I heard a man chuckle briefly somewhere behind me. I turned quickly, knife in hand, but saw no one. No, a quick glimpse of a hand at one of the upper windows of the leper house. A scarred, misshapen hand. Then it was gone.

"Well?" I said sternly, slipping the knife back up my sleeve. "Are you coming?"

"Yes, Maman," whimpered Helga.

We entered the bordel.

Helga took in the lewd decor without changing her expression. I looked around, then shouted, "I demand to see the one who calls herself an abbess!"

There was a soft, deliberate tread down the stairs; then she appeared in the doorway. Her feet were bare, and they were lovely indeed, I noted with chagrin. The body was one I would have given my eyeteeth to possess when I was younger, but the face in the daylight looked haggard.

We appraised each other from across the room, and I found myself tensing for another fight.

"I have a man who is supposed to keep the likes of you out of here," she said.

"He failed," I said. "I have a man who is supposed to keep away from the likes of you."

"He failed," she said.

"Yet he claims he did not tarry," I said. "That he was in and out of this house quickly. Although I suppose many men here are in and out quickly."

"He was here, and then he left."

"I know that. It is what happened in between that concerns me."

"What is it that you want?" she asked.

"Your word that my husband did not betray me last night."

"Why should I tell you?"

"Because I asked."

"Why should you believe me?"

"Because I asked."

The guard staggered in, looking sheepish.

"What happened, Carlos?" asked the Abbess.

"She—I don't know," he said.

"Go back to your post," she ordered. "Try to keep any more tiny women from coming in."

He slinked out.

The Abbess turned back to me. "I have no time for wronged wives," she said. "I must needs bury one of my women."

"I heard," I said. "I am sorry. Did she have family?"

"She had us," she said. "Once you come here, that's all you have."

"Then I am sorry for all of you," I said.

"Don't ever feel sorry for us," she said, biting off each word. "We take care of our own."

"You didn't last night," I said.

The Abbess looked me up and down, appraising me. "I have customers who might pay well to be manhandled by the likes of you," she said.

"No thank you," I said. "Being paid would take the fun out of it. Answer my question."

"Your husband did not dishonor your bed," she said. "But he thought about it."

"He may think whatever he likes," I said. "So long as the thought remains unfulfilled."

"I'm sure he fulfilled it with you last night," she said. "You should thank me for providing him with the inspiration."

I laughed in astonishment. "You dare to speak to a married woman in that manner?" I asked.

"In here, I speak how I like," she said. "No matter how the rest of the world treats me, in this house I am the Abbess."

"Then the Fool has the advantage over the Abbess," I said. "I speak how I like everywhere I go."

"Then I envy you," she said. "Are you satisfied?"

I looked at her and nodded.

"Depart from here," she said. "As a friend."

I turned to leave, then hesitated. "May I come to the funeral?" I asked. "I could play my lute."

"Why would you want to do that for a woman you have never met?"

"Because a woman died at the hands of a man," I said. "And all such women should be mourned."

She looked at me for a long time, expressionless. Then she nodded. "Yes, we should," she said. "We will be at the church of Saint Agnes, down the road about a half a mile. Tomorrow morning."

"We will be there," I promised.

The guard flinched as we passed by him. I didn't give him so much as a glance.

There was another chuckle from the rear of the leper house. I looked up.

"Well done, lady," called a hoarse voice. "Best entertainment I've had in years."

I curtsied grandly, then continued on.

"Why are we going to the funeral?" asked Helga.

"Two reasons," I said. "One is to see who shows up. Always interesting, always useful."

"And the second?"

"You'll see tomorrow."

Theo was curled up on our bed amidst several sheaves of parchment covered with small, cramped writing. These were Balthazar's notes, which his late predecessor as Chief

Fool of Toulouse had kept for over thirty years. We had found them useful on more than one occasion, but as they were in chronological order, one sometimes had to go through thirty years of the past to find anything helpful for the present.

"Any luck?" I asked.

"The Count of Foix has been in and out of favor," he said. "Balthazar actually had a great deal of respect for his intellect, which surprises me. I've only seen him be a parasite and a lecher."

"But a successful parasite and lecher," I said. "That demands a kind of skill."

"Says he's a decent poet," snorted Theo. "A poet! All I have ever heard him rhapsodize over is the charms of his latest conquest, and that was expressed in the most lurid of prose. It lacked only a few equally crude illustrations to make a book worth banning by the Vatican."

"Perhaps only women hear his poetry," I said. "Some women like to be wooed by poetry."

"Nothing rhymes with Claudia," he said. "Or Viola."

"I'll settle for Gile," I said.

"There once was a woman called Gile," he began.

"Stop immediately," I said. "Anything else in there?"

"Well, the most interesting thing about him is his wife," said Theo.

"That's the most interesting thing about most men," I said. "What about her?"

"He said she was a Cathar."

"The Countess of Foix a Cathar? For how long?"

"Doesn't say. But that would make her one of the more prominent members if so," he said.

"Is she one of the Perfect?" I asked.

"Have to find out," he said. "Interesting if she was. If she had renounced her husband's bed to become one of the

Perfect, then that might explain his running around with so many women."

"It could be the other way around," I said. "Something to console her for his constant infidelities."

"You always take the woman's part," he pointed out.

"Someone has to," I said.

"Well, I'll follow up on that with Hugo down at the Yellow Dwarf," he said, yawning. "He knows all the gossip on the Cathars."

"And the ale is good," I said.

"And the ale is good," he agreed. "What will you be doing?"

"Going to a whore's funeral," I said.

"Hmph," he said. "My day sounds like more fun."

The church was small and simple, serving the small cluster of shops outside the gate and the vegetable farmers who worked within sight of the city walls. I suppose the ministry included the bordel and the leper house, more than enough challenge for the sole priest who presided over the area. I wondered which of the city parishes had jurisdiction here. I hoped it was Saint Sernin, as our current relations with the bishop at Saint Étienne were frosty. Understandable, given recent events.

The priest turned out to be a young beleaguered-looking man who sighed with exasperation when he saw us. "A jester. Wonderful," he said. "Bad enough to have those wretched women parading in here. Now all of Toulouse will know that Father Bonadona is the whore's priest."

"You see, girl?" I commented to Helga. "Fools are worse than prostitutes in the eyes of God."

"That isn't what I meant," he said.

"Will you be preaching the funeral Mass?" I asked him.

"Oc," he said.

"Then we will sing for it," I said. "A fool's mite."

"None of your bawdy songs in here," he said angrily.

"I have never heard *Igne divini radians amoris* described as bawdy," I said. "Depends how you sing it, I suppose."

He looked at me in surprise, then bowed his head and put his palms against his chest. "Forgive me my wrong assumptions," he said.

"Forgive us our motley, and we shall call it even," I replied, returning the courtesy.

We sat on a bench by the side. I tuned my lute, and Helga took a flute from her bag.

"You know the hymn?" I asked Helga.

"I knew it before I joined the Guild," she said. "I knew it from my mother."

"Then you shall sing it," I said.

"Shouldn't you?" she asked in surprise. "You're the jester. I'm only an apprentice. And you sing much better than I do."

"You have a lovely voice, girl, so don't use that excuse again," I said. "You shall sing the hymn."

"Is this part of my training?"

"No," I whispered as the doors to the church swung open. "I want you to sing it for your mother."

I had expected the denizens of the house to make a show of respect for the church, some semblance of mourning. I was wrong. In strode the Abbess, still barefoot, still in a gown that would have raised the dead, or at least one part of them. Behind her, six ladies, each scandalously clad, carried in a coffin. I scanned their faces—sorrow and resignation on some, anger and defiance on the others.

At the rear was the guard I had so recently given a tumble in an entirely different way than he was used to from a woman, followed by a small collection of people—whether passersby, curiosity seekers, or genuine mourners, I could not say. Some young men were nudging each other and whispering, trying to get a better look at La Rossa, perhaps for the first and only time in their lives. The Abbess turned and silenced them with a glare that had talons.

The priest was taking them in with horror.

"You cannot come in here like this," he hissed at the Abbess.

She stood before him, a scornful sneer on her lips. She was taller, I noticed, even in her bare feet.

"She belongs to God now," she said softly. "For years, she has done things that no woman would want to do because she was paid. For years. Now, you will do what you do not want to do for one hour of your life because you have been paid. Perform your office."

His Adam's apple bobbed up and down rapidly. Then he abruptly moved to the lectern. He took a deep breath and composed himself.

"All that the Father giveth me shall come to me," he began. "And him that cometh to me I will in no wise cast out."

Good, I thought.

"We are gathered in the house of the Lord to consign to him—"

He stopped and looked at the Abbess.

"What is her true name?" he asked. "I cannot call her La Rossa before Our Savior."

The Abbess looked at the rest of the women uncertainly, and they whispered among themselves.

"She said her real name was Julie," said a blonde in a light blue gown. "I don't know if it was her true name."

"We know no others," said the Abbess. "We ask nothing of any who join us."

"Sounds like our Guild," I whispered to Helga.

The priest seemed less than satisfied, but began the funeral Mass, and the women read the responses with fervor. When the hymns came, Helga and I accompanied them, something that seemed new to this priest. The music lightened the air, somehow. At the appropriate time, Helga stood, took a step forward, and began to sing.

Igne divini radians amoris
corporis sexum superavit Agnes,
et super carnem potuere carnis
claustra pudicæ.

"Shining with the fire of divine love, Agnes overcame the gender of her body," I thought. "And the undefiled enclosures of the flesh prevailed over flesh."

The priest joined his voice to hers on the next verse.

Spiritum celsæ capiunt cohortes
candidum, cæli super astra tollunt;
iungitur Sponsi thalamis pudica
sponsa beatis.

"The heavenly host took up her brilliant white spirit," I thought. "And the heavens lifted it above the stars. The chaste bride is united to the blessed bride chambers of the Spouse."

Then, to my surprise, the Abbess and all her women sang. And they sang fiercely.

Virgo, nunc nostræ miserere sortis
et, tuum quisquis celebrat tropæum,
impetret sibi veniam reatus
atque salutem.

O Virgin, now have pity on our lot,
and, whoever celebrates your victory day,
let him earnestly pray for forgiveness of guilt
and salvation for himself.

The singing did not have a forgiving tone. I shivered. I hoped that the count would hang Baudoin, but true justice might better be served by turning him over to these women.

I glanced at Helga. She was looking up at the painting of Saint Agnes standing before the fire that was soon to take her, looking up in her turn at the heavens and salvation. My apprentice, the bordel brat, the rescued daughter, sang the last verses with tears streaming down her cheeks. My own eyes blurred watching her.

I blinked quickly to clear my vision, and glanced around the church. The young idlers had been silenced several times, and were now looking bored. There were some elderly women present who had the look of regulars, kneeling and lost in their own prayers.

Past them all, in the back, a lone man sat, hunched against the wall. He neither spoke nor moved during the service, not even to join in the responses. Our eyes met for a moment, but I continued looking around as if I hadn't noticed him.

Helga sat next to me, wiping her eyes.

"Blow your nose, girl," I whispered, giving her hand a squeeze.

She snuffled, but did as I asked. I noticed the Abbess looking at her curiously.

"Now, back to work," I whispered. "Do you mark the solitary man at the rear of the church?"

She nodded.

"When the service ends, watch him. If he comes to the

burial, stay with me. But if he leaves, follow and find out what you can."

The priest finished the office, then looked down at the coffin. And he spoke. "When Jesus had lifted up himself, and saw none but the woman, he said unto her, 'Woman, where are those thine accusers? Hath no man condemned thee?'"

He looked directly at the Abbess.

"She said, 'No man, Lord,'" said the Abbess.

"And Jesus said unto her, 'Neither do I condemn thee,'" continued the priest. "Go and sin no more."

He looked across at the young wastrels.

"He that is without sin among you, let him first cast a stone at her," he said. Then he raised his arms to include all of us. "I am the light of the world; he that followeth me shall not walk in darkness, but shall have the light of life."

The Mass ended, and the women gathered around the coffin to take La Rossa—no, Julie—to the graveyard at the rear of the church. The young men actually filed behind them respectfully.

The man at the rear disappeared out the front door. Helga nodded to me, then slipped out the side door. I slung my lute behind me and my baby in front and followed Julie to her final bed.

She was buried in consecrated ground, I was glad to see. As the grave-digger covered her up, the onlookers drifted away, their entertainment over. All who remained gathered at the grave: the ladies, the priest, myself, and one of the old women. When the prayers concluded, the ladies knelt and each placed their right hand on the dirt.

"Rest," whispered the Abbess. "At long last, rest."

They stood and began walking back to the bordel. The Abbess came up to me and pressed two coins into my hand.

"One for you, one for your daughter," she said. "Do not insult me by refusing it."

"I understand being paid to do what I do," I said.

"Where is your daughter?" she asked, looking around. "I wanted to thank her."

"Ran off to play with her friends," I said. "I am amazed I could get her to sit still in a church for that long."

"She cried for a woman she never knew," she said. "I saw her."

"She is a sympathetic soul, for all the trouble she gives me," I said. "I worry about that, to tell you the truth. She could be taken advantage of so easily."

"A dangerous age," agreed the Abbess. "A dangerous world. When I was her age, I was already working the streets."

"Not here," I said.

"No, not here. How did you know that?"

"Something in your way of speaking," I said. "Langue d'oc is not your first language, no matter how well you speak it."

"Nor is it yours," she pointed out.

"No," I said. "We came to Toulouse last winter."

"From where?"

"Somewhere else."

"I am from there as well," she said. "Small world."

"Where was La Rossa from?" I asked.

"Here, I think," she said. "She never told me her story. Why do you ask?"

"Curiosity," I said. "A professional habit. A jester seeks out interesting lives like a prospector for silver, and mines them for stories and songs."

"To hold them up to ridicule," said the Abbess.

"Only those who merit ridicule," I said. "Some to hold up for moral instruction. Some to celebrate. I find myself wondering about La Rossa more and more. Do you think I might ask your ladies about her?"

"You can't be serious," she said.

"Sometimes I can," I replied. "And if I don't preserve her story, who will?"

"A whore's story preserved," said the Abbess. "Does the world really want that?"

"I don't know, but I want that," I said. "We'll let the world make up its mind later."

"We are having a small meal in her honor," said the Abbess. "Come join us. I've become curious about her myself."

"I would be honored," I said.

CHAPTER 6

I walked with them back to the bordel, Portia riding my shoulders and looking at the colorful gowns of the women.

"Oooh, pretty," she said, pointing at them, and several of them turned at the tiny voice and smiled.

What a good little spy you will be, my daughter, I thought.

When we arrived, Carlos looked at me, then at the Abbess, a question in his eyes. She shook her head. He shrugged, and resumed his post at the door.

We went in, but rather than sitting in the front parlor, we continued on to the rear, where there was a large homey kitchen, dominated by a table in the center. The ladies took seats around it. The elderly woman who had accompanied us to the gravesite was there as well, and she began to distribute bowls of soup to each of us. I thanked her.

"What's the fool doing here?" asked the blonde who had provided Julie's name at the service.

"She's here at my invitation," said the Abbess. "She will explain herself."

"You're married to that Tan Pierre, aren't you?" asked another.

"I am," I said. "I'm Gile, by the way, and this little fool is Portia."

"Aude," said the blonde.

"Stéphanie."

"They call me La Roqua."

"La Bruna."

"La Navarra."

"Marquesia."

"How many of these names are real?" I asked.

"How real is any name?" asked the Abbess. "How real is yours?"

"As long as I answer to it, it is real enough for everyday purposes," I said.

"Then ours are as real as yours," she said. "We have heard them screamed in passion often enough."

"May I hold the baby?" asked Aude shyly.

I passed Portia over to her. She looked at the woman with interest, then reached for her hair.

"Careful, she'll pull it," I warned her.

"It's been pulled before," said Aude. "And by much larger people. Once, I was— Ow! Let go! Let go!"

"I warned you," I said. "Let go of her hair, Portia."

Portia watched Aude's reaction with what seemed to be scientific interest, then released her.

"Good grip for such a little one," muttered Aude, massaging her scalp.

"Give her to me," said La Navarra. "I know how to handle children."

Before I could say anything, Portia was in her lap. She reached for her hair, and La Navarra caught her hand.

"Pull anything on me, little girl, and I will pull something on you," she said pleasantly. "Do we understand each other?"

Portia looked at her, then withdrew her hand.

"See?" said La Navarra.

"Very maternal," I said.

"My specialty," said La Navarra, and the other women giggled. "Now, why are you here? Truly?"

"I wanted to know more about your late colleague," I said. "I would like to learn her story before she becomes completely forgotten."

"She wanted to be forgotten," said La Roqua. "Else, she'd have kept her name. She became La Rossa, and nothing but La Rossa."

"What was she trying to forget?" I asked.

"I can't remember," said La Roqua immediately. "Will you be asking us about our lives as well, or must we wait until we've all been hacked up like chickens?"

"Stop," Marquesia shuddered.

"And what will you do with these stories?" asked La Bruna. "Will you write them down? Make them into a book?"

"With illustrations!" giggled Stéphanie. "That will get us in good with the Church."

"What if I did?" I asked. "What if I put all of your stories into a book, and made two copies?"

"Two copies? Who would get the second?" asked the Abbess.

"You would," I said. "Your own histories, your lives preserved."

"Our clientele for the most part prefers some anonymity," said the Abbess.

"I will respect those confidences," I said. "Although a book like this might become a useful means of protection should you ever find the tides of fortune ebbing."

"Interesting idea," said the Abbess. "Ladies, shall we take her up on this proposition?"

"What good will a book do me?" sniffed Aude. "I cannot read."

"I could teach you," I said.

"What use is reading to a whore?" scoffed La Bruna.

"It will give you something interesting to do in bed for a change," I replied.

There was a bray of laughter from all of them except Marquesia, who looked down at the table.

"I would like my story to be written down," she said softly. "I would like to be remembered after I'm gone."

The others became quiet, with only the sounds of the servant washing the bowls and knives in a basin behind us.

"Her name was Julie," said Aude. "I never knew her last name. She grew up in Toulouse. She was already here when I came to this house."

"She had been a maid in a big *maison* once," said Stéphanie. "Her master went off on Crusade, but he never came back, so the house closed down and the servants forced to leave."

"No, he came back," said the Abbess. "But the house fell into ruin anyway. So she came here. I took one look at that hair and knew she would do well. And she did."

"Until yesterday," said Marquesia.

"Did she have anyone on the outside?" I asked. "A relative?"

"She stayed here, and went to Saint Agnes on Sundays," said La Navarra. "If she had any relatives, she never mentioned them. She may have been fleeing them; she may have been protecting them. Who knows? Not I."

"Anyone special among her clientele? A secret admirer? A lover on the side?"

"No man was special," said La Navarra. "She held all of them in contempt, and would do none for free."

"A true professional," I said.

"As are we all," said La Navarra. "It's the only way to survive. There is no room for love in this world."

"Yet there are many rooms for love in this house," I said. "And I doubt the walls are thick enough to keep everything private. Someone must have some idea."

"Of what?" asked La Roqua.

"Of why she was killed."

"Ask the man who killed her," said La Bruna. "That filthy Parisian, stabbing her while she slept and sleeping next to her corpse. Who knows what went on there?"

"Who had the room next to hers?" I asked.

"I did," said Marquesia.

"And I was on the other side," said La Roqua.

"And you heard nothing of how it happened?"

"I was occupied," she said dryly. "And then I fell into a well-earned sleep."

"I heard the usual sounds," said Marquesia. "She was a noisy one, full of shrieks and laughs. But there was nothing unusual. I heard them speaking gently to each other after, and then they slept."

"How did you know they both slept?"

"She snores," said Marquesia, and La Roqua nodded in agreement. "And I heard him say something in his sleep. But I heard nothing else in the night, and I am a light sleeper."

"You are not," protested Stéphanie. "You snore louder than any of us. I can hear you from the other side of the house."

"That isn't true," said Marquesia indignantly.

"What about the count's brother?" I asked. "Did you—?"

"The what?" interrupted the Abbess.

"Baudoin, the count's brother. What was he saying?"

"Why do you call him that?" she demanded.

"Did you not know? He claims to be the count's brother, the last child of the same mother, born after she fled Toulouse. Surely you had heard about this?"

They looked at each other, then at the Abbess.

"I swear I did not know this," she said. She was directing this at the other women. "I was told—"

Then she looked at me.

"Nothing," she said. "I was told nothing. We are outside the walls here. We do not receive the gossip of the town as readily as you might."

"If he is truly the count's brother, then he will never see the end of a rope," said La Navarra bitterly.

"What proof does he have?" asked the Abbess.

"They have sent a man to Paris to verify his claims," I said. "It will be several weeks before they know. Meanwhile, he is a guest of the count, locked in the dungeons below the Palace of Justice."

"A dungeon is one thing," said La Bruna. "A noose is another. He'll never hang. Not in Toulouse."

The servant finished doing the dishes and took the basin outside to empty it. I got a glimpse of a garden in back.

"Tell me more stories about La Rossa," I said. "Things that happened here."

They regaled me for the better part of an hour. Tales involving men, of course. Men entertained, men led astray, men besotted, men humiliated. All wanted her; none could stay with her for long.

"She never sought to become a rich man's mistress?" I asked. "I always thought that would be the ambition of such a woman."

"I would in a second," said La Roqua. "But she would not allow herself to be tied down."

"Not in that way, at least," said Marquesia, giggling.

"Did she ever bear anyone's child?"

"No," said the Abbess. "She saw to that."

"How old was she?"

"In truth? Older than she looked," said the Abbess. "I would say in her mid-thirties."

"No!" exclaimed La Roqua. "How did she manage to look like that? She must have sold her soul to the Devil."

"He's collected," said La Navarra.

There was an uncomfortable silence.

"Well, it is past noon," said the Abbess. "Our clientele will be arriving shortly, and no one ever made good money sitting in a kitchen. Come again, and we will tell you tales of the living. And please give our most affectionate regard to your husband."

"What's it like being married to a jester?" asked Aude. "Does he make you laugh all the time?"

"We laugh for a living," I said. "But live a normal life when we aren't entertaining. Most of the time I love him, and the rest of the time I contemplate braining him with a cooking pot."

"The married life," sighed La Navarra. "Never for me."

They rose and filed out of the kitchen, leaving me with the Abbess.

"Thank you for your hospitality," I said. "Especially considering how I barged in earlier."

"You are not the first wife to try that," she said. "Although you are the first to put Carlos on his back."

"You run a good house, from what I can see," I said. "How long have you been here?"

"Ten years now," she said. "If all goes well, I will be able to retire in a few more."

"And do what?" I asked.

"Rest," she sighed.

"Might we see your garden before I go?" I asked. "I got a glimpse out the back. Portia loves gardens."

"Certainly," she said. "Take a flower for her. And one for your other daughter."

"My thanks, Domina," I said.

She nodded and left the kitchen. I hoisted Portia onto my shoulders and opened the door.

I was expecting a simple kitchen garden such as we had in town, but we were no longer bound by city walls here. This one extended back a hundred yards, with vegetables, herbs, and flowers in equal proportions. The flowers were in bloom—lilies and pansies, daffodils and peonies. Off to the side, a trio of goats was grazing, fenced off from the rest. Next to them stood a small shed. A brick wall, six feet high, ran around the entire property. Tall enough to frustrate gawkers, but not to keep out a determined killer.

The servant was standing by the goat pen, a bucket in her hand. She turned to see who had come through the door, wiping her eyes with her sleeve as she did so, doing little to conceal that she had been crying.

"I am sorry," I said. "I did not mean to startle you. The Abbess said that we may pick two flowers."

She nodded, walking toward us. The bucket sloshed with goat's milk. She looked at Portia; then the tears began to flow again.

"I am sorry for your loss," I said. "Was she a favorite of yours?"

"We never should have come here," she whispered. "I told her so, but she never listened to sense. Not once. She—"

"Sylvie!" said the Abbess sharply from the door. "There are linens to be washed. Inside immediately."

"Oc, Domina," said the woman, her head bowed. She hastened inside.

The Abbess looked at me.

I held up two flowers. "They are lovely," I said. "Thank you."

She nodded, then stepped back from the door to let me pass.

As I did, I said softly, "If you are in trouble, I can help."

She started, but immediately regained her composure. "I've never asked for anyone's help in my life," she said.

"Then you shall never receive any," I said. "Enjoy a profitable day, Domina."

I walked through the house. There were already sounds of beds creaking from upstairs. We passed through the front parlor where Aude and La Navarra waved to Portia. She looked nervously at La Navarra, but waved back.

Half a day, I thought. They closed shop for half a day to mourn their sister. Did they carry on last night while Sylvie attended to her body? I didn't want to know.

Carlos gave a formal salute as we left, then resumed his post, his eyes half-closed. As I walked toward the street, a voice hailed me from the leper house.

"Lady Fool, entertain me for a moment," he cried.

I recognized the voice from the day before, but he must have been standing back from the window. I could not see him in the shadows.

"What would you like?" I called. "A song? Some juggling? I do not think that I could persuade Carlos to join me in another tumbling act."

Carlos grunted in agreement from the bordel.

"Or in witty repartee," I added.

"Juggle for me, lady," called the leper.

Clubs are better than balls when your audience is at a distance. I put Portia down, took five clubs from my pack, balanced one on top of my head and another on my right foot. I lifted my right leg straight out and began juggling the remaining three.

"Impressive," called the leper.

"It's nothing, really," I confessed. "Any jester can do three clubs in her sleep. The other two make for a pretty tableau.

But here's the real trick. I don't always get it right, so watch closely."

I took a breath, then simultaneously nodded my head and kicked up my outstretched leg. The other two clubs fell into the pattern, and I had five going now.

"Marvelous!" he cried.

I caught them and bowed to my unseen spectator.

"I would applaud, but it is painful," he said. "No, I will thank you properly."

"Good senhor, do not hurt yourself on my account," I begged him.

"No. I must pay you tribute."

There was a single muffled clap before I could say anything else.

"Please stop, senhor," I said. "I am here to bring you pleasure, not pain."

"That is the supposed goal of the ladies in the house behind you," he said. "I daresay you achieve it more often than they do."

"You are most gracious, senhor," I said. "That solitary clap honors me more than the applause of an entire tavern."

"If only I could see you perform in a tavern," he sighed. "I miss taverns—the taste of new beer, the camaraderie of drunks, the flirting of the maids. Especially the maids. Will you come back here?"

"It seems that I shall, senhor," I said. "I shall perform for you again. Shall I alert the house when I return?"

"No need," he said. "I rarely sleep. The view from this window is my entire world. I will know when you return."

"Until then, senhor," I said, bowing.

I gathered my clubs, then my daughter, and left. It occurred to me as I passed through the gate that I never learned his name.

I sorted out my thoughts on my walk home. The Abbess seemed genuinely caught off guard by the news that La Rossa's last night was with the count's brother. But she knew something about Baudoin.

Or was it La Rossa who knew something? If so, that secret was dead and buried with her. Unless . . .

Sylvie.

Never underestimate the servants. I may have been a duchess once, and a duke's daughter before that, but that was a lesson I knew long before the Fools' Guild brought it back in my training. The servants who hear all, who see all, who mop up the floors and change the sheets after, will have an intimate knowledge of every stain left behind.

Sylvie knew about La Rossa. And that garden was big, but it couldn't supply all the needs of that house. Which meant that someone had to go to the market each day.

I am a jester, and I am a woman. I like markets. I resolved to encounter Sylvie in the market while she made her purchases. Accidentally, of course.

I hadn't arranged with Helga where to meet once we had completed our respective tasks. The usual choices were home and the Yellow Dwarf. I chose the latter. Besides, the ale was good.

The regulars were there when I arrived, greeting me with the regular comments, which I would have regarded as flattering had they come from sober men. Portia waved to everyone, then screamed, "Papa!" at the top of her lungs. Only one man waved back at that, although several looked momentarily panicked. I put her down, and she ran to Theo, who picked her up and tossed her into the air, her head coming just short of striking the rafter.

"The only things that keep me from worrying when you do that is she's getting heavier and you're getting old and weak," I said as our child landed safely in his arms, laughing.

"These are compensating factors," he agreed. "Look who I ran into. And you'll never guess where."

There was Helga sitting by him, wolfing down some stew. She swallowed hastily.

"I found out who the man at the church was," she said. "I followed him through the town. He didn't look back once, so it was easy. He went all the way through and out the other side."

"Which gate?" I asked.

"The Porte Narbonnais," she said. "He went into the château. I couldn't really follow him there."

"But how did you find out who he was?" I asked.

"I watched from outside, and I saw him heading toward the Palace of Justice. And before he goes in, he stops to chat with one of the most disreputable characters in all of Toulouse."

"Really?" I exclaimed. "And who would that have been?"

"That would have been me," said Theo, bowing modestly. "Your mysterious man was none other than our Parisian visitor, Huc."

"Baudoin's man," I said. "But why was he at the funeral?"

"Don't know," he said. "Not yet. How did he behave?"

"He sat at the rear and tried not to be noticed. That's why I noticed him."

"Did he seem to be in mourning?"

"At first glance, I would have said so. But now, I am not sure. I wonder if he was investigating in behalf of his master?"

"Hah! I think that you have found the answer," said Theo. "It will be interesting to see what he discovers. He's a stranger here. We, at least, know the territory."

"We have been here only six months," I pointed out.

"But we are fools," he said.

"Well, there is that," I conceded. "Huzzah for us."

"So, how was the bordel?" he asked mischievously. "Make some new friends? Some new money?"

"I had a better time gossiping with the ladies there than I have on the highest levels of society," I replied.

"I myself go to such places only for the conversation," he said. "Any fresh insights into Baudoin?"

"They all think he did it," I said. "And they would happily tear him limb from limb if they had the opportunity."

"I know which limb they'll start with," chirped Helga.

I summarized what I had heard. He looked thoughtful when I was done.

"No struggle, no argument," he said. "He makes love for as long as he can, waits until she falls asleep, stabs her twice while she lies there, then falls asleep next to her. I have never heard of such a manner of killing. Those times when men have treated women so savagely, there was some rage or madness that came upon them. Those who were clever enough to kill them quietly would never be so obvious about it or so foolish as to remain at their side after. This smacks of neither rage nor cleverness. Which means either he is innocent, or he's a mild-mannered, stupid sort of murderer."

"And you come down on the side of innocence?" I asked.

"Let's just say that I am not certain of his guilt," he said. "You saw the gardens out back?"

"Yes. There was a wall around them, but not one that couldn't be scaled easily."

"So someone could have come in through the rear door," he mused. "But it was barred from the inside."

"Unless someone let the murderer in," I said. "And then rebarred it after he left."

"Or if someone in the house did it," he said. "Either way, one of those women may have been involved."

"A woman who walks barefoot makes the least noise," I pointed out.

"The Abbess would be the likeliest," he agreed. "So, the question becomes, who would want to set up Baudoin like that?"

"What did you find out about the Count of Foix?"

He waved Hugo over. Our tapster, beside being one of the treasured brewers of Toulouse, had been one of the Cathar society until a year ago, when he had been bested in a barroom debate by a Castilian priest who was passing through town accompanying the Bishop of Osma. We were not in Toulouse then, but Hugo had recounted the story enough times that we felt we had front row seats to a divine encounter in a coliseum, concluding with the priest being carried aloft by an angelic host upon his victory. Still, despite Hugo's conversion, he was loyal to his Cathar companions, holding friendship as a cardinal virtue to be valued over dogma.

"Na Gile, good day to you, and to you, my lovely Portia," he greeted us, fondly patting my girl on her head. "How is the ale today?"

"Ambrosia, as always, my good tapster," I said.

"Hugo, tell her what you told me about the Count of Foix," said Theo.

"Was he one of the Cathars?" I asked.

"Never openly," said Hugo. "But he supported them, no question. His wife and his sister are both heavily involved. They received the consolamentum last year in Fanjeaux."

"Was he present?"

"Of course," said Hugo. "He indulges his wife in everything. He owes her his freedom."

"How so?"

"She intervened when he was imprisoned by King Pedro during some dispute with Aragon over territory. It was kept fairly quiet, but the Cathars were involved in the negotiations."

"Did Raimon step into that as well?" asked Theo.

"Not that I heard," said Hugo. "But I am only a poor tapster, living off the leavings of the traveling gossip."

"What do his wife and sister do with the Cathars now?" I asked.

"They support them financially, host their meetings, usually just for the women," replied Hugo.

"And the count supports that as well?" I asked.

"He does," said Hugo.

"He does have an affinity for houses full of women," mused Theo dryly. "Thank you, friend Hugo, both for the gossip and the ale."

"I enjoy dispensing both," said Hugo. "Now, if you will excuse me. I see thirsty men in need of my ministrations."

He left us to digest his information.

"The Count of Foix is devoted to his wife," I said. "Yet he spends his waking hours pursuing other women."

"And not just for the thrill of the chase and seduction," said Theo. "He will take the easy way out and pay for them when he cannot have them otherwise. He is a veritable satyr."

"Which is the truth?" asked Helga. "A man cannot be in love with his wife while sleeping with every woman he sees. Can he?"

"Another paradoxical character," said Theo.

"Unless she has willingly released him from his marital duties," I said.

"Why would she do that?" asked Theo. "Why would any woman do that?"

"Because she has become one of the Perfect," I said. "Even among the Cathars, they are extreme in their devotion. And they regard coition—"

"As anathema," he finished. "So, if she has ascended to this higher state of being, leaving him to an unfulfilled marriage bed, then she may have assented to his quenching those fires in other pools."

"Perhaps in exchange for his supporting her religious efforts."

"A convenient arrangement," he said.

"But what does that have to do with Baudoin?" asked Helga.

"I don't know," confessed Theo. "But if Baudoin is innocent, then Foix must be involved. He picked the whore."

"Who picked the whorehouse?" I asked.

He sat up suddenly. "Damn," he muttered. "Damn, damn, damn. I hadn't thought it through all the way. It was a long way to go to get what could have been gotten much closer. That particular bordel was suggested by my good friend Sancho, who has since turned out to be much more devious than we knew."

"And he's the count's man," I said. "Did this scheme come from Raimon himself? Was he trying to destroy his brother? And if so, why?"

"If he is, then we should back away quickly and quietly and let things play out," said Theo. "It isn't the Guild's business, and this cat hasn't enough lives left to risk on mere curiosity."

"But what if Sancho is working against the count?" I asked. "What if there is some plot here, one involving both Sancho and the Count of Foix? That means two men in Raimon's inner circle could be dangers to him. And that makes it Guild business."

I watched as Theo took a long, slow swallow of ale, his eyes fixed on a point somewhere on the ceiling, his vision somewhere else entirely.

"Then may the First Fool protect us from harm," he decided. "We go after Foix."

"And Sancho?"

"I'd like to find out if he is beholden to Foix in some way," he said. "But not just yet. If we start looking into him now, he'll be on to us in no time. Dear God, what are we getting ourselves into, I wonder?"

"What about the bordel?" I asked. "There is more to be discovered there, I'll warrant."

"There was something," he said. "The Abbess was surprised when you said Baudoin was the count's brother?"

"She swore to the others that she didn't know," I said.

"Raimon Roger greeted Baudoin as the prodigal brother right in front of her," he said. "And Sancho said something about it as well. She had to have known."

"So disillusioning when a whore turns out to be a liar," sighed Helga. "Who will be left for me to look up to?"

"There is always Saint Agnes," I said.

"What is it with whores and Saint Agnes?" wondered Theo. "There were saints who actually started out as whores, yet every bordel I know worships this girl who died rather than become one. Why choose her for inspiration?"

"For the daughters," answered Helga. "It is too late for the mothers, but the daughters can still be saved, so long as they pray to Saint Agnes."

"That makes sense," said Theo. "But why not the sons?"

"Because they grow up to become the men who want the whores," said Helga. "Boys are stupid, useless creatures."

"Hear, hear," I said.

CHAPTER 7

It did not come as news to me that the women in my life, at least those capable of expressing themselves, regarded me, being the nearest representative of my sex, as a stupid, useless creature. I could only hope that Portia hadn't figured that out yet. There would be opportunity enough to disappoint my daughter when she was older. In the meantime, there was a plot to investigate that might exist only in my untrammeled imagination.

It would not do for us to pursue Raimon Roger right away, I thought. I had seen him at the Château Narbonnais that morning, engaging in the usual braggadocio with the count and the other members of that exclusive little wolf pack. I added my usual witty remarks, then left for the afternoon, only to be intercepted by Helga.

So, if we were to descend so soon upon the house that the Count of Foix maintained in town, it would no doubt raise his defenses. We had to find a more natural route to his inner life, to learn what lurked beneath the layers of lard and lechery shielding him.

It would help if he would hold a formal dinner. I knew for a fact that he liked to eat.

Or I could pursue his other vice and show up at one of his amorous adventures, lute in hand, ready to accompany his seductions with a randy melody. I just had to make sure that my own virtue would not be endangered now that every attempt at making love to my wife could be regarded by her as penance for sins unknown.

My own virtue. A recent reacquisition. Three years married, and in some respects, I was still getting used to it after so many years of foolery and fooling around. To say no to a prime piece of female flesh like the Abbess would have been astonishing to the old Theo. The Theo who still lay beneath my own motleyed surface, conjuring up visions of her jumping into bed with me.

Feet first, of course.

I remonstrated sternly with the old Theo and bade him remember all the disasters that littered the landscape of my lusty travels, and returned to my strategizing. The old Theo muttered something about my manhood being locked in a box in my wife's possession, then subsided.

The four of us made the rounds of the taverns that afternoon, doing well with the pilgrim traffic that was resting up for the long walk to Compostela. No sign of the Count of Foix. We ran into Pelardit at the Red Crow and joined him for some wine after he had finished performing for several members of the night watch who were getting their last drinks in before starting on their patrolling.

"Seen the Count of Foix on your tour today?" I asked him.

He shook his head.

"Know where he's likely to be found?"

He batted his eyes, his mouth pursed, and suddenly became something flirtatious and feminine. Then he swelled up his cheeks and became Raimon Roger, huffing and puffing in pursuit. He switched rapidly between the two, enacting the whole chase and capture while never leaving his seat. Then he did something unmistakably lewd with his fingers.

"Any specific target that you know of?" I asked, laughing.

His arms encompassed the entire world and all the women that lived on it.

"That should narrow it down," said Claudia.

He raised an eyebrow, his way of asking why we asked. I gave him a brief explanation. He looked at me skeptically, then gripped the ends of an imaginary rope with his hands and pulled them apart, straining with the effort.

"All right, it is a stretch," I conceded. "But worth investigating."

He looped the imaginary rope around his neck and lifted it, his head sagging to one side, his tongue lolling out grotesquely.

"Oh, someone will swing for it," I said. "But it won't be us, have no fears on that account."

He wagged his forefinger at all of us.

"We'll be careful," promised Claudia.

The next morning, I appeared bright and early at the Château Narbonnais, singing in the hall before I even entered the Grande Chambre to let Count Raimon know that I was there. He was eating his morning meal alone.

"You're here a lot lately," he observed.

"You've needed me a lot lately," I said, grabbing a chair and joining him.

"That's Raimon Roger's chair," he said.

"Then it should have no difficulty supporting my weight," I said, grabbing a muffin. "It may even be grateful for the respite."

"You have empathy even for inanimate objects," he said. "Except for muffins."

"To truly know someone, you must get at their essence," I said, my mouth full. "This is the only way to get at the essence of a muffin. How are you today?"

"Bored."

"I shall cure you of that."

"By eating in front of me? I have seen that before. In fact, I see that more than I see you perform."

"Fuel for the fool," I said. "Have I told you the tale of the fox who fell in love with the hen?"

"Will this be one of those tiresome fables with a hidden agenda?" he asked.

"Well, yes," I confessed.

"Then refrain," he said. "Play me something without words. I grow weary of words."

I touched a finger to my lips, swallowed the remainder of my muffin, then picked up my lute.

For all his quirks and cruelties, this was a count who had a genuine appreciation for music. I could see the tension slip away, his eyes relax, his ever-present guard drop. He became human once again, alive and vulnerable.

If I ever found it necessary to kill him, it would be while playing my lute. I hoped that day would never come.

I quickly shoved that thought deep into the midden of my mind and played on, my expression smooth and bland. When I reached the end, he took a deep breath and let it out slowly.

"I consider myself entertained," he said, smiling for the first time that morning.

It vanished as he heard his friends down the hall. They entered the room in mid-squabble.

"Well, how was I to know you were going after her?" protested Sabran. "You told me you were going after her Friday night. I assumed that by now you had already tired of her and that she was ripe for the picking by a real man."

"My plans changed," growled Foix. "You, of all people, should know that if I had had her Friday, I would have been telling you about it Saturday morning."

"Perhaps he thought you might have been suffering from a bout of discretion," laughed Comminges.

"After knowing him for how many years?" scoffed Raimon. "What happened?"

"This interloper, this blunderer, this fool—"

"Excuse me?" I interjected.

"Not you, Fool, the other fool, the real fool," said Foix.

"Excuse me again?"

"Shut up and let's hear the story," said Raimon.

"Right," said Foix. "He knew that I had been on a sacred quest to deflower the daughter of the ostler who lives by the Porte Montgalhart. I had been courting her for days, learning her father's daily routine, ascertaining the most propitious moment for my foray. And just when I had her half-naked and panting on my knee, in walks this lecherous parasite, and off scampers the wench, screaming to wake the dead."

"We both had to make haste," said Sabran. "The father's a brute, with no respect for one's rank."

"And off we ran, stopping only to collect Bernard in case any unjustified accusations came our way."

"So I am to say that you were with me?" asked Comminges.

"Should the ostler come seeking redress, yes," said Foix.

"Just pay him off, you dolt," said Comminges. "Why raise such a commotion over one cheap slattern of a daughter?"

"Fool, no thoughts on all of this?" asked Raimon.

"I am still trying to master the idea of the Count of Foix

running," I said. "It is beyond even my prodigious powers of imagination."

"I can run fast enough when there is a pretty maid to be chased," protested Foix indignantly.

"Or when there is an angry father to elude," added Sabran. "I am the witness to that. Any less fleet of foot, and he would have had a fresh brand on his buttock."

"I would not have been able to sit for a month," said Foix. "Speaking of which, Fool?"

"Senhor?"

"My chair."

"What about it, senhor?"

"You are in it."

"Just keeping it warm for you," I said, standing and holding it for him. "Though to warm it properly would be the work of several men."

"Or one ostler's daughter," he sighed, plopping his bulk onto the seat, which shuddered but held under the onslaught. "That piece will be under lock and key for a goodly time."

"She wasn't that good, truth be known," said Comminges.

Foix and Sabran looked at him in astonishment.

"When?" asked Foix.

"This morning," said Comminges smugly. "I saw the ostler pursuing the two of you. I thought, aha, his daughter is alone, unguarded and no doubt disappointed. I consoled her for her loss."

"You are no friend of mine," growled Foix.

"Neither is she, anymore," said Comminges. "But as I said, no great loss."

"There you have it," said Foix. "I do all of the hard work, the research, the reconnoitering, and just when I am about to achieve success, in swoop the raveners to pick up my gleanings. You are both parasites."

He grabbed the last two muffins and popped one into his mouth to assuage his sorrow.

"You usually have more of these, don't you?" he asked Raimon.

"You were late this morning," I said. "I was forced not only to occupy your chair, but your role."

"You let him eat my muffins?" wailed Foix, crumbs spewing from his mouth.

"My château, my muffins," said Raimon. "One of the benefits of being count around here."

"By the Holy Mother, Fool, if you come between me and a muffin again, there will be a reckoning," said Foix.

"Tell you what," I said. "I shall race you for the last one."

"No contest there," said Sabran.

Raimon Roger rose to his feet and placed the muffin on the table.

"I accept your challenge," he said. "Once around this room, and to the victor belongs the muffin."

"And the penalty?" asked the count.

"If I lose, I shall perform at your next dinner gratis," I said.

"Hardly a penalty," said Comminges. "Just try getting him to open his house and purse for the rest of us."

"That is not so!" protested Foix. "Why, I had a dinner party only—"

He stopped and thought, then looked sheepish.

"It has been some time," he admitted. "Very well. I shall have you all over, and the fool will entertain."

"And your penalty, senhor?" I asked.

"What would be the equivalent of a free performance, I wonder?"

"I have it," said Raimon. "His penalty will be to run ten more laps around this room in front of all of us."

"Done," I said.

We took positions at the head of the table.

"At your command, Dominus," I said.

"Go!" shouted Raimon.

To my surprise, Foix took off at a fox's pace. The others might have anticipated me to have an easy victory over the fat man, but no one expected the quick start. And, for all my bravado, running was no longer my forte, since I had injured my leg a few years back.

Foix also knew the terrain. It was a large room, but it was littered with trestles and chairs thrust against the walls. With the lead he had, he was able to grab them as he passed and send them crashing into my path. The sprint for him became a steeplechase for me, and as we passed the last corner, he had increased his margin by a good five steps.

Sabran and Comminges cheered him on, while the count merely watched, a slight smile on his lips. Foix bounded toward the table, one hand outstretched to snatch his prize. But as he was about to reach it, Comminges leaned forward, grabbed the muffin, and popped it into his own mouth. Foix sprawled against the table, howling in chagrin, and I crashed into him a second later.

"You never learn, do you?" said Comminges with his mouth full.

The count and Sabran laughed uproariously, and in moments, we had all joined them, Foix and I collapsing onto the floor in an exhausted embrace.

"I am at your mercy, my good master," I gasped. "How is tomorrow night?"

"Should be enough time," he said, still chuckling.

He stood, dusted himself off, and bowed to the others.

"My friends, will you do me the honor of joining me for dinner tomorrow evening?"

"Of course," said the count, and the other two nodded.

The count clapped his hands, and Anselm appeared immediately. "To the kitchen, and bring up an entire platter of muffins for my friend, Raimon Roger."

The servant bowed and left.

"With your leave, Dominus," I said. "I must go lick my wounds."

"Can't bear the sight of me eating more muffins, eh?" taunted Foix.

"Oh, I have grown used to that, senhor," I said. "To truly astonish me, you would have to refuse one."

"You may go, Fool," said the count. "Thank you for the diversion."

I bowed, and left.

I did not leave the grounds of the château immediately, but directed my steps instead to the Palace of Justice.

Baudoin was sitting in a corner of his cell, his hands out in prayer. I waited until he was done.

"Any results?" I asked.

"You are here," he said.

"Your night with La Rossa," I said.

"Yes?"

"Tell me more about it."

"A great deal of it is . . . intimate," he said.

"Keep the retelling to the conversation," I said.

"A great deal of that was obscene."

I sighed.

"Did she ask you any questions about yourself?" I asked.

"Yes," he said. "Much of it general. Where are you from, how was your journey, how long did it take, was the weather good?"

"Did she know who you purport to be?"

"I see you have gone from pretend to purport," he observed. "That's an improvement."

"You are a purporter to the throne," I said. "Answer my question."

"She said nothing that indicated she knew," he said. "But she did ask me about my time in Paris."

"Specifically?"

"What I did, who I knew," he said. "Goings-on at court, gossip of the high and mighty, that sort of thing."

"Anything about your being brother to the count?"

"No," he said. "In fact, nothing at all about my purpose here. Only about Paris."

I thought about that for a moment.

"If you are the son of Constance, and Constance was the sister of the late King Louis, then that makes you first cousin to King Phillippe Auguste," I said.

"Yes," he said. "When I was born, I was actually third or fourth in line for the throne of France, according to my mother."

"Are you and your cousin close?"

"It has been up and down," he said. "A great deal of down lately."

"Which is why you came to Toulouse," I said. "To try your luck with your other family."

"So far, it's worked like a charm," he sighed.

"Is there anything that you told La Rossa that you should not have told her?" I asked. "Anything, if overheard, that would have made her a threat?"

"All I told her was Parisian court gossip," he said.

"Was she impressed?"

"She kept asking for more. I had to start inventing things, just to keep the conversation going. Have you discovered anything?"

"Where are you right now?"

"In a dungeon, awaiting the noose."

"Then you have your answer," I said. I started down the corridor to the steps.

"Is there any hope?" he called after me.

"If you are truly innocent, then you will go to Heaven when they hang you," I said. "That's more than most of us can say."

I visited with the prisoners on the higher level of dungeons, telling some jokes and singing a few songs. Afterwards, I climbed back into daylight. Huc was coming to the palace.

"Going to see your master?" I asked.

"I am," he said. "Have you just been to see him?"

"I have," I replied.

He looked around so ostentatiously to see if anyone was listening to us that he probably drew the attention of the guards on the Grand Tower; then he leaned forward and whispered, "How goes your investigation?"

"Fine," I said in a normal voice. "How goes yours?"

"Mine?" he said in surprise.

"You were at the funeral of La Rossa yesterday," I said. "My wife and daughter saw you there."

"I did not know that they knew me," he said. "Yes. I was curious to see who else would appear there."

"Any surprises?"

"No," he said. "Gawkers and gossips, as far as I could tell."

"Well, let me know if you turn up anything useful," I said.

"I will," he said. "And thank you for your efforts."

"No effort at all," I said. "I am a gawker and gossip, too. I'd be asking questions anyway."

I passed through the gates to the city, then paused.

"What do you want, Sancho?"

He emerged from the shadows to my right. "You were visiting the prisoner," he said accusingly.

"It's Tuesday," I said. "I normally visit the prisoners on Tuesdays. Which did you have in mind?"

"Baudoin."

"Yes," I said. "So what?"

"You told me you wouldn't be investigating this incident," he said.

"There is nothing to investigate," I said. "How can I investigate something that isn't there?"

"Because that is precisely the sort of thing you would do," he said.

"And yet I spent yesterday lounging around my house, as you very well know since you had two of your men watching it, and I spent this morning entertaining the count and visiting prisoners. Hardly an efficient way of pursuing an investigation, wouldn't you say?"

"You're up to something," he said. "I am certain of it."

"If you are certain, then I know that nothing will dissuade you. But why, if I may ask, are you so concerned, good Sancho? Especially if there is nothing to look for?"

"Because you stir things up," he said. "The water is nice and clear and drinkable, and then you shove your stick into the muck at the bottom and it all becomes murky and confused and tastes of death and decay."

"Sancho, you are a poet," I said in surprise. "I had no idea."

"I just want things to settle back to the bottom so I can get on with my life," he said. "It's wearying worrying about you."

"I am touched that you care, my friend," I said. "But do not fret. I assure you that I will do no harm. And as for disturbing the peace, that's what a jester does for a living. Now,

I am off to have an ale. I will be at the Yellow Dwarf, so tell your men they can have the best view of me through the east window."

"Since you know they are there, I'll tell them to have a drink inside the damn place," he said.

"Hugo will be glad of the business," I said. "In fact, I should incur more suspicion and demand a commission for each watcher I draw into the place."

"Go on," he said. "I am going to have a nap."

"Dream of anything but me, my friend," I called as we parted.

My family was already there when I arrived, along with Pelardit, who was demonstrating some sleight of hand involving colored kerchiefs to Helga.

"So that's how it's done," I said as I slid onto the bench next to my wife.

Pelardit indicated to Helga to give it a try. She put her hands under the table for a moment, setting things up, then folded them on top of the table again.

"I am going to cry," she announced, and sure enough, a single tear trickled down her right cheek. She snuffled loudly, then plucked a blue kerchief from her sleeve and dabbed at the tear liked she was blotting up the sea. When she brought the kerchief down, it had changed to green. She looked at it in bewilderment, held it up for inspection, then crumpled it up in her right hand. She pulled one green corner out through her fist, then grabbed it with her left and removed it with a flourish. The kerchief was now yellow.

There was applause from Hugo from the other end of the room. Helga bowed grandly.

"Not bad," I said.

Pelardit sighed and tapped Helga's sleeve, where the green kerchief was still visible.

"Damn," she muttered, deflating visibly.

Pelardit looked at her sternly, then directed her to do it again.

"It's coming along, Apprentice," I said reassuringly. "It took me weeks to get that one down."

"Pelardit makes it look so easy," she said.

"And you will as well," said Claudia. "What impresses me is how easily you cry on cue."

Pelardit suddenly looked grief-stricken, his face in agony. In seconds, tears were rolling down his cheeks. This, of course, aroused our competitive instincts. Moments later, all four of us were a group portrait of woe.

"Will you stop that?" complained Hugo. "People will think it's my cooking."

"Tears of joy over the fineness of today's ale, my good tapster," I called, wiping my eyes. "Now, to business. We have an engagement tomorrow night."

"Where?" asked Claudia.

"The house of the Count of Foix. He's having a dinner, and I am to provide the entertainment."

"Well, for one whose purse has·been sewn shut with threads of iron, it will be interesting to see how much he pays us," said Claudia.

"I can tell you that in advance," I said. "Nothing."

Pelardit winced.

"You volunteered our services?" exclaimed Claudia.

"I lost a wager," I said, and I told them of my morning race.

"You lost to him on purpose just to get inside his house," said Claudia accusingly.

"Yes," I said.

Pelardit heaved a sigh of exasperation.

"Pelardit, if you would rather perform somewhere for money, that would be fine," I said. "I would understand entirely. However, we would, at least, be fed, and I suspect that a man of Foix's stature, or anyway a man of Foix's circumference, provides a decent table on those occasions when he is forced to fend for himself."

Pelardit drummed his fingers on the table, then shrugged his acquiescence.

"Thank you," I said.

"I notice that you are not offering me the same choice," said Claudia.

"I am not married to Pelardit," I said.

Pelardit gave a look of relief and offered a quick prayer of gratitude to the Heavens.

"I am a jester in full," she said. "You should at least do me the courtesy of asking."

"Want to come?" I asked. "Free food."

She drummed her fingers on the table, then shrugged her acquiescence in perfect copy of Pelardit.

"Thank you," I said. "I particularly need you to worm what you can out of his wife. The Perfect woman."

"There is no such thing," said Claudia.

"I disagree," I said, patting her hand.

"Oh, stop," she muttered. "I am too old to blush."

"Anything new on your investigation?" I asked.

"I waited to see what market Sylvie frequents," she said.

"Sylvie?"

"The maid at the bordel," she explained. "I didn't want to run into her accidentally yet, so I just followed her. I will see if I can get her talking."

"All right," I said. "Here's something. I spoke to Baudoin this morning. I wanted more details about his night with La Rossa."

"Perverse of you, dear husband. Don't you hear enough of that bragging from the count's coterie?"

"Too much," I said. "But I was intrigued by the nature of La Rossa's pillow talk."

"Sweet nothings? Insincere praise and odious comparisons?"

"More like grilling on the goings-on at the Parisian court."

"Hah!" said Claudia. "Either she's a romantic, or she's a spy."

"Spy," said Helga. "There are no romantics in bordels."

"Not necessarily a spy herself," I said. "But definitely working on Baudoin for information. The question is, for whom was she working? And who is that person working for that she would be working for someone by working on Baudoin? Wait a second before answering, because I think I've just confused myself."

"Let's say she was working for the Count of Foix," proposed Claudia. "He wants to know about goings-on at the Parisian court. Why? And if that's what he wants, why doesn't he want to know more about Baudoin himself?"

"Because he already knows about Baudoin's identity, whichever one is true," I said. "Unless he also suspects Baudoin of being a spy for the French court."

"But why would Foix be the one to set this up? You would think that would come directly from the count, or if not him, Comminges."

"Maybe the count doesn't want to show any direct involvement in someone who may actually be his true brother," I said. "But he's willing to let the flunkies take care of it for him. Like Foix and Sancho."

"And you," said Helga.

"I am no flunky," I protested.

"Sometimes you are," said Helga. "Sometimes a jester has to be. That's what they taught us at the Guild."

"Very well. I am a flunky. But that doesn't mean you should call me one."

"And jesters tell the truth," said Helga. "Especially when it's unpleasant. They taught us that, too."

"They should have given me an apprentice who was not such a good student," I said.

"I heard that you asked for me in particular," she said.

"On the contrary," I said. "You were foisted upon me as penance for my sins."

"Then I shall be with you for a long time," she said. "Here is my question: What sin am I being punished for that they should have assigned me to you?"

"Is this because she's a fool in training, or because she's a twelve-year-old girl?" I asked Claudia.

"The two are so similar, it's difficult to know where one ends and the other begins," said Claudia. "Keep jabbing, girl. You are doing fine."

"Right," I said. "Now, I feel like singing something Castilian."

"What fit brought that on?" asked Claudia.

"The arrival of two of Sancho's men," I said, grabbing my lute.

I strolled over to their table, strumming away, and launched into a ballad that would have made the local women blush if they had understood the language. Except for my wife, but she already knew the song. In fact, she had taught it to me.

The two men, clearly soldiers but in civilian garb, pretended to ignore me, which is how I knew they were watching me in the first place, but the song got to them after a verse, and they started chuckling. By the end, they were joining in on the choruses, doing quite passably with the harmonies.

"Go to, you rogue," said one when we had finished. "We're supposed to be watching you."

"Then watch me," I said. "In fact, I insist. A jester craves attention, so having a full-time audience such as yourselves is a golden opportunity, and I thank you for it. Will you be seeing Sancho soon?"

"When our relief gets here," he said. "Might as well tell you, since you keep spotting us."

"Would it help if I gave you my schedule in advance?" I asked.

"Do you ever know where you're going from moment to moment?"

"Not usually."

"Then no thanks," he said. "We'll do it the old-fashioned way."

"Right then," I said. "Best of luck to you. We'll be at the dinner at the Count of Foix's maison tomorrow night. Sancho probably knows that already, but you could bring that tidbit to him just to show you're on the job."

"Thank you," he said. "Would you like us to give you a head start, just to make it fun?"

"Very sporting of you," I said. "Let me say good-bye to my wife."

I rejoined my fellow fools.

"Don't look, but I suspect that I'm being followed," I said.

"You think?" said Helga.

I kissed Claudia on the mouth, Portia on the nose, Helga on the cheek, and stopped myself just in the nick of time from kissing Pelardit. He pouted in disappointment. I waved to my two watchers, and they waved back as I left the tavern.

They didn't follow me, but I quickly noted their two replacements who were waiting for me to emerge so they could take up the task. I walked for two blocks just to give them a fair chance.

Then I lost them.

CHAPTER 8

The Count of Foix. The Abbess. La Rossa. Sancho.

All with their secrets. What they knew, what they wanted to know, whom they worked for. One, at least, had already taken her secrets where no one would ever find them. Well, no one except for that bloodhound who called herself my wife. Even the grave might prove no barrier to her curiosity.

It made sense to leave the women to the woman. I considered the men.

Sancho concerned me more and more. He was obviously afraid that I was on the verge of some unpleasant discovery, in which case he was giving me too much credit. The constant surveillance was hampering my abilities. Even now, sitting on the rooftop that I had climbed to avoid his men, I sensed the many sets of eyes this spider had deployed in my direction. My escape was only temporary.

And the increase in his fear served only to increase my apprehension at the scope of the threat that I might uncover.

If he was working against Count Raimon, then whom was he working for? What could have corrupted this man? A week ago, I would have said nothing. Sancho was what he seemed to be: a simple, stolid soldier.

Well, mercenary. But one who honored his commitments to his master. Would he actually gamble on a betrayal this—

Gamble. Of course he would. This was a man who would hazard a month's salary on a single throw of the dice. I had seen it. No different from any other mercenary, quartered in a strange city far from home with too much peace on his hands. I have seen more than one incorruptible soul, even one immune to the pleasures of flesh and drink, pick up a pair of dice and sink into that particular pit, never to reemerge.

If Sancho was such a man, then it would be useful to know who held his debts.

I peered over the edge of the rooftop. Sancho's men were trudging back toward the Château Narbonnais, no doubt dreading the tongue-lashing they would receive for losing me. I scanned the area for others, saw none, and dropped lightly into the alley, frightening a small boy who was playing with a pile of sticks.

"I was on the roof," I explained.

"Why?" he asked.

"Excellent question," I said. "I couldn't think of a good reason to be there either, so I came back down."

"Oh," he said.

I pulled a piece of candy out of my pouch. "It's what fools do," I said, holding it out to him.

"Oh," he said, taking it.

He went back to his work. I went back to mine.

The Toulousan dicemakers had their own guild, something they maintained to put a patina of propriety on a depraved profession. There was no guildhall. As far as I could tell, the leadership passed from man to man on an irregular basis and without election. I suspected that this was done by rolls of the dice at their occasional meetings at a tavern called the Knuckles in the Comminges quarter.

The current head of the guild was named Antonio, whose shop was around the corner from the tavern. I was hoping he would be at the Knuckles, where the drink might loosen his tongue, but he was a craftsman who took his working hours seriously. When I came in, he was bent over a plane, meticulously smoothing the surface of a single wooden cube, then holding it against a perfect stone one to compare. I waited until he had it to his liking, then cleared my throat.

"Ah, Tan Pierre," he said, looking up and smiling. "Welcome to my humble shop."

"May I see?" I asked, holding out my hand.

He tossed it to me, and I held it up to the sun. Each corner was perfect. Each surface was as smooth as water in a silver chalice.

"It's magnificent," I said. "And then you will dab it with black spots, and it will become the very decider of someone's life. I see now that the difference between a thing of geometric beauty and an instrument of seduction are the spots."

"Do you approach everything in life this philosophically?" he asked, taking it back and placing it in a box of similar blank cubes awaiting their transformation.

"Always seeking the truth," I said. "That's what a fool does."

"Does it pay well?" he asked.

"The truth is priceless," I said. "Which means that no one can afford to hear it. No, it doesn't pay well at all. Does dice-making pay well?"

"The demand is constant," he said. "They are much desired, and easily lost."

"Like women," I said.

"Only you can't put a woman in your pouch and travel with her," he said.

"The moment God creates one, I shall be on her doorstep with a bouquet and a ring," I said.

"Would you like to see my wares, good Fool?"

"Actually, I have a pair already," I said.

"Let me see," he said.

I pulled them out of the recesses of my pouch and handed them to him. He hefted each in his hand, then held them up to the light and inspected each corner critically.

"Better not let the baile catch you with those," he said, tossing them back to me.

"I'm not a gambling man," I said.

"I can see that," he replied. "A gambling man would have honest dice. Why are you here?"

"Information," I said.

"Why?"

"I am on a mission of mercy," I said. "Mercy to a mercenary, of all things, but he is a friend, and I am hoping to bail him out of trouble before things get any worse."

"He is a gambler."

"He only thinks he is," I said. "What he really is is a man of considerable bad luck. I suspect that he has stumbled into a game where the dice were like mine. I seek to retire his debt before it becomes a threat to his position, and I hope to accomplish this with some discretion."

"Using those?" he asked, pointing to my dice.

"Hopefully, the offer of money will be enough," I said. "But I have these as a secondary line of attack."

"A very Christian thing to do," he said. "However, as the head of the Dicemakers' Guild, I cannot sanction the disruption of a game by a dishonest set of dice, no matter how worthy the motives are."

"The game has already been disrupted, if my suspicions are correct," I pointed out. "I would be restoring balance to a loaded world."

"Who is this soldier of misfortune?" he asked.

"Sancho of Castile," I said. "A good man at heart."

He sat at his table, thinking. Then he took the die he had just finished, shook it in his fist, and rolled it. It bounced several times, banged off the plane, and came to rest. He looked at it, then back up at me.

"Very well," he said. "From what I have heard, your friend fell into a game run by a man named Higini, who works by day in the stables in Saint Cyprien."

"I know those stables," I said. "Thank you. Did that die determine your decision to help me?"

"Of course."

"But there aren't any spots on it yet," I said. "It's blank."

He smiled. "Only to you," he said.

I crossed the Daurade Bridge to the neighborhood of Saint Cyprien. We had lived there when we first came to town, the rents being cheaper outside the protection of the city walls. The area was notable mostly for its cemetery and for the barracks for the count's mercenaries, but many of the city-dwellers stabled their horses there. I decided to pay a quick visit to Zeus, my own recalcitrant beast.

He had been imposed upon me by Brother Dennis, the ostler for the Fools' Guild, when I needed to travel in disguise as a merchant for a particular mission. He was a vicious, petulant, violent, and sometimes uncontrollable animal, but he was fast and strong, and there were occasions when I needed him to be both. Nevertheless, he was the terror of the stable boys—indeed, of any rational human being. The only one that he tolerated was me. The only one that he truly adored was Portia, who returned his love threefold. The same horse that could throw an unwary rider twenty feet through the air or put a well-placed hoof through a steel visor would walk along as gently as a lamb when my daughter sat on his back, embracing his neck and tugging on his mane.

I bought a bunch of carrots and stopped by the stables.

One of the stable boys saw me and waved. "Have you come to make sacrifice to the great god Zeus?" he called.

"I am on that holy pilgrimage," I said, holding up the carrots. "I hope that I am deemed worthy."

"Approach the holy stall with humility and gifts, and he will receive you," he said. "Will you be riding him? He could use the workout. He has a lot of pent-up energy today."

"That is precisely when I do not want to ride him," I said.

"Please," he begged me. "We could use a laugh."

Well, that was an appeal I could not possibly refuse. One of the perils of being a jester: One is expected to be entertaining anytime and anywhere. If I couldn't handle that request, then I had no business being in the business.

"Follow me at a safe distance," I said, "and send my body back to my wife when it's all over."

I passed the row of stalls as their inmates watched with interest, each hoping a carrot would land in the straw at their feet. From the shadows of the last stall, my shaggy gray steed cast a malign eye in my direction.

"Feeling cooped up and sorry for ourselves, are we?" I chirped. "Let me comfort you with carrots."

I dangled the bunch invitingly at the edge of the stall. A moment later, the gate shivered under the impact of Zeus's body hitting it. I stepped back in time to avoid being horse food. Two of the carrots were less fortunate.

"Two more once I've saddled you," I said. "The rest when we're done with our ride."

He looked back and forth from me to the remaining carrots. I hung them on a hook on the opposite wall where he could see them, then took his saddle from its shelf over the stall. I took a deep breath, then slid quickly through the gate to his side.

The side of a vicious horse is the safest place to be, with the exception of nowhere near him. Equidistant between kicking and biting, so all he can do is try to crush you against the wall. Which he did.

"No saddle, no carrots," I reminded him once I was able to inhale again.

Having made his point, he settled down, and I was able to get the saddle in place and cinch it firmly. I vaulted over the gate before he could bring his teeth into play, and gave him two more carrots.

"As you can see, I am a man of my word," I said. "Now, let's put on a show for the stable boys."

I stuffed the rest of the carrots into my pouch and grabbed his reins. When I opened the gates, the stable boys, who had been watching from a safe distance, scattered. I led Zeus out to the field where a few other horses were being exercised. Even they stopped when they saw Zeus.

"Any last words?" one of the riders called.

I thumped my chest in salute, then climbed up.

He had this nasty habit of lurching forward before I could get my other foot into the stirrup. I pulled back hard on the reins before he could launch into a full gallop, and managed to locate the stirrup with my free foot as it swung wildly. He reared, and I gripped hard with my knees until he came down again. I secured my foot, then leaned forward.

"Is that all you've got?" I whispered.

The next thing I knew, we were at the other end of the field. I prepared myself for the inevitable leap over the fence, but he stopped abruptly, nearly catapulting me over his withers. I thudded into his neck instead, jarring my teeth together.

"That was new," I muttered. "Good one. Now, let's see how fast—"

He was off again, veering so perilously close to the fence that I feared for my leggings. And my leg. I urged him away, and he made the turn without colliding with anything and continued on. I got a brief glimpse of the grooms watching from the other side of the fence, coins changing hands. Then I was off to the races again.

We made five more laps before he deigned to be reined in again. I wasn't aware that I had been screaming until I ran out of the wind needed to sustain it. He was barely breathing hard. I had sweated through my motley, and didn't even want to know the condition of my whiteface at this point. When I finally brought him to a halt by the stables, the collected group applauded. I dismounted and signaled to the stable boy who had first greeted me.

"Enough entertainment for one day, I hope," I said, handing him the reins. "Oh. Wait."

I took the rest of the carrots, gave one to Zeus and the rest to the boy.

"Make sure he gets all of them, and a bucket of water to cool him down," I said, tossing the boy a penny.

"Would you like one for yourself?" he asked. "You smell worse than he does right now."

"Get on with you," I growled.

One of the exercise riders, a wiry young man with a nose that had been broken more than once, came up to me and shook my hand heartily. "Thank you," he said.

"For the entertainment?" I asked.

"That, and for making me enough money to last a month," he said. "I won the pool."

"And what was the subject of this wager?"

"How long you would stay on," he said. "I took the position that you would not be unhorsed at all."

"I am not sure I would have bet on that outcome myself," I said.

"I've seen you ride him before," he said. "You're quite the horseman."

"It helps that I had training as an acrobat," I said. "When I was your age, I could have ridden him standing on his back, playing my lute, and singing a chivalrous song."

"We could set that up as a bet," he said, brightening.

"The key phrase in that brag was 'when I was your age,'" I pointed out. "That was a long time ago."

"Then we should come up with a challenge more suitable to your declining years," he declared.

"My years and I decline your kind offer, thank you," I said. "Do you often set up these strange betting opportunities?"

"I have bet on horses, donkeys, ducks, turtles, and cockroaches," he said. "I have bet on twigs floating down the Garonne, how many monks will fall asleep during a sermon, and whether or not a man will swing after Assizes. If I had been on the Ark with Noah, I would have made my fortune off his three sons betting on which day we would have found land."

"Surely that was God's decision, not a random date," I said.

"I believe that God is a gambler," he said. "What else can explain the randomness of our fates but the vicissitudes of chance?"

"You have thought about this deeply," I said. "You should teach."

"Anyone who bets with me will learn a lesson," he said modestly. "Care to try?"

"As a fool, I fear any man with greater knowledge, which is to say, all of them," I said. "Besides, if I was to bet on anything, it would be on the roll of a pair of dice."

"I spent many happy years in unlit alleyways relieving drunks of their wages by means of those treacherous cubes," he said. "I have never seen you participating."

"I came to town only six months ago," I said. "I promised my wife for last year's resolution that I would stay on God's path. But it's a new year, and I don't see the harm of one little game. I heard there's a fellow named Higini who runs one around here."

"Higini?" he said in surprise. "I thought you were interested in gambling."

"I was. I am."

"Higini's game is not a gamble," he said. "Higini's game is a complex mechanism for taking away Paradise without any hope of redemption. It is a trap for the unwary and the simple-minded."

"You could not have described me any better if you had been my own mother," I said. "Higini, it is. Take me to him, if you'd be of a mind."

"I bear no ill will toward you, good Fool," he said. "May I not take you instead to a true game of chance?"

"No, though I thank you for your charitable impulse," I said. "I will have Higini, and no other. Guide me to him, if you are truly grateful for the money you have made wagering on my death and dismemberment today."

"My gratitude is to God, the Great Gambler," he said piously. "He who kept you in the saddle and me in silver."

"Then it is God's will that we meet, and that you lead me to my next station," I said.

"There may be something in that," he conceded. "Very well, Fool. Follow me."

There were several stables in that section of Saint Cyprien, built with no particular regard for order. My new guide led me through them like a bee through a hive, shouting out greetings and friendly insults to ostlers, smiths, grooms, and stable boys without missing a step. I was treated to the sights and smells on this little tour. The sights were fine, if you have an eye for horses. The smells were those you get when you have an eye for horses: mounds of hay being piled into lofts, waiting to be gulped up by equine mouths; heaps of dung being piled into wagons, the end product of hay and horse; burning charcoal from the blacksmiths, a smell that never failed to remind me of a man I once encountered in—but I have told that story before.

Many of the stable boys and grooms seemed to live here. I doubted that any of them had ever seen the inside of a church since baptism. Based on their appearances, that may have been the last time any of them had been bathed as well. There were sudden turns into narrow alleyways that then opened up into unexpected enclaves where women nursed infants or stirred bubbling pots over small fires. They looked at me in my motley and whiteface curiously, even fearfully. I made my usual funny expressions to the children to no avail.

My guide took one last turn, and I was in an alley that led to a dead end. He turned to me and held out his arms in triumph. I became very aware of the sounds around me, wondering if I had been set up for an attack.

"We have arrived," he said.

"And Higini?"

"He is here."

I looked behind me at the alley, then up at the stable walls around me, then back at my guide, who was grinning like an idiot.

"You are Higini?" I asked.

"At your service," he said, bowing low. As he did, a pair of white dice rolled into his hand from his sleeve.

"Where is the rest of the game?"

"The game is wherever I am, and it is up to those who wish to play to seek me out."

I looked at him more closely. His face was smooth, as though no hair had ever pushed up through its surface. His fingers were long and supple, and he rolled the two dice between his knuckles like a conjurer. His smile was guileless and welcoming. His eyes showed nothing.

He may have been the most devious man I had ever met in my life, and I doubted that he was more than twenty-two.

"Let me show you my arena, Fool," he said, and he pointed to his feet.

While the rest of the alleyway was dirt, there was a section of hard clay laid down there, about nine feet square and tamped smooth.

"Even ground for an even match," he said.

"Which, according to you, cannot be possible."

"There are more honest games in town," he said. "But those who come to Higini come thinking they can outfox the fox. What is your game, Fool?"

"I came to help one who thought he could outfox you," I said. "I want to pay off his debt."

"Noble," he said. "Who is the man?"

"Sancho, of the count's guard."

"A friend of yours?"

"Why else would I be here?"

"Because you like the challenge of facing the fox," he said. "You are a fox yourself. Sancho was a wolf in sheep's clothing. Higini fleeced the sheep, then skinned the wolf."

"How much to redeem his two coats?"

"It cannot be done," he said.

"Why not?"

"Because Higini sold Sancho's debts to another."

"Wonderful," I sighed. "I thought myself on a simple errand of charity, and it has turned into a epic quest. Who now owns Sancho's debts?"

"Why should Higini tell you?" he asked. "What does Higini care for a soldier of misfortune?"

"Would a coin or two help?"

"Higini has already been paid by the master of debts. Higini's discretion was part of the bargain."

"Commendable," I said. "And I know where this ends. We roll for it."

"You truly are a fool," he said.

"I brought my own dice," I said, producing them from my pouch.

He laughed.

"Higini has seen fools before," he said. "Pelardit has come to the heart of the stables to perform for us. He is a master of sleight of hand, so fast and so adept that not even Higini can spot the pass. And Pelardit defers to you."

"Pelardit is the master in that respect," I said. "But I am not without skills. Nor is Higini, I expect."

He sat cross-legged at one edge of the clay surface and placed his dice down at the edge. When he lifted his hand back up, there were two sets. He passed his other hand over, and there were now four pairs. He waved again, and they had changed from white to red.

"All crooked in some fashion or other," I said, applauding.

"Maybe," he said. "Maybe yours are as well. Now, what can you offer Higini for your stake in this contest?"

"If you will not take money, perhaps a performance?"

"Higini can see you in any tavern he wishes, working hard for the price of a tankard of ale."

"That's just the tavern routine. You haven't seen the material I save for the lords."

"Do you fart in a richer, more noble tone when you play for them?"

"Oh, you saw that routine. What else may I wager?"

"Your motley," he decided.

"What? This is my only pair. And I need it to make my living."

"Your mission to save your friend is not worth so much as a suit of patches? For shame, Fool."

This was becoming serious. I couldn't bet my motley against a cheat to gain a small piece of information for an investigation that may have been senseless from the beginning.

Only a fool would do such a thing.

"You're on," I said.

"Well done," he said. "Now, we shall roll."

"Wait a second. Using whose dice?"

"I will use mine, you will use yours," he proposed. "High number wins."

"But I don't trust your dice."

"And I don't trust yours. Are we at a standstill?"

I thought for a moment, then sat opposite him and put my dice forward.

"Select a pair of yours," I said. "Then I shall take one from that pair, and you will take one from mine. We will each roll a mixed pair, and that will make it at least half a random outcome."

He lit up, the smile reaching his eyes for the first time.

"You are a clever fool," he said. "Higini accepts."

He looked at his dice, selected one pair, and placed them by mine.

"And to keep things clear, place all those other dice in that corner where I can see them," I said.

"Done," he said, moving them. "And you roll up the sleeves of your motley, soon to be Higini's. I will do the same."

I complied. His eyes widened when he saw the two daggers strapped to my forearms. I shrugged.

"I do a knife-throwing act as well," I said. "Let us now hold out our hands, fingers spread, and turn them slowly."

We watched each other's hands like hawks would a scurrying mouse, then placed them on the clay surface.

"You are my guest," said Higini. "You may choose first."

I took one of his dice. He took one of mine. Then we picked up our remaining cubes.

"We throw together," he said. "One, two . . ."

"You smell like a sweaty horse," said my wife as we snuggled together later in bed.

"I almost came home naked tonight," I said.

"Who was the wench?" she demanded immediately. "Give me my rival's name, so that I may curse it properly as I strangle her."

"No wench," I said. "Merely a talented young cheat whom I tempted with a rare moment of fairness."

"Explain?"

I told her of Higini and the maze through which he led me.

"But how did you beat him?" she asked.

"I beat him when I gave him an opportunity to gamble

for real stakes," I said. "His discretion against my profession. I reminded him of the true thrill of the wager, the joy of the dice. The reason he became a gambler in the first place."

"And the dice came up favoring you?"

"Fool's luck."

"I see," she said. "I suspect that he was not the only one in that alleyway who lives for the gamble."

"I am not like him."

"No. You gamble with your life. Which, I must remind you, is also mine. Please take better care of it."

"I haven't risked our lives much lately."

"In the last few days, you've been off to a bordel, and when I deprived you of that, you turn around and go to a gambling den."

"Best investigation I've ever had," I agreed.

"Did you become this degenerate recently, or were you like this all the time, and I was too blinded by love to notice?"

"I became degenerate only when I married you," I said.

"Likewise," she purred. "Anyhow, you won. What did you find out? Who purchased Sancho's debts?"

"The Count of Foix," I said.

CHAPTER 9

"Y ou go to sleep with a man who smells like a horse, you wake up smelling like a horse yourself," I grumbled to Helga the next morning.

"You said 'horse'?" asked Helga uncertainly.

Theo was still asleep upstairs, his snores shaking the rafters. I was attempting to feed Portia, who had decided that her oatmeal was some type of sculpting material.

"Your lord and master decided to follow his nose yesterday," I told her.

"And he smelled horses?"

"He was looking for the gambler who had ensnared Sancho," I explained. "An infamous runner of moving games with fixed outcomes."

"Oh, Higini," she said matter-of-factly.

"Are you truly a twelve-year-old girl?" I asked, glaring at her. "Or are you some ancient malevolent demon who prowls the dark corners of the human soul?"

"You've already told me that there is no difference," she said.

"Apparently not," I replied.

"I'm going to be thirteen in June," she said cheerfully.

"The world trembles in fear," I said. "How did you know about Higini?"

"I go to the stables to visit Zeus," she said.

"And the stable boys?"

She smiled dreamily, then shook herself. "Stable boys?" she asked innocently. "Anyhow, I heard all about Higini. I hope Theo isn't going to match dice with him."

"He already has."

"Oh, no!" she cried, her face falling. "What have we lost?"

"He won."

"He beat Higini at his own game?" she exclaimed.

Her face was as awed as if she had seen a vision of the Virgin Mother appear in Portia's oatmeal. As a matter of fact, the shape Portia had fashioned in it did bear a passing resemblance.

"Did any of that actually get into your little belly?" I asked my daughter.

Portia thought seriously for a moment, then nodded.

"That is a lie," I informed her, and she looked at me guiltily.

I looked at the mess that my daughter had made, and the larger mess that was my daughter, and the largest mess that pretended to be my daughter.

"I think that we are all due for a bath," I said.

"But it's only Wednesday," protested Helga.

"Come on," I said, scooping up the baby. "I smell like a horse, and Portia smells like oatmeal."

"What do I smell like?" asked Helga.

"Fire and brimstone," I said. "We must wash you clean and douse you in holy water before you may pass safely amongst the citizens of Toulouse."

There was a women's bathhouse in the Comminges quarter, patronized, or rather matronized, by those who stayed nearby. This meant that one's bathing partners were most likely to be pilgrims or prostitutes. Or both, occasionally—I had met many a fallen woman on her way to Compostela to gain absolution for her many sins, and not a few pilgrims who fell from grace in Toulouse after making a pragmatic if desperate choice to fund the rest of the journey.

I paid for a tub of fresh hot water, soap, and cloths, and we piled our motley and linens on the bench. A team of maids ran back and forth with steaming buckets to fill the oaken tub. One tested the water, winced, and added two buckets of cold water to bring the temperature down to a tolerable level. I stepped in and lowered myself until I was completely submerged, then surfaced and took Portia from Helga.

"Do my hair, girl," I directed my apprentice, and she worked it to a fierce lather while I scrubbed Portia, who squealed with frustration. I plunged her down and up quickly, and she spluttered in indignation. Then I did the same with myself, holding her above the surface and blowing bubbles at her.

"Your turn, Helga," I said.

Helga put her hands on the edge of the tub and kicked up into a handstand as the women in the other tubs gasped and clapped in delight. Then she flipped into the water, sending a geyser ten feet into the air.

"You're supposed to leave some in the tub for washing," I reminded her. "Hold Portia."

She took the baby, and I washed her hair. Around us, women were happily exchanging gossip, recipes, stories about children. All of the currency of women. From different corners, songs suddenly arose, to be joined by others. There was freedom in this room that didn't exist outside it.

I finished washing Helga's hair and rinsed it with a bucket of water. "I remember now—you're a blonde," I said as I inspected the results.

She groaned in exasperation at the old joke.

"There's nothing in this world that's going to untangle this," I said. "Do you ever comb it?"

"I do," she said indignantly. "Sometimes. Every now and then. Ow!"

"They say Alexander solved the Gordian Knot by splitting it with his sword," I said as I worked one cluster out. "Alexander would have taken one look at you and fled, screaming in terror. There, that's another one loose."

"I've seen gentler handling of horses by their grooms," she grumbled.

"I've been meaning to speak to you about that," I said.

"About my hair? Or about horses?"

"About your running around to those places when you're not with us."

"I'm not doing anything I shouldn't," she said.

"Not yet," I said. "And you may not want to do anything you shouldn't. But no matter how much you like Zeus, and no matter how friendly the stable boys act, you may find yourself in a dangerous situation."

"Unlike the ones you and Theo keep putting me in."

"That's different," I said, working another knot loose.

"Following deadly men through dark alleys, fending off attacks by ruffians in the woods, spying in great houses. All of these could get me killed, yet you worry about stable boys?"

"You are training to be a jester," I reminded her. "A member of the Fools' Guild. All the tasks we assign you are part of that training, and we would never send you into anything before you were ready."

"If I can go into the seediest tavern in Montpellier alone, what makes you think I can't hold off an amorous stable boy?"

"Because when you act as a jester, you keep your guard up," I replied. "But when you are wandering off on these explorations, you don't. And it's when you let down that guard that you are at risk."

"I am not," she insisted. "And I'm not a jester all of the time. There should still be time for me to have some fun."

"When you are overcome by several men who carry you behind the stables and have their way with you, fun will be the last thing you'll be having."

She looked at me in shock. "That wouldn't happen," she whispered. "I would never let that happen."

"No woman ever thinks it will," I said. "But it does. Women have to be on their guard all the time, just like jesters."

"What about now?" she pointed out. "We're naked, sitting in a tub of water. How are you on your guard?"

I showed her the washcloth in my hand, then let it fall open slightly to reveal the dagger concealed under it.

"I didn't see you do that," she said.

"No one did," I said. "Remember—just because you think you know all about evil doesn't mean that you'll be able to avoid it. Lesson learned?"

"You're not my mother," she said.

"No," I said. "I am your teacher and your guardian. Where is your dagger, by the way?"

"With my clothes on the bench," she sighed. "Too far away to be useful. Lesson learned."

"Good. No more gallivanting about. Understood?"

"Oc, Maman," she said. She looked at me, her eyes brimming with tears. "Sometimes, I wish you had been my mother. You would have been a better one than the one I had."

"The mother you had protected you from harm and molestation, then spirited you out of that bordel to the Fools'

Guild," I said. "She must have been a courageous and re-sourceful woman to do that, and she passed those qualities on to you. You should honor her memory."

"What was your mother like?" she asked suddenly.

"I never knew her," I said. "She was carried off by a fever when my brother and I were but a few months old. Our father died when we were thirteen."

"Theo's mother died when he was born," she said.

"Yes," I replied, a little surprised at her knowledge.

"He's always on his guard, isn't he?"

"It's what has kept him alive so long," I replied.

"It must be hard being married when both of you are on guard all the time," she commented.

I worked through the last knot and ran my fingers through her hair. "You see too much sometimes," I said.

We dried ourselves and dressed. I did not observe where she concealed her knife on her person, and was pleased with that.

"Where to now?" asked Helga as I applied my whiteface.

"Back to the bordel," I said.

"Right," she said. "So that we may continue my righteous upbringing and education."

"As a matter of fact, educating is exactly what I will be doing," I said.

We stopped by the market on the way to the bordel, but saw no sign of Sylvie, so we continued on. As we crossed the yard between the leper house and the bordel, we were hailed from above. I turned and looked up at the window, shading my eyes from the late morning sun.

"Good day to you, Fools," called my leprous admirer.

"And to you, senhor," I replied, making courtesy.

"You are too early," he said. "The ladies will not be at their posts until midafternoon. They are still asleep."

"They are fortunate to have you watching over them," I said.

"I did not watch enough, alas," he said mournfully. "I will miss that fiery redhead. Will you perform for me when you are done with your errand?"

"Certainly, senhor," I said. "But it will have to be dumb-show, for my music may wake the slumberers."

"If they can sleep through a murder, they can sleep through your music," he said.

"I thank you for the comparison," I said, bowing again.

Carlos didn't even bother raising both eyelids this time. One bleary eyeball acknowledged our existences, then was hidden again. We took that as permission and went inside.

The only stirrings we heard came from the direction of the kitchen, accompanied by some wonderful aromas. We followed them in to find Sylvie up and cooking.

"Good morning, Na Sylvie," I said. "I have come in my new capacity of tutor."

"A waste of time," she muttered. "These women are good at one thing, and one thing only, and reading will not make them any better at it."

"On the contrary, a mistress who can read to her patron may find that she may soothe him just as readily as by love-making," I said. "Or she may arouse him to new heights. It all depends upon the subject matter being read. Do you read and write?"

"Enough to copy down my recipes," she said haughtily. "More than that, I have no time for."

"So, you are a veteran cook?" I asked.

She nodded.

"I am not surprised, given the tantalizing odors emanating

from those pots," I said. "I take it that you haven't worked in this house in its principal activity?"

"Certainly not," she snapped. "And I will thank you to show some respect for my station."

"As a consumer of food, I respect all cooks," I said. "Helga here has been showing some promise in that area. Could she assist you in exchange for some tips?"

"Can you stir a pot, girl?" asked Sylvie.

"One with each hand," said Helga. "And a third with my right foot if necessary."

"We have only two pots to stir," said Sylvie, handing the girl two long spoons. "Keep your feet away from both of them."

"Has the Abbess replaced La Rossa yet?" I asked.

"Why, do you want the job?" sneered Sylvie.

"Not I," I said.

"Then what business is it of yours?"

"Curiosity," I said. "Having avoided bordels all my life, I am fascinated to find myself actually in one. I want to know everything about it."

"You have children," said Sylvie.

"Obviously."

"You know how that happened, don't you?"

"Of course."

"Then you know what happens here. There's just much more of it, and with money changing hands."

"And partners changing beds," said Marquesia as she entered the kitchen, not bothering to conceal an enormous yawn. "Speaking of which, Sylvie, I need my bed linens washed."

"Oc, milady," muttered Sylvie, leaving us.

Marquesia grabbed a handful of nuts from a bowl and started cracking them.

"Good morning," I said.

"I hate mornings," she said. "I hate the light, I hate the birds singing, I hate how I look before I have my face together."

"That's where whiteface has an advantage," I said. "There is no need for subtlety in its application. Are you ready for your lesson?"

"My what?" she asked.

"You wanted to learn how to read," I said.

She looked at me, her mouth hanging open for a moment, a half-chewed nut visible. Not the most attractive prostitute at that moment, but she was off duty.

"You actually meant it when you made that offer," she said, swallowing quickly. "I didn't think you were serious."

"An obvious conclusion, since no one ever thinks that we're serious," I said. "Do you know your letters?"

"Of course," she said indignantly. "Well, most of them."

"Let's start with a quick review," I said, pulling out a sheet of parchment. "Which is this?"

"*A?*"

"Good. And this?"

"Um . . ." She hesitated.

"*R,*" said Portia confidently.

"That's right, Portia," I said, turning to her in surprise. "Which one is this?"

"*P!*" she exclaimed happily.

"Wait, aren't I supposed to be doing this?" asked Marquesia.

"I'm sorry, but I didn't know Portia knew her letters," I said. I looked at my daughter. "Did Papa teach you that?"

"No," said Portia.

"Who did?"

"I did," said Helga.

"You did? When?"

"I don't spend all my time running after stable boys," she said, grinning. "I get stuck with my sister an awful lot while you and Papa are off performing. So I taught her her letters and numbers."

"You sweet, thoughtful girl," I said, pulling her into an embrace.

"Maybe she should teach here," said Marquesia.

"She could, but I would worry about what she might learn in exchange," I said.

"Things that will serve her well when she finds a husband," said Marquesia. "Or a stable boy."

"That's what worries me . . . ," I began.

Then Sylvie charged into the room, an accusing finger pointing in Marquesia's direction. "You took her room!" she shouted. "You slept in her bed, you filthy, selfish whore."

"It's a much nicer room than mine, and the Abbess said I could have it," sniffed Marquesia. "I'm sorry that you lost your favorite, Sylvie, but that room belongs to me now."

Sylvie stood for a moment in helpless fury, then stormed out the back door.

"Guess I'll be making my own bed for a while," said Marquesia.

"And lying in it," muttered Helga.

"What was that, little girl?" asked Marquesia.

"Nothing," said Helga.

"Back to our lesson," I said.

We went over the letters one by one, Portia and Marquesia seated side by side while poring over them. The proficiency of the toddler aroused Marquesia's competitive instincts, and by the end, they both had them down. Sylvie did not return from the garden.

"That's enough," said Marquesia. "That's as exhausting a workout as I have had lately."

"If I were a man, that would be a compliment," I said. "How has it been here since the—incident?"

"Busy," she groaned. "The notoriety draws men like manure draws flies. The room was the main attraction—the blood on the wall, the holes in the coverlet. But the Abbess didn't want that to be the center of attention, so she had it cleaned up, and now I'm there."

"Aren't you frightened, sleeping in La Rossa's bed?" asked Helga. "I would be."

"She was my friend," said Marquesia. "I do not fear her ghost. If anything, I think that she would protect us."

"Too bad no one protected her," said Helga.

"Has the Count of Foix been in since then?" I asked.

"Why do you want to know about him?" asked Marquesia.

"I am to perform at his house tonight," I said. "Any inside knowledge as to his likes or dislikes would be useful."

"He likes women and food, not necessarily in that order," she said. "He dislikes spending money. Oh, and closed doors. He always has us with the door wide open. It's quite shameless."

"Is he here frequently?"

"More for—"

"Marquesia, it is time for you to prepare," said the Abbess, standing in the doorway.

"I shall come again," I said.

"Thank you for the lesson," said Marquesia. "I must wash. We do that every day here."

"Cleanliness is next to godliness," I said.

"It will take more than a bath for us to achieve that," said the Abbess. "Get going, girl. There will be customers soon."

Marquesia fled, and the Abbess glided in.

"How was her lesson?" she asked.

"Good," I said. "She is a quick learner."

"Quick learners make good earners," said the Abbess. "At least in this house."

"And now she has a better room," I said. "Any candidates for the vacant one?"

"Why? Are you interested?" she asked, smirking.

"I do fine as a jester, thank you," I said. "I was just wondering how easy it is to replace someone like La Rossa."

"I have been besieged by whores with their hair dyed red seeking her place," she said. "I have no need for anything that garish in this establishment."

"I am glad that you maintain your standards," I said. "Helga, how is the cooking coming along?"

"I think the stew is ready," she said. "But Sylvie should decide that, not me."

"I will go and fetch her from the back, milady," I said, picking up both Portia and my cue. "No doubt you have household matters to attend to."

I was out the door before the Abbess could question why I bothered.

Sylvie was at the rear of the garden, digging up onions. "What do you want?" she snapped without even looking up at me.

"To find out more about La Rossa," I said. "Julie, I mean. She was your favorite, wasn't she?"

She said nothing. I put Portia down, who waddled over to watch the digging. Sylvie looked at her, tears trickling down her cheeks.

"That can't be from the onions," I said.

"I remember when she was born," said Sylvie, wiping her eyes with her sleeve. "She had that red hair from the start. The Devil's hair. We all told her mother that she was going to be trouble someday. Thank God she didn't live to see it. But she wouldn't have been surprised."

"Who was her mother?" I asked.

"A servant, like me," said Sylvie. "A beauty, which I never was. Ambitious. Stupid to be ambitious when you're a servant."

"Where was this?"

"Here. In town," said Sylvie.

"Sylvie!" called the Abbess from the rear doorway.

"I came to tell you the stew is ready," I said.

"No, you didn't," said Sylvie. "But I will tell her that."

We walked back together, Sylvie holding the onions in her apron.

"Thank you for the recipe," I was saying as we passed the Abbess into the house.

"Will you remember it all without my writing it down?" asked Sylvie, dumping the onions on the table.

"I will come back if I forget anything."

Sylvie took the spoons from Helga and tasted the stew. "It's ready," she said to the Abbess.

"Time to feed the ladies," said the Abbess. "They will need their strength tonight. I will walk you out, Fool."

It was no request.

As we passed through the front parlor, I saw Aude and Marquesia on display in full makeup and costume. Marquesia gave a furtive wave.

"*M*," said Portia, pointing to her.

"*P* for Portia," Marquesia called back.

We passed by Carlos, who was up and stretching now.

"That reminds me," I said. "We haven't had juggling practice yet today. Shall we do some four-handed work for our invisible audience?"

"Absolutely," said Helga.

I plunked my daughter down to play in the dirt, and Helga and I hauled out three clubs each and began our warm-ups. Once we were loose, we marched ten paces from each other and turned.

"Breathe," I commanded her. "And . . ."

We began passing them back and forth. She was good, this young girl, and she had started young, unlike me. But I had been taught by Theo, who had been taught by Amleth, who had been taught by Theo's father, who reportedly was . . .

It occurred to me that I didn't know who La Rossa's father was.

"First forfeit to you," called Helga. "After only eight passes, too."

I looked at her blankly, then down at the club lying at my feet. I wasn't even aware that I had dropped it.

"Sorry," I said, picking it up. "I lost my concentration for a moment."

"After all that talk," she said. "Be on your guard now."

"Be on yours, Apprentice," I growled.

We made it through twenty passes before she caught one awkwardly and dropped a second while trying to recover.

"Better," I said. "Next one to drop cooks dinner."

"Not a fair wager at all," she protested. "If I lose, I have to cook, and if I win, I have to eat your cooking."

"Nevertheless," I said, starting the pattern.

I felt loose, the bath having unknotted my muscles more than it did Helga's tresses. I inhaled the warm spring air, filled with the scents of blooming things. My newly literate little girl played happily by my feet, wordlessly singing something she had heard in the bathhouse that morning, and the clubs flew to my hands like trained falcons.

Brother Timothy, the Fools' Guild's juggling master, once told us that there comes a point where you become one with the pattern, and it was in that moment that you knew God. I had scoffed at that at the time—not to his face, of course, for he took the subject very seriously, but today I felt it. I was not even aware of my arms moving. There could have been a hundred clubs flying at me for all I cared. I would have caught them all. I was on the verge of something, a discovery, a revelation. . . .

"Damn," muttered Helga as she fumbled one.

I fell back to earth with the club.

"I counted forty-three passes," called our friend from his aerie. "Very good."

"Ah, but that was just an exercise," I said. "Now, you shall see a show."

And we launched into our street routine, playing to an audience of a leper in front and a bodyguard behind. A few furtive daytime customers passed by on their way to the bordel. They watched briefly, but moved on to their destinations.

"I thought you said juggling was better than making love." Helga pouted.

"To watch, Apprentice," I replied. "Not to do. For now, stick to juggling."

"Thank you, ladies," called the leper. "I look forward to your next performance."

We bowed, then turned and bowed to Carlos, who was caught by surprise.

"You have no excuse for not applauding," I said.

He got to his feet quickly and clapped.

"Better," I said. "I hope that came from entertainment and not fear."

"You took me off guard that time, woman," he said with a thick Catalan accent. "I will not underestimate you again."

"Bravely spoken, senhor," I said. "Let us part in peace."

He nodded. We collected our gear and Portia and left.

"We have worked very hard, it's only midday, and we have no money to show for it," sighed Helga.

"We have taught a prostitute her letters, given ease to a leper, and nearly met God through juggling," I said. "If we died now, we would have our place in Heaven."

"Let's not put that to the test," she urged. "Do you really believe what Brother Timothy always told us?"

"I am beginning to," I said.

"Then I'm sorry I messed up," said Helga. "I kept you from divinity."

"I have a feeling that there will always be a dropped club standing between us and perfection," I said. "Let's get something to eat."

There was a small tavern near the gate that was reasonable. As we finished our meal, Helga gave a slight nod toward the window. I looked, and saw the Abbess going by.

"You would think she would be minding the store," commented Helga.

"You would," I agreed. "Are you tired of following dangerous men?"

"Never," she said. "But a dangerous woman would be a change of pace."

She was off before I could even tell her to go.

I put Portia up on my shoulders and headed home. Theo was in the lower room, sitting by the window and picking a tune out on his lute.

"You're up early," I commented.

"You're not so pretty when you're being snide," he replied, putting his instrument down and hoisting Portia from my shoulders.

"And you still smell like a horse," I said. "You can't perform before the nobility smelling like that. They may think it's the act."

He sniffed the air suspiciously.

"I think that's Portia," he said.

"Your daughter has had a bath today," I informed him as Portia looked hurt. "So have I."

"Really? All that extravagance for a nonpaying job?"

"It's not my fault that we're not getting paid," I said. "But on that topic, I gave a reading lesson to a prostitute and a performance to a leper, and am out what I spent on luncheon. There had better be some food for us tonight at the very least."

"What a disastrous profession we're in," he sighed. "We'll have to make sure Portia marries someone with a regular income."

"Nonsense," I said. "She will earn her own way."

"Send her to the Fools' Guild?"

"Anywhere but," I said. "We will send her to a proper university when she's of age."

"A girl at university? That's a waste."

"The one at Bologna takes them," I said. "She can even study law there."

"Now you're just trying to frighten her," he said, shuddering at the idea.

A quick series of short and long knocks, then Helga came through the door.

"Who is this?" exclaimed Theo. "She knows the knock, but I swear that I do not know this girl."

"It's Helga," she said.

"But the Helga I know is a dust-covered demon," said Theo. "You are a blond angel from Heaven."

"This is another bath joke, isn't it?" said Helga.

"Are you quite certain that I am her father?" Theo asked me. "She doesn't look anything like me."

"No, her father was a handsome man," I said.

Theo walked over to her and took her chin in his hand. He perused her face seriously. "You are on the verge of being a very pretty girl," he said. "That can be dangerous."

"I have already had this conversation today," said Helga.

"Ah, good," he said. "My wife knows too well the pitfalls of being a beautiful woman. You end up marrying penniless fools like me."

"That's not true," I said. "You had a penny when I married you. I know because I gave it to you. Apprentice, report."

"The Abbess went through the gate, then put her cloak up once she got into the city," said Helga.

"You were following the Abbess?" asked Theo. "Why?"

"Be quiet, husband," I said. "Continue."

"She went to the Robin's Egg near the Dalbade and went straight to a back room."

"An assignation for the Abbess," mused Theo. "One would think her own establishment would be sufficient."

"Remember being quiet, husband?" I reminded him.

"Right, you did mention something about that," he said, subsiding.

"Well, I couldn't just walk through a tavern and peek inside," said Helga, shooting me a sidelong glance. "It wouldn't be proper for a young lady like me."

"Just so," I said. "Your solution?"

"There was no window I could look through," she said. "No door, either. I went to the rear to see if I could hear through the walls, but they were too thick. So I came back to the front and stood where I could see through the door."

"Did anyone go in to see her?" I asked.

"No," she said, looking disappointed. "And after a few minutes, she left."

"Oh, well," I said. "You tried."

"But after she left, someone did come out," Helga said in triumph. "A large man, also cloaked. So, I followed to him to his *maison*, which is a very fine one indeed. After he went in, I asked at one of the stalls who this very fine *maison* belonged to. And he told me, why, to none other than the Count of Foix."

CHAPTER 10

The Count of Foix is looming large in our investigation," I said to Theo after I recounted my morning with the ladies.

"He looms large wherever he is," said Theo. "He is a large-looming man. The Abbess spent only a few minutes with him?"

"Yes," said Helga.

"And did not emerge with her dress in any noticeable disarray?"

"No."

"It could still have been the normal transaction of a prostitute and a patron," said Theo. "A few minutes would be sufficient."

"For the man, anyway," I said. "But he has not hidden his visits to the bordel. Why the sudden need for secrecy? Why the Robin's Egg, and not the bordel itself?"

"Something set the two of them off," speculated Theo. "And I have an idea what it might have been."

"What?"

"You," said Theo. "Your questions about him at the bordel. The Abbess wanted to let him know that you're poking around in his life."

"That should make tonight's performance at the house of Foix particularly interesting," I said.

"I can't wait to see it," said Helga excitedly. "The expression on his face when—"

"You're not going," said Theo.

"What?" she exclaimed, her face falling.

"You're staying here with Portia," he said. "You will bar all the windows and doors, and you will rig as many trip lines as you think you need. If anyone gets through, take to the rooftops and go to the room at the Yellow Dwarf."

"But, Theo—"

"Not another *but Theo* out of you, Apprentice," he said. "I am the Chief Fool of Toulouse and your master. You do as I say without protest."

"Yes, Theo," she said with nary a pout.

"And you, Master, will take a bath," I said to my husband.

"Yes, dear," he said. He was pouting.

He pouted less when I came in to scrub his back, but still complained.

"You had hot water and a room full of naked women," he said. "I get a couple of buckets from the cistern and—"

"If you ever want to see this woman naked again, you will choose your next words wisely," I said.

"A goddess," he said quickly. "That's what I was about to say, of course."

"Of course," I said. "Goddess of what, exactly?"

"Of loving, living, and laving," he said.

"And now, the goddess of leaving," I said, pouring the last bucket over him to rinse off the soap. "Get yourself dry and dressed. We have work to do."

I kissed Portia good-bye as Theo came down to the lower room, then handed her to Helga. Our coded knock came on the door, and I opened it to see Pelardit. He bowed with an awkward flourish, several balls tumbling out of his sleeves.

"Everything ready?" asked Theo.

"At your command, my lord high master," I said.

"Bar the door, Helga," said Theo.

She stepped forward immediately, and he grabbed her shoulder.

"Wait until we've gone through it first," he instructed her.

"Ohhhh," she said in dumb comprehension.

Pelardit cracked a smile, and she broke character to smile back for a moment.

The moment the door closed behind us, we heard Portia start to howl in protest.

"Go into danger, or back to our screaming daughter?" asked Theo.

"Danger's much easier," I said. "Let's go."

Pelardit lifted an eyebrow at the mention of danger, so we brought him up to date. He was shaking his head by the time it was over, and held up his hand, his thumb and forefinger almost touching.

"No, it isn't much," conceded Theo. "But I've been going over Balthazar's notes on the Count of Foix. Seems that his relationship with Raimon has always been tenuous. He owes his presence at the court more to the Duke of Comminges than through his own importance, although he is Raimon's cousin. And not an illegitimate half brother, for a change."

"That's refreshing," I said. "Is he very important? Foix is just this little place up in the Pyrenees. How much power can one have being the Count of Crags?"

"He gets by on charm and flattery," said Theo. "Not so different from us, if you think about it. He lets himself be the butt of their gibes, brings them amusing stories of his escapades, and gets to keep feeding at the golden trough as a reward."

"When did he first show up?" I asked.

"On a regular basis, not that long ago," said Theo. "He had gotten into that little fracas with Aragon about four years back and ended up being held hostage by King Pedro for a while. After his wife, along with Comminges, intervened, he began frequenting Raimon's court."

"I guess home is too close to Aragon for comfort," I said. "Here, he can pretend he isn't afraid of anyone. There's the *maison* up ahead. How do you want to play it tonight?"

"Get what gossip we can from the servants," he said. "If you can get the lady of the house alone, it might be interesting to learn her take on Toulouse and Baudoin."

"Do you know what occurs to me?" I asked.

"What?"

"If Foix has been here only a short time, how could he possibly care about Baudoin? All of that happened forty years ago."

"But Baudoin's arrival started Foix on this path," he said. "If you see a man react as if he's been threatened, then you know that the threat must exist even if you can't see it."

"But is that what he's reacting to?" I asked. "Is he even the principal here? What if he's just one more rung up the chain of command?"

"Do chains have rungs?" he mused.

"I meant one more link in the ladder," I said.

"Ohhhh," he said, imitating Helga. Then, "Ow!"

"So sorry," I said. "My fist slipped."

Pelardit took a large step away from us and started to whistle nonchalantly.

"What I meant is what if Foix is following someone else's orders?" I asked.

"Do you think he's done all this for Count Raimon?"

"No," I said. "Raimon wouldn't need all this subterfuge to set up Baudoin. He could simply banish him, or fob him off on some minor holding, or do whatever counts do when annoying long-lost relatives show up."

"If not Raimon, then whom would the Count of Foix owe to this extent?" speculated Theo. "Comminges helped bail him out of Aragon's dungeon, but Comminges is closer to Raimon than anyone."

"You are missing an obvious possibility," I said. "The wife."

"Who also helped get him out," said Theo. "And who needs all his influence and protection because she is a Cathar, and quite open about it."

"And because all husbands owe a debt of obedience and deference to their wives," I said.

"Right, I keep forgetting that," he said. Then, "Ow!"

"Damn this pesky fist of mine," I said. "I apologize."

Pelardit moved to the other side of the street.

"I will need this arm to function if I am going to earn a living," said Theo.

"True," I said. "I promise not to hit you again until after you get paid."

"Lucky for me we're performing for free tonight," he sighed. "That gives me an extra day without pain."

We passed through the gates into the courtyard, then made our way to a door on the side. This let us in through the kitchen, which was in full bustle. But there was disorder and disarray where one would expect to see the military precision of a great house. The cook, a tall woman with a short temper, was berating everyone in sight, while the assistants scurrying around seemed to have no idea where to find the ingredients she was screaming for or where to place the pots that they were carrying. There were a couple of near collisions in the short time we passed through, and Pelardit had to duck a saucepan that the cook flung at a boy who was not heeding her call quickly enough.

"You get the feeling that most of them were hired today?" muttered Theo.

"I was so counting on a decent meal to make up for the lack of payment," I grumbled.

"I'll cook you one tomorrow," he promised. "Ah, that looks like someone who knows something."

He stopped a harried-looking manservant who pointed us in the direction of the great hall. We went up a flight of stairs, stepping gingerly around the maids who were frantically scrubbing it, their cloths already black with removed grime. At the top of the stairs, a man stood wearing the yellow-and-red striped livery of the house of Foix, a silver chain of office around his neck. He was speaking to a woman wearing a plain black gown.

"Excuse me, senhor," said Theo, nodding to him politely. "We are the fools, here for the entertainment."

The man looked at him severely and barked, "Show the proper courtesy to the countess, fools!"

Theo blinked once, then turned to the woman and bowed deeply. We followed his lead.

"Good day to you, fools," said the countess.

Her voice was slightly hoarse, as if it normally did not receive much use. Her accent was from somewhere west of the Pyrenees. As we rose, I looked at her more closely. She wore no trace of adornment. Not a jewel, not a comb, not a hint of makeup. Her hair was gray; her nails were her own. Had she walked down the street, I might have first thought her a washerwoman.

Yet, as I looked at her more closely, I realized that I would have seen my error quickly. There was intelligence in her eyes, an inner light that she took pains to conceal. And her bearing was proud, for all the accoutrements she had forsaken. This was a woman who had grown up with the nobility, and would forever be a part of that world.

I should know. It was my world once as well. I wondered if anyone could still see it in me, or were the makeup and motley sufficient to hide my earlier life?

"Good day to you, Domina," said Theo. "I am Tan Pierre. This is my wife, Domina Gile, and our colleague, Pelardit."

"I have heard tell of you, Senhor Pierre," she said, smiling at him. "My husband tells me he won your performance in a footrace."

"Too true, alas," my husband said, shamefaced.

"I should thank you for providing him with the exercise," she said. "He runs to stoutness."

"Yet he is a stout runner for all that," said Theo. "Had I known he was so fleet of foot, I would never have challenged him."

"Do not blame yourself," she said. "He is too fast for me as well. Richard, show them to the great hall."

Her man beckoned to us without speaking. We bowed to her once more, then followed him.

The great hall took up half this level of the *maison*. Three musicians had already claimed the best corner for themselves. They were not a trio we had worked with before, although we had heard them play. They nodded to us while they tuned their instruments.

"Always a good sign when they tune first," said Theo. "Where do those fellows usually perform?"

Pelardit became birdlike and gently cradled something small and round in his hands.

"The Robin's Egg, right," said Theo. "Where Helga saw Foix meet the Abbess. Maybe he was only there to hire the band. Mediocre musicians from a disreputable establishment. Rather low-class group to bring before the Count of Toulouse, don't you think?"

"Yet as cheap as they are, they will still be paid more than us, I wager," I said.

"Please, keep reminding me of that," said Theo. "It will put me into such a good humor for this performance. What did you make of the wife?"

"I was trying to remember if we have seen her before," I said. "I don't remember her being at the dinner the count had before Christmas."

"Unless she dressed like the other ladies," said Theo. "Was she at the main table with her husband then, Pelardit?"

Pelardit thought, then shook his head.

"Her choice or his, do you suppose?" I asked.

"The most public of public events," Theo said. "The one time to show your love for your count where everyone may see it. Even the Count of Foix would want her at his side, if only for appearance' sake."

"At least he did not bring a mistress in her place," I said.

"Then it must be true love between them," he snorted. "That was a rather pointed comment she made at the end of our meeting just now. How much do you think she knows about her husband's goings-on?"

"Everything," I said. "He doesn't even make a show of secrecy."

"It is quite the blatant performance," agreed Theo. "I wonder if that's what it is?"

"What?"

"A performance."

"You mean all his whoring is a cover for something else?"

"It's a thought. But let us put it aside for now. The guests will be arriving soon."

We finished unpacking our gear and stowed our bags with those of the musicians. We had a hurried consultation with them to coordinate our performances, or at least not step on each other's toes, then launched into our dinner modes. As the guests entered the room, they were greeted by music, clubs flying through the air, and the usual brilliant patter from my husband and myself. Pelardit somehow managed to leer at the ladies while maintaining the utmost deference to their husbands, all without uttering a solitary word.

It was a small gathering as these affairs go. Eight couples in all—Raimon and Éléonor; Comminges with Indie, Raimon's half sister; Sabran with his wife; Peire Roger, the viguier, and his wife; and a few of the lesser nobility who hovered around the inner circle like flies, hoping for a chance to feed without being flicked away.

While the ladies did not compete in costume so much as they might at one of the balls at the Château Narbonnais, they still kept enough jewelry on display to finance a small army among them. They had to make a careful calculation as to how much they could wear while stopping short of sur-passing Éléonor. It would not do to arouse her jealousy. She had wisely chosen a necklace of bloodred rubies that empha-sized the exquisiteness of her unlined neck, her hair plaited behind and up to further expose it. She made every woman there look older, and the smiles they bestowed upon her barely concealed their envy.

Except for Phelipa, still unadorned, still in her plain gown. She should have looked ancient in this company, a hag in Paradise, yet she sat in serenity, chatting cheerfully with the others, and somehow seemed more at home with herself than did any other person in the room.

There was only the one central table, so we played directly to it as the servants scurried around us with their own juggling act, balancing bowls and trays, pouring from ewers with both hands. The Count of Foix for this occasion sat directly by the Count of Toulouse, regaling him with feeble anecdotes that had Raimon smiling wanly. Theo observed the strained amusement and leapt in.

"Lords and ladies," he cried. "I stand before you in shame, as you very well know. A fat man outran me. I have been searching within my soul for the reasons that this happened, and I think that I have found the answer."

"It is because I am the faster man," bellowed Foix.

"No, senhor," said Theo. "That was not the reason. If you look back at the great stories of footraces in ancient lore, you will find that they are not merely about who won and who lost, for that would merely be a simple matter of fact at a given place and time. No, my noble friends, the stories that are handed down from generation to generation are tales of moral instruction, fables that ferret out the fatal flaw of the fleet-footed favorite. I would be a poor loser indeed if I could not learn from my failure, and pass that learning on to you."

"School us, then," commanded Raimon, leaning back in his chair.

"I shall, Dominus," said Theo, bowing. "Now, for this dramatization, the Count of Foix must be portrayed by one of impeccable character."

Pelardit stepped forward and bowed.

"He looks nothing like you," Comminges said to Foix.

Pelardit, on hearing this, looked wounded, then thoughtful. He strode over behind Comminges and tapped him on the shoulder. Comminges looked up and Pelardit shoved him forward gently, then seized one of the large cushions from his seat. He came back around to us and held it up for all to see. Then he lifted the tunic of his motley and shoved it underneath. He leaned back, the cushion bulging in front of this stomach, and puffed out his cheeks grotesquely.

"Oh, that's him, to the life," said Sabran as the rest of the company laughed. Even Foix joined in, although it seemed forced.

"Very good," said Theo. "Now, to play me, I have selected a paragon of virtue, a superbly handsome and gifted fellow, to wit, myself."

He swept forward into a magnificent bow as I applauded madly and cheered from the side. As he straightened up and then bowed again, I increased in volume and enthusiasm until I was whooping with adulation. He straightened again and glanced over at me. I kept it going until he cut it off abruptly with an obvious hand signal.

"May I add that the quality I value most in my wife is her sincerity," he said.

I started up again at that, and cut off a split second later after an even more obvious signal, accompanied by an irritated glare.

"Now," he said as Pelardit stood by his side, "we shall depict the race as it actually happened."

They stood for a moment, then bowed.

"But you did nothing," said Raimon.

"On the contrary," said Theo. "The actual race was at such a blinding pace that you could no more see it than you could the beat of a hummingbird's wings. In the time that you thought that nothing happened, we completed our five circuits of the room and are, as a result, quite exhausted."

Pelardit mopped his brow and grabbed a goblet of wine from the table to ease his thirst from running so far and so fast.

"So, my lords and ladies, to properly show you how this

mound of flesh triumphed over me, we shall have to slow the actual pace down to one that the human eye may perceive. Pelardit?"

Pelardit took one last gulp of wine, wiped his mouth with his sleeve, and nodded. The two of them stood ready to run.

"One, two," Theo counted slowly. There was a long pause. "Threeeee..."

They turned slowly and took an exaggerated step forward, then another. Each moment could have been a study for a painting, a living tableau of a footrace, only moving at a snail's pace.

Well, snails don't have feet, but you get the idea.

As they rounded the first corner and started to head my way, Theo was two steps in front of Pelardit. He looked back at him and thumbed his nose. As he did, I held my lute by the neck and swung it slowly into his path. It caught him in the stomach, and he doubled over and went into a somersault that took forever to complete as Pelardit passed him.

Theo got up, glared at me, and took off in leisurely pursuit. He caught Pelardit by the next lap, at which point I grabbed a pair of stools and slid them into his path. He hurdled them both, a smug look on his face that lasted until I retrieved them and sent them across the floor to the other side of the room just in time to collide with him. He ended up plastered against the far wall, then peeled himself away and caught up with Pelardit in a determined effort.

On the third lap, I stuck my leg out. It snagged his outstretched foot, and he went tumbling in a series of complicated rolls that carried him out the door and into the hall as Pelardit, puffing mightily, continued on.

Theo reappeared immediately, churning his legs until he reached the other fool. This time, I stepped in front of him, and we both ended up in a lethargic tangle of limbs on the floor that I rather enjoyed, truth be known. He got up, and I lay there, my face in an expression of lewd bliss as he made his next lap, looking back over his shoulder at me as I slowly got to my feet.

It was the final lap. The entire room looked to where I was standing, waiting to see what I would do this time. As Theo approached, I simply looked at him and smiled.

He stopped, swept me into his arms, and kissed me hard. Pelardit made his turn and crashed slowly into the table right in front of Raimon, then raised his arms in victory.

Theo kept kissing me to the hoots of the guests. Finally, he came up for air and turned to them with a hangdog look.

"So, my lords and ladies," he said. "I lost the race. But right now, I don't care."

And he kissed me again until I swooned in his arms. He picked me up and slung me over his shoulder.

"It looks like you have some serious eating to do," he said to the table. "We shall leave you to it."

He carried me over by the musicians and dumped me on the floor, then plopped down next to me. Pelardit joined us a moment later.

"That went well," murmured Theo.

"Especially considering we never rehearsed it," I said. "I liked the bit with the cushion, Pelardit."

Pelardit acknowledged the compliment with a nod, then slapped his forehead. He stood, removed the cushion, and whistled across the room. As the diners looked up, he spun like an athlete throwing a discus and hurled the cushion back to the Duke of Comminges, who caught it and put it back on his seat. Pelardit sat back down.

"We'll have to perform this again," said Theo. "Maybe pass it on to the Fools' Guild. They could use some new material. What shall we call it?"

"The Fat Man, the Fool, the Footrace, and the Flirt," I suggested.

He smiled and put his arm around my shoulder. "You know alliteration arouses me," he growled in my ear.

"I prefer kissing," I sighed. "And rolling around the floor."

"In front of everyone like that?"

"At the moment it happened, you were the only one in the room," I said.

Pelardit let out a long, dying whistle as one of the maid-servants passed by. She shot him a momentary smile, then went back to her duties.

"Is she your chosen one for tonight?" asked Theo.

Pelardit shrugged, his eyes never leaving her.

"How he woos and wins them without talking is beyond me," said Theo.

"A man who doesn't speak is every woman's dream," I said. "It's when you open your mouths that—"

Phelipa abruptly stood up, looking at the table in horror. "How could you?" she whispered to her husband.

Then, clutching a napkin to her mouth, she ran from the room. The guests looked at Foix in puzzlement.

"My apologies, my friends," he said. "You know how she is. Please, pay it no mind. I have more of this feast waiting for you."

There was a pause; then Raimon turned back to his plate. The others followed his lead.

"What just happened?" wondered Theo.

"Chicken," I said. "They are serving chicken. You enter-tain them. I am going to see if she is all right."

"Chicken," muttered Theo as I left. "Of course."

With all the household servants in attendance at the din-ner, there was no one to stop me from wandering around the *maison* on my own. I sought out the tower and climbed the steps.

Two floors up, I heard a low voice sobbing. I tracked it to a room off the stairs. The door was slightly open. I listened for a moment, then knocked. The sobbing continued.

Well, no one told me to go away. I went in.

Phelipa's room had no more decoration than its mistress. The bed was a plain affair, a simple assembly of pine planks and a thin pallet. It did not look strong enough to support the Count of Foix. Or his marriage.

She was curled up on top of the covers, her face buried in her hands, somehow seeming like a little girl rather than the matriarch that she was. She took no note of my entrance into her chamber.

"Domina, I am here," I said.

She looked up in surprise at my voice. "What are you doing here?" she asked. "Your job is to entertain the guests."

"The guests are the responsibilities of my husband and Perlardit," I said, sitting on the bed next to her. "My job is to entertain my hostess. Apparently, you did not enjoy the act."

"No, it wasn't that," she said.

"I know," I said. "It was the chicken. Nothing consumed that is born of coition. That is your belief, is it not?"

"I have never kept it secret," she said. "All know that Phelipa is a Cathar."

"Not just a Cathar," I said. "You are one of the Perfect, are you not?"

She was silent.

"It was cruel of your husband to serve this meal," I said. "He could have honored your beliefs and kept it simple."

"He was entertaining the Count of Toulouse," she said. "He felt he had to provide an appropriate meal for a corrupt lord."

"Did you not know that he would do so?"

"I thought we had agreed that he would honor my beliefs," she said. "He may do as he likes outside this house, but in here, even the Count of Toulouse is only a guest."

"I hope that the Cathars don't have anything against jesters," I said. "As it happens, we, too, are the product of coition."

"You mock me," she said, but there was a momentary smile.

"I mock everybody," I said. "It is strange. We have entertained all manner of folk, from the nobility of God and men to the lowest of the low. We have performed for Christians, Jews, and Mohammedans. But we have never performed for Cathars. At least, not specifically. Do they have senses of humor?"

"Of course," she said indignantly.

"Tell me a joke, Domina," I said.

"What?"

"You claim to have a sense of humor. Show me."

"A countess does not tell jokes," she protested.

"I don't see why not," I said.

"And how should I amuse a jester?" she said.

"A paradox," I said. "Very well, I will let you off the hook this time. But before this life is over, you will tell me a joke. I prophesy it."

"How did you become a jester?" she asked.

"I fell in love with a jester," I said. "How did you become a countess?"

"I fell in love with a count," she said.

"This falling in love is a tricky business," I said. "One really must be careful about it. You never know where you will end up. How did you become a Cathar?"

"That was a long and thoughtful process," she said. "The very opposite of marriage."

"There," I exclaimed. "That was a joke. How would I go about becoming one?"

"Are you serious?"

"Curious, I would say. I have become increasingly disappointed with the Church, and God knows the bishop here does little to sustain one's faith. Do you think I could become one of the Perfect?"

"In time," she said. "Faith is easy. Keeping faith over time—that is the difficult part. There are so many distractions."

"Dinner parties and such."

"Wandering husbands with wandering eyes," she sighed. "He is a good man at heart. And he loves me, I am sure of it."

"But he serves chicken to the count. Does your husband share your beliefs?"

"He supports them," she said. "But he does not share them. I hope someday that he will. He fears losing his influence with the count. I don't know why my husband continues with him. The count didn't lift a finger to help him when he was held captive. It wasn't until Peire Roger spoke in my husband's behalf that Comminges even got involved. All because their dear friend is married to a Cathar."

She wiped her face with a cloth from a washbasin by the bed.

"Do I look like I have been crying?" she asked.

"Yes," I said.

"Then I must stay here," she said. "Thank you for seeing to me. It was kindly done."

"No more than any wife would do for another," I said. "We share that understanding."

"Do you know what I truly wish to do?" she asked.

"What, Domina?"

"To establish a house of Perfect women. Only women. And in that refuge, we may pray and follow our beliefs without the interference of men."

"A Cathar nunnery?"

"Nunneries are beholden to the corrupt pile of stones that is Rome," she said. "I wish to build a simple place, and retreat there from the complications of the world."

"Will jesting be allowed in this house?"

"I shall give it some serious thought," she said. "Leave me now, Domina Gile."

"I will come see you again, Domina," I said.

I left her, still on her bed but no longer weeping. Sometimes that is all a jester may do. But at least I could accomplish that much.

As I reached the main floor, I saw the Count of Foix approaching, a look of concern on his face.

"Have you been with her? Is she all right?" he said quickly.

"Oc, senhor," I said. "Although, speaking as a wife, I would say not inclined to set eyes upon you ever again."

"Damn," he muttered, glancing up the stairs toward the living quarters.

"Or at least for tonight," I continued. "I would recommend that some effort be put into the apology."

"What can one do for a woman who wants none of the world?" he sighed.

"Give her something not of the world," I suggested.

"And what could that possibly be?" he asked me, looking at me directly for the first time.

"I am of the world, senhor," I said, shrugging. "My knowledge ends at its borders. I leave the otherworldly to others."

"Huh," he said, looking at me more intently. "I never noticed this before."

"What, senhor?"

He pulled open a door. "A word with you, Domina Fool," he said, beckoning to me.

"Alone with you in there?" I asked. "It would be unseemly."

"We shall leave the door open," he said, smiling. "This world will still be very much with us."

He held it open for me.

I went in.

I am not sure why I went in. But I went in.

It was a small office, with a simple maple desk and a shelf with documents piled in untidy heaps. He directed me to a chair in front of the desk. I sat. To my increasing discomfort, he chose to sit on the front of the desk, directly before me.

There was a pair of lit candles illuminating the room. He picked up the candlestick and held it between us so that he could examine my face better. "I was right," he said softly.

"About what, senhor?"

"Underneath all of that whiteface, you are a beautiful woman."

"Right, thanks," I said, hastily getting to my feet. But quicker than thought, he was standing between me and the doorway.

The open doorway.

He always has us with the door wide open, said Marquesia. It's quite shameless.

"Milord, should we not be returning to your guests?" I asked.

"I left them so that I may attend to my wife," he said.

"And I?"

"You did the same."

"She is a very well-attended woman, your wife," I prattled on. "Perhaps we should go attend her now."

"My attentions have turned to you, Domina Fool," he said. "What do you look like without your whiteface?"

"Haggard, old," I said. "That's why I wear it. The beauty is only an illusion. Not even skin-deep, just painted on."

"I have never made love to a jester before," he said, moving toward me.

"Not really worth the experience," I said. "We make fun of you."

"I could use a good laugh, then," he said.

My problem was that I knew many ways to kill an attacker, several of which were available to me right now. But I knew fewer ways to fend off an amorous aggressor without killing him, and that was what I needed to do.

"I have no desire to become another conquest for you to brag about to your friends," I said. "Especially considering that my husband will end up hearing about it."

"You, I will not brag about," he said. "You, I will keep to myself. Let me add that as a lover, I am legendary."

"The problem with legends is that they are unworthy of belief," I said, backing up, which only placed me against the far wall. "Perhaps you could submit some references? A testimonial or two?"

"You know of La Louve de Pennautier?" he asked me. "A woman of such exquisite beauty that all men desired her the moment they beheld her, and the failure to possess her led many to madness."

I had a memory of poor Peire Vidal, one she had so entranced, tied to a bed soaked in his own filth, gibbering in fourteen languages and howling at a moon only he could see.

"I know of her," I said softly. "I know of that madness."

"Then know that her child is mine," he said. "She chose me of all possible lovers, and when we parted, the madness became hers."

"I could hardly accept the testimonial of a madwoman," I said as he closed the gap between us.

His balls, I thought. Grab them and squeeze them until his eyes pop out of his head.

Unless he liked that sort of thing.

"Give yourself to me," he whispered, leaning forward.

My hand inched toward my dagger.

"I will compose a poem for you every day," he whispered, his lips grazing my throat. "Only for you."

"Interesting," said a voice from behind him. "What exactly rhymes with 'fool'?"

My husband was standing in the doorway. Of course.

CHAPTER 11

I am not a jealous man. I have occasionally had concerns over
my wife disappearing on some impulsive investigations
rather than discussing them with me first. But I have done
the same and we have, up to this point, always found our
ways through thickets of danger back to each other again.
Nor has she ever given me any cause to suspect her of stray-
ing from our marriage.

So, I was taken aback to see her pinned against the wall
by one of Toulouse's leading lechers, and I confess to having
a pang of fear—well, more like a stab wound through my
heart—irrational though it may have been.

Then I saw the glint of steel in her hand as she replaced
her dagger, and I felt better again.

The Count of Foix took his time releasing her. He did not
appear in the least flustered by my arrival on the scene. "Aren't
you supposed to be juggling or something?" he asked.

"I work with a partner," I said.

"There's Pelardit," he offered.

"How about I bring him here, and we could swap?"

"I would be the loser in that deal," said the count.

"Don't underestimate his talents," I said.

"You don't expect me to explain this, do you?" asked the
count.

"I can see what is happening without explanation, thank you very much. An apology, on the other hand—"

"I do not apologize to inferiors," he said.

"My wife is superior to you in every way," I said. "Apologize to her."

"Or what?" he smirked. "You will protest my conduct to the authorities?"

"I don't bother with the authorities in circumstances like these," I said.

"Will your honor require you to challenge me to a duel?"

"Nor do I give a fig about pretty little chivalries," I said. "But I have occasionally been known to kill people when they irritate me."

He sat on the edge of the desk and leaned back, his throat exposed. "Do it, then," he said.

My wife took advantage of the moment to run to my side.

"Are you all right?" I asked.

"I am, now that you're here," she replied.

"Touching," said the count. "The gallant husband comes to the slut's rescue."

"If you intend for me to leave you alive, you have a strange way of going about it," I said.

"How far do you think you will get if you kill me?" he said. "You won't make it to the city walls, much less out of the Toulousain."

"The entertainment portion of the evening is over, senhor," I said. "My payment for the wager has been met. We will take our leave of you."

"I am not done being entertained," he said. "I shall decide when it's over, not you."

"We're going," I said to Claudia.

"About time," she replied.

"I know who you really are," he said.

"Enlighten me," I said, exasperated. "A fool is always in search of self-knowledge."

"Your name isn't Tan Pierre," he said.

"A name means nothing," I said.

"I saw you perform before," he continued. "A long time ago, in a different place."

"I have traveled to many places," I said. "And I've been performing for nearly thirty years. Could you narrow it down a little before I completely lose interest?"

"Acre," he said. "You called yourself Droignon then."

I winced before I could bring my reactions under control. He saw it and smiled. It was not a winning smile.

"Acre," I said slowly. "There may have been a tavern there where I sang a song or two. When were you Beyond-the-Sea?"

"Must have been, oh, twelve or thirteen years ago," he said.

"The Third Crusade."

"Oc," he said. "I was with the King of France."

"Not very close to him," I said. "I would have noticed you. I noticed everyone who was of importance."

"You were with some ridiculous boy who called himself a king over a bit of land no bigger than my thumb," he said.

"Yet he was closer to Phillippe Auguste than you were," I said.

"And you were closer still," he said. "You wormed your way right up to the King's ear and whispered evil things."

"You make it sound so dirty," I said. "All I did was tell jokes and sing songs. That's what a jester does."

"Your jokes and songs undermined him more than any sapper did the walls of Acre," he said with contempt. "Then off to home went France, with all of his troops. You have no idea what damage you did to our most holy cause."

"I doubt that anything a fool could say would cause a king to take such a momentous step," I said. "He merely came to his senses, that's all. It had nothing to do with me."

"Then you ran off when the Lionheart decided to take the battle to Jerusalem. What was the matter? Weren't you funny enough to have him betray us further?"

"You truly overrate my importance in the world," I said. "I thought for a moment that you were going to say something interesting, but I was wrong. Let us depart this dull man, my dear."

"It may not be interesting to you, but I think it will interest Count Raimon," he said as I turned to leave. "He should know the poison you could work on a man. It should have quite the deleterious effect on your ability to make a living in this town."

I stopped. "I would rather you not do that," I said.

"This information is something I could keep to myself, of course," he continued.

"There will be a price extracted for this silence, I suppose?"

"I haven't as yet determined what it will be, but yes, there will be a price," he said. "For now, I wish for you to stop nosing about in my affairs."

"Difficult," I said. "It's hard to throw a stick in this town without hitting some woman you're sleeping with."

"Then stop throwing sticks, Fool, or I may change my mind."

I glanced at Claudia. She nodded slightly.

"Very well then," I said. "No nosing about in your affairs. Just don't let my wife be one of them."

"As for that, I promise no pursuit," he said, leering at Claudia. "But if she chooses to stray into my path, I will not hold myself responsible for what happens."

"I'm very careful about where I walk," she said. "Otherwise, I might step in something vile."

"Pity," he said. "You missed a chance for something beyond your dreams tonight."

"If my dreams ever include you, then I shall abandon sleep forever," she said. "Husband, let us go find some civilized company. Surely there is a tavern nearby."

"Sounds like a worthwhile quest," I said. "Good night, Senhor Count. My very best wishes to your gracious wife."

We returned to the great hall, where Pelardit was in the midst of his sleight of hand routine. A minute later, the Count of Foix followed us in.

"My wife sends her regrets," he said. "She has taken ill."

"I understand entirely," said Raimon. "Please tell her that we wish her a speedy recovery, and thank her for her hospitality."

The musicians kept playing as the guests took their leave of their host. We simply packed up and vanished out the door.

"All right, tell us everything," I urged Claudia as we left the courtyard.

By the time she was done, Pelardit was shaking with rage.

"Calm yourself, my friend," I said. "She repelled the onslaught unscathed."

"That's all you have to say about it?" she asked.

"Do you wish me to kill him?"

"No," she said after considering. "But I would like you to be angrier."

"It's all on the inside," I said.

"And you played the scene oddly," she said. "Why did you let him bully you like that? He has nothing to coerce you with. Count Raimon already knows about Droignon and his secret self."

"But the Count of Foix doesn't know that," I said. "Only Count Raimon and Bernard of Comminges know about me. The inner circle of two."

"So you deliberately allowed the Count of Foix to think he now has a hold on you?"

"Yes," I said. "It's how he operates. He bought up Sancho's gambling debts so that he could control the man, although to what end, I do not know. We may find out more about Foix's intentions when he decides how he wants to use me."

"Could we kill him once we find out?" asked Claudia hopefully.

"We'll see," I said. "The main thing we learned is that he sees us as a threat to some plan of his. Which means that he does have a plan worth threatening. And we know that his meeting with the Abbess today was not a carnal encounter."

"I agree," she said. "He kept the door closed with her. So, since we have agreed not to nose about in his affairs, what shall we do?"

"Nose about in his affairs, of course."

"Good," she said with satisfaction. "Now, who is in favor of finding a tavern?"

Pelardit and I raised our hands immediately.

It was late morning when I awoke. I had a pounding in my head that for a change was not from Sancho beating on our door at dawn. Refreshing to feel abysmally hungover with the sun approaching its zenith. One of the best parts of a jester's job is the hours.

Helga and Portia were playing with a ball at the table when I came downstairs. Our daughter still hadn't chosen which hand she liked to use, and I did not want to force the issue. Quite the contrary, ambidexterity being a gift to a jester.

That was assuming she became one, of course. Claudia had her visions of her having a real education. The University of Bologna, and nothing less for our daughter. I humored my wife in this fantasy, but I couldn't see the point. The education at the Fools' Guild was much more practical, in my opinion. No time was wasted on studying law, except for methods of evading it.

Claudia came in with two buckets of water. She was in motley, but had yet to put her makeup on. I looked at her and sighed fondly. She smiled at me.

"You have a lovely face when there's no makeup hiding it," I said.

She stopped smiling. "I heard something similar from the Count of Foix yesterday," she said.

"Curse him for stealing my lines," I said. "And more for trying to steal my wife."

"He tried to what?" asked Helga.

"Our host attempted to seduce me yesterday," said Claudia.

"And you warn me about stable boys," grumbled Helga.

"Avoid all men for now," advised Claudia.

"Sound counsel," I agreed.

"What did he really want?" asked Helga.

"Enough leverage to coerce me into working for him," I said.

"How would seducing Claudia do that?" she asked.

"Well, he would—," I started, then stopped. "Why did he want to seduce you?"

"Because I am so desirable, of course," said Claudia.

"You've been desirable ever since we've come to Toulouse," I said. "Long before, in fact. Why did he wait until last night to let loose the charm?"

"Opportunity," she said. "Or perhaps it was my turn on the list. I really don't care at this point."

"We have been here for six months," I persisted. "There have been ample opportunities for him to catch you alone if he was of that mind. Why last night? Why seduce you at all? What did he want from you?"

"You think that his simple mind believed that I would easily succumb to his allure, and that he could then learn what I had found out about him."

"I do think that. Don't you?"

"My vanity would have me say otherwise," she said. "All right, yes. There was no reason for him to go after me like that unless he's the sort of man to jump on anything female and breathing, and the latter may not even be a requirement."

"Eww," said Helga.

"Which means that he was worried about my talking to either La Marquesia or his wife," reasoned Claudia. "The only problem is, I haven't learned anything worthwhile from either one."

"Not yet," I said. "Some return visits may reveal more."

"Tricky to do without alerting Foix," she said.

"Good thing you're a tricky woman," I said.

"Thanks," she said. "What will you be doing while I am consorting with courtesans and countesses?"

"I have been thinking about Paris," I said.

"Wonderful. Let's go immediately. Why Paris?"

"I have been considering the Third Crusade, and the Count of Foix's role in it."

"Not a major one," she said.

"No. But I find it interesting that he was attached to the King of France back then."

"He certainly bears no love for him now," she observed. "No one in the Toulousain does."

"Does the Count of Foix strike you as the crusading type?"

"Not at present," she said thoughtfully. "But the crusade was years ago. He might have been a different sort of man then."

"Wars do change people," I agreed. "That one changed everyone who took part in it. They went in filled with holy desire and returned feeling betrayed. If they returned at all."

"You were there," Helga said. "How did it change you?"

"It made me want to never see a slaughter like that happen anywhere ever again," I said.

"The Count of Foix seems regretful that there wasn't more of a slaughter," said Claudia. "He blames France and you, and not necessarily in that order."

"I wonder if our friend Baudoin was on that little misadventure," I said. "If he is who he says he is, then he's cousin to Phillippe Auguste. It would have been natural for him to accompany the King. I wonder if Foix could have known him there. Or learned about him."

"Did you see Baudoin there?"

"I don't remember every single parasite latched to the king, just the larger bloodsuckers. What with the three main contingents bumping into each other, I was bound to miss a few."

"So if Baudoin was with France in Acre, he might have made an enemy among the Toulousans there," said Claudia. "One who held a lasting grudge. That's no more implausible than any other idea you've come up with lately."

"Thank you for your confidence in me," I said.

"What is a wife for?" she said.

"Would you like me to answer that?" I asked.

"Not in the least," she said. "Get your foolish face on, then it's off to the dungeons with you."

"I'll trade you for the courtesan and the countess," I offered.

"No deal," she said.

I put on my whiteface, grabbed my gear, and left the house.

I didn't bother ditching Sancho's men this time. I waved as I passed them, whistling as I walked. They glared, then fell into step behind me, not even bothering to conceal themselves.

It probably did not help their irritation that I simply strolled down the Grande Rue to the Château Narbonnais. They stopped in the courtyard while I entered the Palace of Justice, no doubt to alert Sancho to my arrival.

Huc was standing outside Baudoin's cell when I reached that level. He turned when he heard me coming, and whispered excitedly to Baudoin. The Parisians looked at me expectantly.

"Good morning," I said.

"It is nearly noon," said Huc.

"Therefore, still morning," I said.

"Good morning," said Baudoin. "Any news?"

"The sun rose again today," I said.

"Was there ever any doubt that it would?"

"Since you don't know if you will ever see it again, I thought that it would reassure you," I said. "I am always happy to see the sun. It means that I have survived yet another night."

"True enough," he said. "Thank you for that information."

"Well, I'll be off, then," I said.

"Is that it?" asked Huc. "Nothing but the sun?"

"Had you already told him about it?" I asked Huc.

"No, but—"

"Did you have anything more important to tell him?"

"Anything is more important than that," said Huc.

"Actually, now that it has been put in its proper perspective, nothing is more important than that," said Baudoin. "Thank you, Fool."

"Now that I think of it, I do have a question for you," I said.

"Finally," sighed Huc.

"What is it?" asked Baudoin.

"Ever been to Acre?"

"Acre?" he repeated, puzzled. "No."

"Did you go on crusade with Phillippe Auguste? Or make a pilgrimage Beyond-the-Sea?"

"No and no again," said Baudoin. "I was never of a crusading mind. I liked Paris, especially when my cousin was away."

"Why then?"

"I had little to justify my existence other than our kinship," he said. "I received whatever stipend he was willing to give because of my mother, but accompanied by his constant reproaches over my draining his vast resources."

"Can't really blame him," I said. "And you came to Toulouse because that well had run dry."

"Yes," he said. "My mother died many years ago, and the time had come for Phillippe and I to part ways. A leech is less amusing at forty than he is at twenty."

"That's right, you're forty," I said. "Quite a lengthy run of uselessness. I almost admire your tenacity."

"I should have been a jester," he grinned.

"Oh, but that's hard work," I reminded him. "How about you, Huc? Ever been to Acre?"

"Me? Why me?" asked Huc.

"It came up in conversation," I said. "Have you?"

"No," he said. "I was not even in Paris then."

"Really? When did you arrive?"

"When was it, around '97?" Huc asked Baudoin, counting on his fingers.

"You have been in my employ for nine years," said Baudoin. "That would make it '96."

"Where were you before?" I asked.

"I had worked as a servant for a great house in Rouen," said Huc. "But my master died, so I went to Paris to seek my fortune."

"Did you ever find it?" I asked him.

"I found this gentleman," he said. "I have served him faithfully ever since."

"Very well," I said. "That completes my questions."

"Do our answers give you any help?" asked Baudoin.

"They shot down a theory, and that saves me the effort of looking into it," I said. "Good day to you. May you live to see another sunrise."

"And you, friend Fool," he replied.

I left them, thinking.

Baudoin was a worthless man who had led an unimposing life. A pleasant man, to be sure, and that must have served him well in maintaining his royally subsidized existence. His mother must have been a good woman to have gained her son such lengthy protection.

I wondered if her memory would still help him here? Raimon would still have been just a child when she left. Baudoin, if legitimate, would be his only surviving sibling at this point. There had been two others, but . . .

What would a full brother of Toulouse gain? What was he entitled to when there were no others competing with him? Was there a county designated for his use? A castle?

An army?

I was thinking too narrowly in my pursuit, I realized. This was not simply a matter of family squabbling. The squabbling family in this case was made up of well-connected nobles. Wars had risen and thrones had toppled over lesser matters than these.

Let's say that Baudoin's return would place him in a position of command, whether he was suited to it or not. He might gain instant access to Raimon's innermost circle, right there with Comminges, something that might take others a lifetime to attain. And once there, he might present one more obstacle between them and Raimon.

In that light, the Count of Foix may very well have had good reason to destroy Baudoin before he got that far.

I was still chewing on that thought when I ascended into the light of the courtyard. Sancho was waiting for me, my two trackers flanking him.

"I am waiting for you to do something subtle," he said.

"I have been doing subtle things all along. Did you not notice?"

"What were you doing down there?"

"Visiting a prisoner."

"I thought you usually visit the prisoners on Tuesdays."

"Today isn't Tuesday?"

"It's Thursday."

"Sometimes, I visit them on Thursdays. Especially when I think that they are Tuesdays. Tomorrow's Friday?"

"Right."

"Then I haven't missed Mass. Thank you for bringing me up to date. Good day to you, whichever it is."

"Not yet," said Sancho sternly. "You see these two fellows with me?"

"I have been seeing nothing but those two fellows lately."

"They are on permanent Tan Pierre detail," he said.

"Punishment for losing you the other day. They lost a man wearing whiteface and motley in broad daylight, can you imagine that?"

"Dear me, I had no idea I was lost," I said. "I certainly hope that I turn up soon. I am quite fond of me, you know."

"I am ordering them to dog your every footstep until you go to sleep tonight."

"Will they be in the bedroom with me? That would douse the romance. Perhaps they could stay in the children's room and tell Portia a story. She likes stories."

"Or you could simply tell me what the hell it is you're doing."

"Tell you what, friend Sancho," I said. "I'll make a wager with you. I will wager that I can lose your hounds within a half—no, a quarter of a mile of the Porte Narbonnaise, and come back to you in this courtyard without them."

"What are the stakes?" he said, looking interested.

"The usual," I said. "I lose, I talk. I win, then you buy the next drink."

He turned to his men. "Think you can avoid fouling this up?" he asked them.

"We'll be so hot on his tail that he'll feel our breath on the back of his neck," spat one.

"That almost sounds pleasurable," I sighed, batting my eyes at him. "Well, then. Let's be off."

I strolled out of the compound and through the gates.

A few minutes later, I rejoined Sancho, who was still standing there.

"Where are my men?" he asked wearily.

"Somewhere in the Comminges quarter," I said.

"How did you do it?"

"Cloak, hay wain, rain barrel, ladder, rooftop," I said. "There were a few other steps. It happened so fast, I can barely remember it myself. Nearly dried my eyeballs out in the whirlwind. Now, about that drink . . ."

The two men came dashing into the courtyard, out of breath. They looked at me in chagrin.

"Go guard something that isn't moving," ordered Sancho. "Try not to lose it."

They trudged off.

"Don't get too smug about this," warned Sancho.

"I shall only be the right amount of smug," I said.

"Someday, you will run into someone who will beat you at one of these contests."

"I already have," I said.

"What did you lose?"

"I married her."

"That was her loss," snorted Sancho. "Let's get that drink."

He took me to the same tavern as the last time we had shared a drink. The day of La Rossa's death, I thought gloomily.

"The murdered courtesan," I muttered.

"What's that?" asked Sancho, returning with a pitcher of ale and two cups.

"An unfinished ballad about a finished lady," I said.

"La Rossa? Why are you still going on about her?" he asked. "She's done for, and the man who did for her is now in a dungeon with only fools for company."

"Yet I cannot let it go," I said. "I don't think Baudoin killed her."

"He was lying in bed next to her fresh corpse, his knife in her breast," said Sancho.

"In a house full of whores, any one of whom could have crept in there and killed her while they slept," I said. "Which makes more sense than Baudoin doing it."

"Why?"

"Because a man would not leave a city where he had lived for forty years to risk his comfort on slight expectations of welcome, only to throw it all away on a useless murder."

"This man did," insisted Sancho stubbornly. "And you didn't answer my question. Why are you so interested in all of this?"

"I don't know," I said. "But why is the Count of Foix so interested in my interest?"

"The Count of Foix?"

"Come off it, Sancho," I said impatiently. "That's why you've been following me, isn't it?"

"The Count of Toulouse ordered it," he said.

"No, he didn't," I replied. "The Count of Toulouse would be as curious as I am to know what happened to La Rossa, especially if Baudoin turns out truly to be his brother. No, Sancho, the Count of Foix is the one making you interfere with my investigation. You are merely one more line of attack."

"Why would I do anything for him?" scoffed Sancho.

"He bought up your gambling debts, didn't he?"

"I don't know what you're talking about," said Sancho, dropping his voice down.

"Sancho, I heard this from Higini himself," I said. "The Count of Foix owns you."

"He does not!" Sancho shouted. Then he brought his voice back down. "How the hell did you get Higini to tell you that?"

"I won the information from him at dice."

"You conquered Higini? How? Please, tell me the secret," begged Sancho.

"We both used loaded dice," I said. "It made the bet fair again."

"Hah!" he said. "Beat him at his own game. I must remember that."

"Sancho, you are evading the point," I said. "The Count of Foix is squeezing my wife and me so that we are constrained to do his bidding. If I am going to get us out from under his thumb, I will need your help. And I can help you do the same. We can work together."

"Maybe, maybe," he said, looking around to make sure no one was in earshot of the conversation. "Let's say I agree. What is it that you are looking for?"

"A reason the Count of Foix would fear Baudoin so much that he would set him up for La Rossa's murder."

"There is none," said Sancho. "He didn't do that."

"How do you know? I think Baudoin posed a threat to him."

"He may have," said Sancho. "But not to the point that Foix would have La Rossa killed to eliminate him."

"Why not?"

"Because La Rossa was too important to him," said Sancho.

"As a spy?"

"As an earner," explained Sancho.

I stared at him in confusion.

"You don't know?" said Sancho, seeing it. "You honestly don't know?"

"Know what?"

"That bordel and every woman in it pay tribute to the Count of Foix," said Sancho. "He owns the whorehouse."

CHAPTER 12

W hy would the Count of Foix own a bordel?" I asked.

"Why does anyone own any business?" returned Sancho. "To make money."

"But a nobleman—"

"Still needs money," said Sancho. "Lots of it, in fact. It takes much more to sustain the life of a nobleman than a humble soldier like myself. Look around the city and you'll find lots of decaying gentry who can't even keep a decent house, much less one that can entertain the Count of Toulouse. And when you are paying off the Church and the viguier to look the other way while your wife practices her cute little heresies, then that will cost you a few pennies by itself."

"How much does he pay for that?" I asked.

"The bishop came cheap, as you might have guessed, but the abbey didn't," said Sancho. "The viguier, on the other hand, is an old friend of his, so he got a bargain rate, but there are all the bailes to think about. And Foix is not the most lucrative county around, so it's no surprise that the count had to cast about for some profitable enterprises."

"He's a whoremonger," I said, shaking my head in amazement.

"Well, there's worse things," said Sancho. "Although he's probably done a few of those as well. And to be charitable, he treats the ladies very well compared to some of the other places in town. He should. He was running through all his money there before he realized that he could buy the whole thing at once instead of with daily installments. So he did. The Abbess is just a front."

"Although the front is spectacular," I said. "When did Foix make this investment?"

"You remember when—no, you weren't here then. But you know the story about him being held prisoner a few years back?"

"I did. His wife and the Duke of Comminges negotiated his return."

"Right. So, anyhow, there's the Count of Foix imprisoned for six months or more, and you can imagine what that would do to a man of his appetites."

"They didn't feed him?"

"They fed him a normal man's diet, which nearly starved him to death. And they don't bring you women in places like that."

"He must have gone mad."

"Oh, that barely covers half of it." Sancho grinned. "He emerged from captivity half his girth and randy as hell. Once he showed up in Toulouse, there was not a table or a bed that was safe from his hungers, both belly and prick. Bernard and the viguier finally had to take him aside and steer him toward the Abbess's bordel because he was embarrassing them and Raimon. And it was love at first sight."

"He fell in love with an entire bordel?"

"Rumor has it that he went through every woman in the place the first day. Then he bought the place out and kept it exclusively his for a week. They say when it reopened for business, none of the ladies could do more than lie in bed and wave weakly at their customers."

"Nonsense," I scoffed. "He paid them to spread his legend."

"Probably," agreed Sancho. "But it makes for a good story. Once word of his prodigious skills in lovemaking got around, more of the town women took an interest. Made his pursuits more successful. And, of course, it brought word of the bordel to the men who came out of curiosity."

"Which made things lucrative all around," I said. "Whom did he buy it from?"

"Don't know."

"Might be worth finding out. That night we went there with the Parisians?"

"What about it?"

"You were working for Foix then."

"I was with Baudoin on Raimon's orders," he said. "But because of Foix, I will steer anyone who's interested to that bordel."

"You get a commission?"

"It is the best one in town," he said indignantly. "And, yes, I have debts, as you have said. It helps pay them down."

"And that's all that was going on," I muttered. "Damn, damn, damn, damn, damn. Sancho, I have thought you capable of great evil in the past few days, but all you turned out to be was a gambler and a panderer. Forgive me."

"I suppose that counts as an apology," he said.

"How about I buy the next drink?"

"That's more like it," he said, holding out his hand.

"That's two theories gone in a day," I sighed, shaking it.

"What was the other one?"

"I am not going to embarrass myself further by wild speculations," I said.

"Turning over a new leaf, are we?" snorted Sancho. "The minute your speculations stop is when I check your heart to see if it still beats."

"Sometimes I'm right," I said petulantly as the tavern maid came with a new pitcher.

"You're buying this round, so I agree with you," said Sancho.

"How much would it take to buy your way out of the Count of Foix's control?" I asked.

"More than a year's wages," he said.

"I could lend—"

"Shove your loan," he said. "Then I would owe you."

"I wouldn't make you do anything for it," I said.

"I'm just tired of shuffling from one master to another," he said. "I am going to do what I have to do to pay it back, throw my dice in the Garonne, earn my pension, and buy one of the Abbess's castoffs when she no longer has any use for her."

"One of the better retirement plans I have ever heard," I laughed, pouring us another round and raising my cup in salute. "To your future bride. May she still have some energy left."

"I figure cutting back to one man a day will be like a vacation for her," said Sancho.

"Which one do you have in mind?"

"La Navarra," he confessed.

"Why her?"

"She frightens me the most."

"Why is that your principal consideration?"

"I need to be kept on the straight and narrow," he said.

"She is wide and curvaceous," I pointed out.

"But with a short temper and long nails," he said dreamily.

I poured another cup and held it up. "To your taloned, talented, temperamental temptress," I said.

"You will perform at our wedding," he said, knocking his cup against mine.

"But not gratis," I said. "I have done too many free performances lately."

We drank and refilled our cups once more.

"To making our fortunes," he said.

"Amen."

We drank again.

"Our cups are empty," I observed.

"And so is the pitcher," he said, peering into it. "If the pitchers are empy, then we must be full. I have to get back to my post."

He sagged to the floor. I put my hands under his arms and hauled him to his feet.

"How did you manage to outdrink me?" he mumbled as I helped him walk out the tavern.

"I'm taller," I said.

"I should have been taller," he said, staring intently at something no one else could see.

I managed to get him back to his quarters. By the time we arrived, I was exhausted and he was comatose. He collapsed at the base of his cot. I looked at him, wondering if it was worth the effort getting him in. I decided that it was not.

I wandered over to the Grande Chambre, which was empty, then up to the count's office. Raimon was not there. Peire Roger, the viguier, was sorting out some documents and making meticulous entries in a ledger book.

"Good morning, senhor," I said.

"Good afternoon, Fool," he replied.

I looked out the window. "Sure enough," I said. "Is the count about?"

"Off riding with the countess," he said.

"By which you mean riding horses," I said.

"Oc, I do," he said. "None of your smutty insinuations, thank you very much."

"I am happy to hear that they are enjoying each other's company in any way, shape, or form," I said. "It's a lovely day to ride. Do you ride, senhor?"

"I am at an age where things that once gave me pleasure now cause me pain," he said, never taking his eyes from the ledger. "I used to sit a horse with the best of them, fully armored with a lance in one hand and a sword in the other."

"I always felt sorry for the poor horses, carrying all that weight," I said. "Bad enough wearing your own armor, but carrying another's on top of it."

"A motley fool like yourself could get by riding a donkey, I suppose."

"I have had one on occasion," I said. "An ass with his ass on an ass, I used to say. Always good for a laugh in the small towns."

"Do you have any particular business here?"

"None here, none anywhere else," I said cheerfully. "Do I detect within you a desire to have me leave?"

"I do not wish to offend," said Peire Roger. "I do have work to do."

"As do I," I said. "I am doing it now. This is me working."

"Work somewhere else, then," he said.

"As you wish, senhor," I said, bowing.

He had not looked up once during the conversation. Oh, well. I turned to leave; then a thought struck me.

"Senhor?"

"What is it, Fool?"

"You were on the last crusade, were you not? I mean, the real crusade, the one to Beyond-the-Sea, not the farce that is playing out in Constantinople."

"I was there," he said shortly. "I do not like to visit those memories."

"I am not asking about them," I said quickly. "I was just wondering, did you know the Count of Foix back then?"

"We served together the entire time," he replied. "We have been friends ever since."

"And did you know the French king?"

"I was not part of his inner circle," he said. "I was not so well-established as you see me now. Why do you ask?"

"Well, I was wondering if you ever heard about Count Raimon's last brother back then. Did you know nothing of Baudoin?"

"Nothing," he said. "Not by name, not by title, not by existence."

"Yet you accepted the possibility of his legitimacy upon his arrival here without question."

"Possibilities are a wise man's playthings," he said.

"I like that," I said. "May I steal it?"

"Be my guest."

"Do you actually think that Baudoin is the real brother?"

He looked directly at me for the first time. "I think that he is a possibility," he said. "No more, no less."

"What happens if the possibility turns out to be a reality?"

"Why do you care?"

"I have been his tutor, his helper, his confidante," I said. "If he takes his place at the count's right hand, then my fortunes will increase with his."

"You are already the count's favorite. What more could you want?"

"To add to my own possibilities," I said. "Sometimes fools fall out of favor."

"I cannot imagine why," he said, turning back to his ledger.

I watched him for a while.

"That was a cue for you to leave," he said at last.

"Ohhhh."

I was stealing from Helga now, I thought. It had come to that.

I went back to the Palace of Justice and descended to the lower dungeons. Huc was gone. Baudoin, unsurprisingly, was right where I left him.

"Greetings, Fool," he said. "How goes the sun?"

"Past its zenith, on its way to the western horizon," I said.

"Good," he said. "I would fear to hear otherwise."

"Tell me about your mother," I said.

"My mother? What does she have to do with anything?" he asked.

"I don't know," I said. "But, from all I can determine after several days of investigation, you pose no threat to anyone."

"How disappointing," he sighed. "One likes to think one is at least slightly dangerous."

"But you are not. I am wondering if this could be some long-held grudge against your mother."

"Her sins visited upon me? Sounds implausible."

"I am running out of ideas," I confessed. "Paris. Your mother. The King of France. How did he treat her when she came back from Toulouse?"

"I cannot say how she was first received," he said. "My earliest memories are of playing in the palace courtyard."

"Did she live with the king?"

"He was her brother. He provided for her."

"Sumptuously?"

"We did not live extravagantly by royal standards," he said. "She only had four servants to call her own. I had a nanny as well."

"It must have been a struggle for her to get by on so little," I said.

"That was meant to be sarcastic, wasn't it?" he said cheerfully. "Good. Nothing a condemned man likes better than being told by a fool that he should have appreciated his good fortune at the time. Well, we did appreciate it. But we were treated as charity cases at the court, I will tell you that. My mother, the woman who could not keep a husband even after bearing four of his children, who could not do her duty to France by hanging on to the leash of Toulouse. We may have been in the lap of luxury, but we were outcasts in the palace."

"Poor you. Did she have any contact with Toulouse after she came to Paris? Any conversation with embassies or casual visitors?"

"Not that I noticed," he said, thinking. "She was bitter and angry about being discarded like that. She never wanted to have anything to do with Toulouse or its inhabitants ever again."

"And you? What did she tell you?"

"That I was nephew to the King of France and might someday take the throne myself."

"That must have raised your hopes," I said.

"Well, she did mention that I was fourth in line at that point," he said. "That I had two brothers and a sister in a mythical place in the south, who dwelled in a castle with an evil man whom she prayed every day would die a quick but painful death."

"That would be the bitterness and anger you mentioned," I said. "Understandable under the circumstances."

"She took to spirituality more and more as I got older," he said. "Brought in priests, nuns, mystics, not a few who claimed to be sorcerers who could speed up the death of her husband. But he lived on a good long time."

"He was a bull, from what I observed," I said. "I saw him once. It was toward the end of his life, but you could see—"

Baudoin was looking at me strangely, his eyes glistening.

"Please, go on," he said. "You are the first person ever to tell me about my father other than my mother."

"I never knew him to speak to, senhor," I said. "It was only that one time while I was passing through with an earlier master."

"Do I resemble him?" he asked eagerly.

"It's difficult to say after so many years," I said. "Maybe in the set of your mouth. You resemble your brother in that."

"You called him my brother," he said. "Thank you for accepting that."

"I don't know that I truly have," I said. "It's only that it's easier to call him that rather than attach the string of adjectives I would need otherwise. Is that the end of your mother's story of Toulouse? Did she tell nothing else?"

"She said that there might be one man here I could trust," he said.

"Who?"

"She never told me his name," he said. "And she died fifteen years ago, so I cannot say who it is now."

I couldn't say why, but I had the sudden thought that this was the first real lie he had told me.

"Well, I must go off and ponder," I said.

"Ponder?"

"It's a fancy word meaning drinking," I said. "See you when I see you."

"Thank you, Senhor Fool. For everything."

I left the prison and walked out the gates. By the second turning, I knew that I was being followed again. I hadn't thought Sancho was sufficiently recovered from our liquid luncheon to arrange for my new tail, but perhaps he had left standing orders.

This one, whoever he was, was more skilled at the job than the previous fellows. I could not get a good glimpse of him. I wondered if it would be worth the effort of ditching him.

I hadn't been followed by anyone good in a while. I thought I could use the practice.

I quickened my pace slightly, reaching into my bag for my cloak. As I turned a corner, I whipped it out, threw it on, and ducked through an alley. I came out the other side into the flower market and slid through the crowd, staying slightly hunched over to conceal my height, always the thing that gives me away the most. I reached an alley at the other side and ran through it, ducking into a doorway when I turned the next corner.

I waited a few minutes, then glanced cautiously around. I saw no one.

I resumed my journey, feeling smug. The feeling vanished soon after as I realized that he was still on my path. This fellow really knew what he was about.

The game was getting tiresome. I wasn't going anywhere that I truly needed to conceal, but I didn't like someone being better than me on general principle. I decided to head toward the Yellow Dwarf to see if any of my colleagues were about.

Pelardit was there. I sat by him and muttered, "I'm being followed."

He shrugged. He'd heard that before.

"It's different this time," I said. "I can't see him, and I can't shake him."

That got his attention. He glanced toward the door.

"I doubt he'll come inside," I said. "But I would like to know who it is. I am going to have a drink, then I am leaving. Try to pick him up, but don't let yourself be spotted."

He nodded, his face serious now.

I had a drink to cover my visit there, then a second one for luck. I considered a third one for authenticity, but I was still feeling the effect of my time with Sancho, so I decided to let that be enough.

"Until tomorrow, Hugo!" I bellowed as I lurched out the door.

I wove back and forth on my way home, taking twice my usual time to get there. Maybe I could bore my pursuer from his objective.

Once at my front door, I sorted through my bag until I found my key, then went inside. Claudia and the girls were still somewhere else. I peered out the window, but saw no one.

After a while, the coded knock came. I opened the door and admitted Pelardit.

"Did you see him?" I asked.

He nodded.

"Did you see who it was?"

He shook his head, then pulled his cloak over it and hid his face with his hands.

"Show me," I said.

He sat at the table, then walked two fingers across it, taking a stumbling, serpentine route.

"That's me?" I asked.

He nodded, then indicated for me to continue the journey. I touched my fingers to the table and walked them around. He then had the two on his right hand start following mine.

"That's the tail," I said.

He nodded. Then he brought the fingers of his left hand into play, tiptoeing them behind the right, stopping and diving for cover.

"And that's you," I said.

He nodded.

We continued until my fingers decided that they were home. His right hand stood and watched for a while, then proceeded away, his left still following. Then his right hand suddenly flew off the table, fluttering into nothing. He lifted his left pointer which looked around in frantic confusion. Then the hand collapsed.

"You lost him?"

He hung his head.

"I must pay Sancho my compliments," I said. "He found a man good enough to follow me and to lose you. I didn't know any such existed in the count's forces."

Another knock, and the ladies were home.

"Dee! Dee!" squealed Portia on seeing my colleague, and the fool swept her up and danced her around the room.

"We have earned dinner," said Claudia, putting her basket down on the table. "A brace of rabbits, a loaf of bread, a skin of wine, and a bunch of carrots. Pelardit, as long as you can keep Portia entertained, you are welcome to join us."

Still holding her to his chest, he bowed low in response, which turned her upside down. She shrieked.

"Entertained, but not overstimulated," I cautioned him. "So, ladies. How was your day?"

"Only profitable financially, I'm afraid," said Claudia as she skinned the rabbits. "I tried to visit at our favorite bordel, but I was barred from entry."

"They don't want your tutelage anymore?"

"We arrived after noon, thanks to our late rising," she said. "The ladies were already at work, so Carlos sent us packing. Then we tried the Countess of Foix, but were told that she was indisposed. I suggested that if she needed cheering, we were some of the best cheerers in town, but once again, we were asked to leave."

"Politely, I hope."

"Oh, we were kicked out with the very best of manners," she said, chopping away. "So, we turned our efforts to the practical side of foolery. Hence, the rabbits. How about you?"

"I have drunk much, learned some things, unlearned several more, and now have a shadow worthy of the title."

"Start with the last part," she said, tossing some onions into the pot.

By the time I was done, the stew was bubbling away, and my wife and Helga were seated across from me, their chins resting on their hands.

"Sancho is really taking you seriously now," said Helga. "I wonder what he thinks you know?"

"I wonder if you actually know something already," said Claudia. "Only you don't know that you know it."

"If only my elusive tail could follow the wanderings of my mind," I said. "Maybe he could find it for me."

"There are still too many possibilities to narrow it down," said Claudia.

"Possibilities are a wise man's playthings," I said loftily.

"Did you make that up just now?" asked Helga.

"Of course," I said.

"Right," said Claudia skeptically. "But if they are a wise man's playthings, they'll be of no use to you."

"Oooh," said Helga.

"Ooooh," echoed Portia.

Pelardit grinned.

Claudia ladled the stew onto slabs of bread and set them down before us.

"Delicious," I said. "Wonderful how you can make a stew out of anything you throw in."

"We could call it Anything Stew," said Helga.

"Or Possibility Stew," said Claudia, winking at me. Then she suddenly looked thoughtful.

"What is it?" I asked.

"A glimmering of an idea," she said. "You've been thinking about Raimon's mother as the root of all of this."

"Raimon and Baudoin's mother, if the latter tells true."

"Raimon's father, the old Raimon, repudiates her after three children. Why?"

"Something political. She was no longer of use to him, and he wanted to marry someone else. That's usually how things work in Toulouse."

"And he was willing to repudiate all of France along with her," she mused. "Risky maneuver. That could make someone angry for a very long time."

"Her, to pick the obvious example. She could have raised Baudoin to embark upon a long-term course of vengeance."

"I was thinking about someone local," she said. "It must have been a huge scandal when it was happening. There is nothing about it in Balthazar's notes?"

"Predates his time here," I said. "This was, what, forty years ago?"

"Who would still be around who would have been aware of it at the time?" she asked. "Someone in the inner circle for over forty years, so in their sixties or more."

"Well, the viguier's up there," I said. "Only he hasn't been the viguier the entire time."

"But he was an advisor to Raimon the Fifth," she said.

"True, but not that far back, from what I know."

"There may have been others who were in favor with the old Raimon, but fell out with the current one," she said. "We need someone with a long memory. A gossip."

"We should ask Hugo," I said. "If he doesn't know himself, he will know someone who does."

"Then that will be our next task," she declared.

We looked at each other happily.

"And his ale is good," we said at the same time.

In bed later, as I was drifting off, Claudia sat up.

"What is it?" I asked sleepily.

"Where did she go when he threw her out?" she wondered.

"Who?"

"The Countess of Toulouse. Where did she go?"

"Is that important?"

"It's another possibility," she said. "Go to sleep. We can't find that out now."

I settled back down and commenced the serious business of sleeping. Then I noticed that she was still sitting up.

"What is it now?" I asked.

"I just thought of the strangest possibility of them all," she said. "One we have completely missed."

"Which is?"

"Which is so strange that I am not going to bother you with it," she said, leaning down to kiss me. "Go to sleep."

Well, that was both intriguing and irritating. But I was too tired to pursue it. I fell asleep at last, with my wife sitting beside me, thinking into the night.

CHAPTER 13

M en. They always think everything is about them, because they have the wealth, the power, and the long, sharp, pointy metal things to keep the wealth and the power.

Which is why they think that they are the only real source of trouble in the world. Oh, they can blame us for their lapses into imperfection, we daughters of Eve, but for a woman to actually wreak havoc on her own? Impossible. We do not have the will, the initiative, or the courage.

So they think.

I had let my husband rope me into this investigation because I love him, and because he believed in Baudoin's innocence. But innocence of what? Killing La Rossa—very well, he may have been innocent of that. But of being a parasite, a spoiled brat even at forty years of age, a man who thought nothing of coming to a new place and expecting to be pampered like the lapdog he had been all his life, and then to go one day after his arrival to use and despoil a woman who had been driven to that life because . . . well, I did not know her reasons. No woman chooses that world easily. But if Baudoin was innocent, it was only of murder.

Theo thought him the target of this attack, the pawn in the greater game, because of the larger piece he might become if he made it to the last rank. Exactly what a man would think of another man in this situation. And the poor woman,

buried and forgotten, was just a means to that end. I had allowed myself to be carried along in this thinking, but it had
gotten us nowhere. It was time to do some thinking of my
own.

I did not sleep more than an hour that night. When the
cock crew, I was already up and in costume. Not in makeup
and motley. Not today, not yet. I needed to disappear, to become someone that no man would watch or take seriously.

To be a woman in a crowd of women.

So, my face free of powder, chalk, and rouge, my body
clothed normally, with a cloak over all and a basket on one
arm, I did what a woman was expected to do, hoping to find
another woman doing exactly the same.

I went to market.

I reached the Porte Villeneuve right as the guards were
pulling the gates open for the morning. The farmers' wains
were lined up outside, bringing in vegetables, milk, and
cheese for the hungry city. I watched them roll by, and
waited for my quarry.

There she was, the old woman in the house of the young,
the hag amidst the beauties, the one who stayed in the back
where she couldn't frighten away the customers, sleeping
alone, sweeping up the remnants of sin every morning.

Sylvie entered Toulouse, carrying a basket like mine.

She did not mark me. Most people live their lives without expecting someone to follow them, because most people live their lives without being followed. But I was not
most people. I checked constantly to see if I was being
tailed while I dogged Sylvie's footsteps.

Of course, if the man who followed Theo so successfully
was now after me, then I doubted I would be able to lose him.
Or even spot him. But as far as I could tell, no one was after
me now.

I made some minor purchases—a loaf of bread, two

bunches of grapes—while watching her shop for her ladies, no doubt hungry after a hard night's work. As she crossed the square to a wain filled with turnips and parsnips, I did the same, arriving at the same time.

"Oh, Sylvie, is it not?" I said in surprise.

She looked at me uncertainly.

"Well, of course, you wouldn't recognize me without the whiteface," I laughed. "It's Gile, the fool."

"Oc, now I know you," she said shortly.

"Are you feeling any better today?" I asked. "You seemed quite upset about Marquesia taking Julie's room."

"All the ladies are allowed their feelings," she said bitterly. "But not the servant."

"That isn't fair at all," I said sympathetically. "Don't you have any friends there now that Julie is gone?

She shook her head sadly.

"Have you no friends outside the household?"

"The house is all we have left since the old master—," she started, then stopped.

"We?"

"Julie and I," she said. "All I had left was her. And now she is gone."

"Will it help to talk to me?" I asked. "I am a good listener."

"So you may tell her story in taverns?" she sneered. "No one cares about her story anymore."

"I do," I said. "You do. And you have your own story. When you pass from this life, both will be lost."

"Then let them be lost," she said. "Let us fade from the world without leaving a trace. Isn't that what happens to most people?"

"Most people leave families and friends," I said.

"Well, I have none, so let that be an end to it," she said.

"Did you ever have a family?"

"I was born to servants, grew up a servant, and will die a servant," she said. "I have never known anything but service."

"But you served another once," I said. "A master in a great house, you said. Along with Julie."

"Oc," she said.

"Who was your master then?" I asked.

She looked at me, suddenly afraid. "Why do you want to know that?" she asked, looking around.

"I was wondering why she was killed," I said.

"She was killed by that man they locked up," she spat. "The one who slept next to her after he did it."

"I don't think so," I said. "I don't think he killed her, and I am beginning to wonder if it ever had anything to do with him."

"Who then?" she stammered. "Who could have—? Why would any of them—?"

"Any of who?"

She was silent.

"Who, Sylvie? The other women? The Abbess?"

"They wouldn't have," she said slowly. "None of them. None had any reason."

"Are you certain about that, Sylvie? These are not nuns we are talking about. For that matter, I have known nuns who were more than capable of murder. There is not a woman in that bordel who could not stab someone in the heart. The question is, did any of them?"

"How would I know?" she asked numbly. "I stay in back. I sleep next to the kitchen. I have long learned to ignore the sounds coming from the rooms upstairs."

"Who among the ladies hated her? Enough to kill her?"

"None of them," she insisted.

"Who among them could have been working for someone on the outside?"

"Could have been? Any of them, I suppose. What about me? You think me incapable of murdering her?"

"I do, Sylvie," I said softly. "I think you loved her like a daughter, and she broke your heart every day she was there. You raised her, didn't you?"

"I had to," she said. "No one else would. Her mother died when she was young."

"And her father?"

"He provided for her," she said.

"How? How did he do that? Who was her father, Sylvie?"

"I won't talk to you. I shouldn't be talking to you. She's dead and buried, and nothing can bring her back."

"And if the wrong man swings for her death, Sylvie, what then?" I asked. "Will her soul ever find peace? Will yours?"

"I won't talk to you," she cried, and she turned and ran.

People were staring. I don't know how much they overheard. I walked after her. She was old, she couldn't run fast or for very long. And she had only one place to run in the world.

I caught up with her just before she reached the leper house.

"Leave me alone," she said tearfully.

"What if Julie's murderer still walks among us?" I asked her. "What if she lives in the house where you sleep every night? How safe will you be?"

"It was that man who killed her," she said. "That's what everyone says."

"He had no reason to," I said. "He came for the pleasures she could give him, and slept like a spent, drunken lecher afterwards."

"How could you know this?" she asked.

"I don't," I said. "But I think I know one who does. If I can prove that Baudoin fell asleep while Julie still lived, will you tell me everything you know?"

"How can you do that?"

"I must ask you to be brave," I said, nodding at the leper house.

"No," she whispered as she saw my intent. "Not in there."

"Just the front parlor," I said. "We will not risk contagion."

"But they are cursed," she said.

"They are afflicted," I replied. "But they are in God's care."

"God is not in that house," she said.

"Will you not learn the truth?" I asked.

"I know the truth," she insisted.

"I think not," I said. "But let us find out who is right."

I held my hand out to her. She looked up at the leper house, took a deep breath, and placed her hand in mine, pressing a kerchief to her mouth and nose with the other.

We walked to the door set in the high brick wall. I pulled the cord that snaked through a small hole to the side, and a bell rang somewhere. There was a wait; then a door opened and footsteps approached. A tiny slat slid back, and one blue eye peered at us through the peephole.

"What do you want?" said a man.

"To visit one of the unfortunates in your care," I said.

"Your name?"

"I am Domina Gile, the jester," I said. "This lady is Domina Sylvie."

"Whom do you wish to see?"

"The curious thing is that I do not know his name," I said. "But I have spoken to him several times. He lives on the upper floor in the back. The middle room."

"Senhor Montazin," he said, his voice softening with affection. "He will be pleased to have visitors."

A bolt slid back, and the door opened.

I braced myself for the sight, but the man who stood before us was not afflicted by anything but age. He was gaunt and gray, and his hands shook with a slight tremor.

"I am Adhémars," he said. "I am the caretaker for this house."

"You have earned your place in Heaven, senhor," I said, making courtesy. "As well as my respect and admiration."

He nodded, then beckoned to us to enter. I went through immediately. Sylvie hesitated, then followed as I tugged at her hand. Adhémars closed the door securely behind us and slid the bolt back.

"Not the sturdiest bolt," I observed.

"No one seeks to break in here," he said wryly. "We have nothing to steal but disease. Come, I will seat you in the parlor. There are some preparations to be made."

The parlor was plain, especially compared with that of its neighbor to the rear, but it was pleasant. The windows were large, allowing both breeze and sun. He showed us to a bench by the front window, then unfolded a large screen and set it up in front of a chair by a door opposite us.

"I do not fear to look upon him," I said.

"I appreciate that," he said. "But Senhor Montazin does not wish to be looked upon."

"I understand," I said.

Sylvie was trembling beside me.

Adhémars walked behind the screen. We heard his footsteps ascending stairs, then silence. Then he returned, poking his head around the screen.

"He will be with you soon," he said.

He left, the footsteps receding into the rear of the house. Then came a soft shuffling step, followed by a long pause. Then another.

He took an excruciatingly long time to come down, and

we could hear him wheezing with the effort when he reached the ground floor. There were a few more tentative steps; then we heard him collapse into the chair behind the screen with a sigh of relief.

"That's my full daily regimen of exercise," he said with a choked laugh. It was the voice that had hailed me from that upper window so many times.

"Senhor Montazin, it is a pleasure to learn your name at last," I said.

"It is gracious of you to see me, Domina Fool," he said. "It has been an eternity since my last visit. Is that Domina Sylvie from the whorehouse with you?"

"Oc, Senhor," muttered Sylvie, not looking up.

"I was wondering what was taking you so long at the market," he said. "You are usually back before now. I should be smelling the cooking aromas. You must be a marvelous cook."

"I—I have been told so," she said.

"You observe a great deal," I said.

"My window is my only view of the world, but it is an active one," he said. "Especially in the evenings."

"How long have you lived here?"

"Eleven years. Since my return from Beyond-the-Sea, my sins absolved and my body destroyed."

"You were on Crusade?"

"Sailed away on a leaky vessel with two hundred Toulousans. Then, when the curse took me, I fought with the Order of Saint Lazare."

"The lepers' order. Brave men."

"Easy to be brave when you know you are dying," he said. "You wish for Death to relieve you of this world, and hope that you will be restored to your body come Judgment Day, as the prophets foretold."

"But you did not die."

"No," he said. "Many is the day that I wish that I had. The pain—well, the pain and I have reached an accommodation of sorts. We keep each other company."

"Tell me more about the view from your window," I said.

"Is that why you are here? To hear of the salacious goings-on of my lovely neighbors?"

"Of one in particular," I said. "La Rossa."

"Ah, how I miss her," he said sadly. "I would have gone to the funeral, only—you know."

"Tell me about her," I said.

"A loud, lusty woman," he said. "Her cries filled the night air, and she never closed her shutters. Not like that peevish girl occupying her room now."

"You could hear her entertain her customers?"

"Hear, see. Sometimes on a good night, I could swear that I caught her scent floating across the yard, a sweet, musky perfume."

"You watched her, you filthy, perverted dog," accused Sylvie.

"I watched her, Domina," he said. "And more than watched in time."

"What do you mean?" I asked.

"There came a night, as she lay pinned to her scarlet sheets by yet another fat, sweaty merchant, that I thought I saw her look directly at me. She smiled, and I caught my breath. For that brief instant, I felt the pain leave my body. It was miraculous."

"Blasphemy!" cried Sylvie.

"Old servant of whores, let me tell my story," he said. "I must tell it now, or I may never tell it again."

"Please, Sylvie, we need to hear this," I urged her. "Pray, senhor, continue."

"When her last customer had left, when the lanterns had

been doused and the front door closed and barred, when the women on either side had collapsed into snores, she came to the window and looked out. 'Senhor,' she whispered. 'Can you hear me?' 'Oc, I can,' I whispered back. 'Can you see me?' she asked. 'I can, and I make no apology for it,' I said. 'I ask none,' she said. 'I know who you are, and what you have suffered for Christ's sake. I have long known you were watching me. It is our secret, senhor, one that thrills me more than any man may do.'

"Well, there was a pretty thing," he said. "All the time I thought I was watching her unsuspected, and she knew. She had left the shutters open—for me. She had screamed her passions into the night—for me. And now, we were speaking without pretense.

"'Senhor,' she said. 'Will you show your face to me? Your true face.' 'It is not a face that bears showing,' I replied. 'It is a twisted, ugly thing, and not deserving of view by one so fair.' 'But I would look upon it,' she said. 'I hear your voice, and I feel the man behind it, underneath the cursed skin. Let me see it.'

"I stepped into the moonlight and showed her," he said. "Waited for her to scream, or laugh, or worse, express pity. But she did none of those things. Do you know what she did?"

"Tell us," I said.

"She said, 'You are beautiful, senhor.' Beautiful! Me, a twisted, scabrous, misshapen remnant of a man, and she called me beautiful. 'It is cruel of you to mock me, lady,' I said to her. She said, 'I do not mock. You have watched over me like a guardian angel, although I deserve none. You look at me, and you do not judge. You do not condemn.' 'I look, lady, because that is all I ever shall do,' I said. 'You think me better than I am. I look because I would touch, but touching would only cause us both untold agonies.'"

I glanced over at Sylvie. She was now looking directly at the screen, still with the kerchief pressed to her face.

"She smiled at me. 'Tell me how you would touch me,' she said. 'Tell me, and I will tell you how I would touch you.' She let her gown fall away and stood in all her beauty at the window. I did the same. And we made love. We were fifty feet apart, but I have never felt closer to anyone in my life.

"It became our evening ritual, our whispered encounters. Her way of letting me know that she had survived the degradations visited upon her body by men, mine of letting her know that I had survived the degradations visited upon my body by Fate. It made her feel safe. It made me feel whole."

He started to weep.

"We were both deceived," he said. "She is gone, and all of my pain is returned threefold. I could not save her."

Sylvie was weeping now, the kerchief moving to her eyes. I thought about poor Julie, spending her best years in a bordel, a blur of bestial men in rut. I saw her through Montazin's eyes, saw her come alive for the first time, and I wept for her death, and for the loss of her life, which happened long before her death. There we sat, the three of us. The only people in the world who still cared enough about Julie to weep for her a few days after the rest of the world had forgotten her.

But I still had a task to accomplish.

"The night she was killed," I said. "Did you see it happen?"

"No," he said. "I wish that I had. I would have staggered across with what's left of my strength and strangled that bastard myself."

"But your evening encounter?"

"Happened as it always did. I watched her with that man with the fancy cloak. He had her wearing it at one point. Just the cloak, of course, nothing else, and she swirled around the room with it like a conjurer's demoness. I watched as she teased, then struck, and then surrendered to him. Then he fell asleep, and she came to her window and I to mine, and we made love and whispered to each other. 'My angel,' she cried out. And when we were done, she lay in bed by the slumbering drunk, and I watched over her until her eyes closed. Then mine closed as well. It was the clamor the next morning that awoke me."

"You never told anyone of this?" I asked.

"No one," he said. "No, wait. I confessed it to Father Bonadona."

"The priest at Saint Agnes?"

"Oc. He comes here once a week. Not the holiest of men, but he's trying. Said that if Jesus could sit with lepers, then so could he."

"He puts us to shame," I said. "Senhor, I cannot be for you what La Rossa was, but if it will ease your pain, I will visit you."

"I would like that more than I can say, Domina Fool," he said. "Thank you for listening to me today."

"Thank you, senhor."

We left him there, and I walked with Sylvie back to the bordel.

"That was nothing but a twisted fantasy," she said. "A sick man's sick mind, wanting a woman he could never have. Wanting any woman."

"Do you really think that, having heard him?" I asked her. "You see how his window faced hers. Is it so difficult to believe that of him? Of Julie?"

"She never loved anyone," said Sylvie. "She was not capable of it."

"We are all capable of it," I said. "Maybe the only man she could love was one she knew could never touch her. Maybe that's why she felt safe with him."

"We will never know, will we?" said Sylvie. "She's dead."

"But not by Baudoin's hand," I said. "And if she was killed because of something in her own life, then I need to find out more about that life. Which means you have to tell me about it."

A bell rang in the distance. She looked in the direction of the church, then back to me.

"I must go to Mass," she said. "I will make my confession there. Come see me this afternoon. I will be tending the garden in back."

"Thank you, Sylvie," I said, taking her hand.

She was startled at the touch. She snatched it back and ran inside the house.

I walked back to the city, thinking about what I had heard. Poor Senhor Montazin. To find a kind of love after love no longer seemed possible, and to have it cruelly taken away. Yet he . . .

Someone was following me. Someone large and male, without making pretense of concealment. That bothered me. Someone only wanting to know my whereabouts and wanderings would have stayed back and let me lead him to my next location. But this man lacked any such subtlety.

All around me, people were going about their daily business. I walked among them like I was one of them and looked about for escape routes. I saw a nice twisty alley off the Montardy Square that suited my purposes. I took a deep breath and turned in, starting to run.

Then I was shoved from behind, sending me off balance into a wall. Before I could turn, someone seized both my wrists.

"Don't get the chance to rough up women the way I like to anymore," said a hoarse voice.

It was Carlos, the guard from the bordel.

"What do you want?" I cried, struggling to break free.

"Better keep quiet, lady, or I'll break your arms, one at a time."

I stomped at his instep, but he shifted quickly to avoid it.

"You have to stay away from now on, do you hear me?" he growled. "No more nosy questions. And just so you learn the lesson real well—"

He twisted my arms behind my back. I gasped in pain. He started groping my body until he found my dagger.

"Thought so," he said, taking it and sliding it into his belt. "Treacherous little bitch like you is bound to have a knife somewhere. I was told to rough you up, but it's up to me how I was going to do it. I got something in mind for you. Don't like being made a fool of like that, getting knocked down by a woman."

"You leave my mother alone!" came a voice from behind us.

He turned, still gripping me. I looked over my shoulder. There was Helga, the fierceness on her face undercut by the fact that she was holding a rag doll in one hand. Her voice, for all the threat contained in it, sounded like a ten-year-old's.

"Oh, it's the little girl," laughed Carlos. "I'm betting you still might be big enough for me to play with when I'm done with your mama."

"I'll stop you," said Helga. "I'll hit you with my dolly."

Carlos guffawed, then forced me down to my knees in front of him and leaned over me. "Go ahead," he jeered.

She grabbed a leg of the doll in each hand, stepped forward, reared back, and swung it hard. Its head smacked into Carlos's jaw with a resounding clunk, and he staggered back into the wall, his grip on my arms loosening. He looked at Helga, dazed.

"If being beaten by a grown woman is bad," said Helga as she walked toward him, "just think how much worse it is to lose to a little girl."

She swung again, and the doll's head crashed into Carlos's temple. His eyes rolled up and he sagged to the ground. I shook my wrists until the feeling returned, then felt his neck for a pulse.

"Is he dead?" asked Helga.

"No," I said.

She raised the doll for another blow.

"No," I said again.

"Even after what he did?"

"Even after what he did."

I took my dagger from his belt and slipped it back up my sleeve.

"Let me see that," I said, holding my hand out for the doll.

She gave it to me. I felt the head. Inside was a round chunk of something heavy and metallic.

"Iron?" I asked.

She nodded.

"From where?"

"From a blacksmith," she said. "By the stables."

"Of course," I sighed. "This isn't the doll that Theo gave you for Christmas."

"Of course not," she said, offended. "That's my special doll. That's the one I play with. I made this one up for just in case."

"Let's get out of here," I said, handing it back to her.

"What about him?"

"He's too heavy to drag. We'll just leave him. People will think he's a drunk sleeping it off."

We slipped down the alley without being observed.

"How long were you following me?" I asked when we emerged onto the street.

"I woke up when I heard you moving around," she said. "By the time I had my clothes on, you were out the door. But I figured out where you were going."

"How?"

"I remembered you wanted to catch Sylvie alone. That early in the morning, it could only mean the market. So, I went in that direction until I saw you."

"I never marked you following," I said.

"Really? You really didn't?" she said, nearly bursting with pride.

"How much did you hear?"

"Nothing in the market," she said. "And I stayed outside the leper house. I didn't want to climb the walls. I listened to you talk to Sylvie in front of the bordel. I waited until you left. I was going to tail you until you got home, but then I saw Carlos going after you, and I didn't like the look of that."

"How long after I left the bordel did Carlos follow me?"

"Almost right away," she said. "But he didn't come from the bordel. He was waiting for you across the road."

"I didn't pick him up until I reached the gate," I said as we reached our house.

"Always be on guard," she reminded me.

"Lesson learned, Apprentice," I said. "Have I thanked you for coming to my aid?"

"It was fun," she said. "First time I've gotten to play with my new doll."

Theo and Portia were not at home, but there was a note on the table: *Gone to see Hugo.*

"Let's go meet them," I said.

"You can't go out looking like that," she pointed out.

"Why not?"

"You look too normal. Everyone will think something bad happened."

"Good point," I said.

I went to change into my makeup and motley, grabbed my gear, and rejoined her.

"Better?" I asked.

"Much better," she said.

Theo was sitting at our usual table at the Yellow Dwarf. Portia was scooting around the tavern, gabbling with the few customers who had nothing better to do in the morning.

"Is she still too young for ale?" Theo asked me as I came up.

"I should think so," I said, sitting next to him.

"Good," he said, filling our cups. "That means there is more for the rest of us. Where have you been?"

"To market," I said. "Would you like some grapes?"

Portia came running up at the sound of my voice and climbed into my lap. "Gwape?" she asked.

I gave her some, and she started cramming them into her mouth.

"One at a time, dear," I admonished her; then I turned to see Theo and Helga, their cheeks bulging with a handful of grapes each, their eyes bugging out wildly in an effort to make each other laugh.

"It will be a miracle if you survive your upbringing," I said to Portia, who was giggling at the sight.

"Did you bring back anything else?" asked my husband after swallowing.

"Bread, information, and an attack," I said.

"Tell me," he said.

When I was done, he turned to Helga and said, "Show me."

She handed him the doll, and he inspected it critically.

"Did you learn this at the Guild?" he asked her.

"No," she said. "I thought of it on my own."

"Clever girl," he said. "You've invented a new trick. I am going to put this in my next report to Father Gerald. Helga's Doll."

"They'll name it after me?"

"It's your invention," he said, handing it back to her.

"How lovely," she sighed.

"Is there anything in Guildlore named after you?" I asked him.

"There's a song about a cow," he said.

"Oh, I know that one," said Helga, wrinkling her nose. "It's disgusting."

"Now, let me understand how all of this started," said Theo. "You got up before dawn to intercept Sylvie because you wanted to find out more about La Rossa."

"About Julie," I corrected him.

"About a whore who has been working out of a bordel since who knows when," said Theo. "Why do you think she matters in any of this?"

"Because she was killed," I said.

"But that was because of Baudoin," he said.

"So you say," I said. "But I say you are wrong."

"Based on what?"

"Based on me saying it," I said. "And because you have yet to come up with a better explanation."

"I could give you one why it isn't her," he said.

"Go ahead."

"Whatever reason to kill her that exists in the world you believe in has existed long before now," he argued. "Yet she didn't actually get murdered until Baudoin showed up in that bordel. Therefore, it was because of him."

"I refuse to accept any explanation that is based upon the logic of a fool," I said.

"And I refuse to accept any explanation that is based upon the intuition of a woman," he said.

"You mean the logic of a woman," I said.

"There is no such thing," he said.

"Oh, now you've done it," I growled. "You've raised my hackles."

"Is that what those are?" he asked, inspecting my neck critically. "Do you really think you are on the right path?"

"I must be," I said. "I received the tender ministrations of Carlos as a result."

"Probably because the Abbess was angry that you were delaying her breakfast by making Sylvie late."

"Has anyone tried to kill you lately?"

"I do have a mysterious follower," he pointed out.

"Hardly amounts to the same thing. Have you accomplished anything today?"

"Hugo, a question for you," called Theo.

Our host came over to join us.

"I'm looking for some vintage gossip," said Theo. "Rare and refined, from the very upper echelons of society going back forty years."

"Llora de Bretanha, if you're feeling brave enough," said Hugo.

"Who is she?"

"She was one of the great beauties of her day," said Hugo. "She was also one of the cleverest. Raimon the Fifth used to run through mistresses and discard them within a month or two, but she hung on for quite a while. He had to set her up for life to get rid of her."

"Set her up how?"

"Nice house in town, and enough properties outside to maintain her in style."

"I should have been a count's mistress," I said. "Much better pay than being a jester."

"But why must I be brave?" asked Theo.

"Sometimes a great beauty of the day forgets that the day has passed," said Hugo. "She has fallen out of favor with current society, but she refuses to accept it. Or believe it. I hear that she can be—aggressive."

"Oh, this I want to see," said Helga.

"You won't see her, little one," said Hugo. "Or you either, Domina. She will only receive men."

"How old is she now?" asked Theo.

"I would guess somewhere in her early sixties," said Hugo.

"Then I shall pay her a visit this very morning," declared Theo.

"Guard your virtue," I said.

"Never had any to guard," he replied. "Here is my challenge, wife. I wager that my investigation will bear fruit before yours."

"What are the stakes?" I asked.

"A month of getting up first with Portia," he said.

"Done," I agreed immediately. "Hugo, you are our surety."

"Ale will be withheld if either of you go back on this," he said solemnly.

"Don't even suggest that," said Theo hurriedly. "Good. The race is on. Whoever finds the killer first wins."

"What if the killer finds you first?" asked Hugo.

"Then the killer has to get up with Portia," said Theo.

"Oooh," said Portia.

CHAPTER 14

Theo was off at a run, leaving Portia staring at me with that look of expectation that veteran toddlers have.

"That's cheating!" I yelled at my husband.

I saw his hand wave at me over his shoulder as he disappeared around a corner. He never looked back.

"Right," I said, scooping up my daughter. "The quickest way is for me to give Portia to you, Apprentice."

"All right," said Helga, trying to hide her disappointment.

"But I would be failing in my responsibility to you if I did that," I said. "Father Gerald told us that nannying was no excuse for missing class, and class has begun in earnest."

"I am ready to learn, Domina," said Helga with a huge grin. "Shall we take Portia with us?"

"I am afraid that she will slow us down," I said. "I cannot afford that when there is a wager at stake. However, salvation is at hand. See who approaches us?"

"An angel sent by God," said Helga.

Portia turned to look, and a huge smile spread across her face.

"Dee! Dee!" she cried.

It took pulling rank, an invocation of his mother's memory, and a small bribe to obtain Pelardit's cooperation. Then

Helga and I were running unencumbered through the city while the silent fool took my daughter back into the tavern.

"Marquesia," Helga said as we passed through the Portaria into the bourg.

"What about her?" I asked.

"Maybe she killed her because she wanted a nicer room."

"No worse a theory than anything else I have heard."

"Yes, it is," said Helga. "Seriously, I think the Abbess did it."

"Why, Apprentice?"

"She runs the place. If there was some violation of the rules—"

"Why do it with Baudoin in the bed?"

"To blame him."

"It brings too much attention," I said. "If there was punishment to be meted out to La Rossa, it would be easy enough to sneak her body out to some place where it couldn't be found. Besides, what's the point of punishing one of your ladies in secret? It should be an example to the rest of them to improve their behavior."

"You're right," said Helga. "But I still think the Abbess had something to do with it. Why sneak off to see Foix otherwise? And isn't the Porte Villeneuve to the east?"

"It is," I said, continuing north.

"And isn't the bordel on the other side of it?"

"It is," I said. "If we were going to the front parlor, that would be the route we would take."

"But we are trying to get in through the kitchen in back," deduced Helga. "So we are taking the long way around."

"Correct," I said. "Only I am hoping that we won't even need to go in the kitchen. This way, Apprentice."

We cut over to the Porte Matabiau, the next gate in the wall enclosing the bourg. Not one of our usual locations, so the guards were slightly surprised to see me in my fool's garb, but there was no reason to question us in the middle of the day.

The road went east through farmland, but that was not our direction. We climbed a fence and walked through rows of vegetables starting to take shape. Another fence, another farm, and then we saw the brick wall that marked the rear of the bordel.

While the fences were built to keep cattle and deer from the vegetables, this wall was built to keep prying eyes from the business of the bordel. I wondered if there were some interesting outdoor events that took place by Sylvie's garden. I thought for a second about the morality of exposing the young girl by my side to such goings-on. Then I remembered who she was and, more important, where she grew up.

"On my shoulders, girl," I ordered, and I leaned into the wall with my palms pressed against the brick.

Helga was standing on my shoulders in an instant, peering carefully over the top bricks.

"No one's there," she reported. "Shall we try for the kitchen?"

"Not yet," I said.

She jumped down, and we sat in the shade of a nearby tree.

"It's noon," I said. "Time for a midday meal for normal people, but the ladies of the bordel should just be getting up. Sylvie will be serving them their breakfast, then will come back to the garden to get what she needs to prepare dinner."

"Which is their luncheon," said Helga.

"Right," I said. "You're getting heavier, by the way."

"Just taller," she said.

"I'm usually the one standing on someone's shoulders," I said. "I am not accustomed to being on the bottom."

"That's another reason why being a jester is better than being a prostitute," said Helga.

"I am glad that you think so," I said. "I still have some grapes and bread. Let's eat."

We sat in silence. The city of Toulouse was quiet, the sounds blocked by the wall. There was little birdsong at midday, but there were bees flitting among the flowers and cows lowing in the distance. I took a deep breath, taking it all in.

"This is nice," I said. "I think it's the first chance I have had to relax since Portia was born."

"I am never getting married," declared Helga.

"Never say never," I said. "But take your time. Sometimes, I wish I had been less impulsive about it."

"You married a duke when you were eighteen," said Helga.

"While caught up in a romantic adventure where I was the instrument of a scheme I didn't know about," I said.

"Sounds like more fun than most arranged marriages," said Helga. "And you got to be a duchess. Did you have many servants?"

"Many," I said.

"And beautiful gowns and jewels?"

"I did."

"Do you miss being a duchess?"

"Sometimes," I confessed.

"You gave up all of that to become a jester."

"By that point, I was no longer a duke's wife. I was a duke's mother, with little to say about how I conducted my life."

"We don't have much choice now," argued Helga. "We go where the Guild tells us to go, and do what the Chief Fool tells us to do."

"We're not doing that right now," I pointed out.

"No, I guess we're not," said Helga. "Although I am doing what you are telling me to do."

"You are still a child," I said. "Children must do as they are told. Some of the time."

"Why aren't you in your castle, telling your children what to do?" she asked.

"It wasn't a castle, it was a villa," I said. "And after my husband died—well, you know that story. It ended with my sister-in-law being appointed regent for my children. All I had left was a comfortably appointed set of rooms and a team of servants to make sure that I could no longer be their mother."

"You miss your children," said Helga.

"Terribly," I said. "Every single minute of every single day."

"But you have Portia," she said.

"Who is a Godsend," I said.

Helga leaned over and put her arms around me. "You could adopt me, you know," she said in a small voice. "My mother is dead. I never had a father. I have been playing your daughter for almost ten months, so it really wouldn't be any different. I would like very much to be part of a real family. You and Theo and Portia are all I have."

"You have the Guild," I said, putting my arm around her. "You are not far off from being made a jester in full. Then they can send you on missions of your own."

"But I would still be your daughter," she said. "We could tell the Guild. Even if I went somewhere else, I would still be your daughter, and Portia's sister, and I could write you letters and come running to your aid from wherever I am because that's what a real daughter would do. And no one would ever know otherwise."

I found myself wondering if the Chief Fool of Toulouse would send his daughter into danger as easily as he sent his apprentice.

And what would happen to Portia if she ended up as a jester?

"I will talk to Theo about it," I said, giving her shoulders a squeeze.

"Thank you, Claudia," said Helga.

We were alone. She did not call me mother. I thought how much that must have hurt her.

From the bordel, a viol began to play.

"I think that's our cue," I said, getting to my feet. "The ladies have begun to work. Shoulder time, Apprentice."

We went back to the brick wall and Helga climbed up my back until she could see the garden.

She ducked down immediately. "She's coming," she reported.

"Good. Get down, and make me a step."

She dropped to the ground beside me and locked her fingers together. I placed my right foot in the cradle, then jumped with the other as she hoisted me up with a grunt. I threw my arm over the top of the wall and pulled myself over it, dropping to the garden in a crouch.

A moment later, to my surprise, Helga landed beside me.

"How did you get over that wall by yourself?" I whispered.

"Younger legs," she replied. "I can outjump you by two feet."

Sylvie had her back to us as she dug up some carrots. I slipped my dagger into my hand, ran up silently behind her and clapped my hand over her mouth.

"Not a word, Sylvie," I whispered, letting her feel my blade. "Behind the shed. Now."

I brought her over to where we would be concealed from the house in the unlikely event that any of the women looked in this direction. I made the old woman sit as her eyes cast about wildly. Then I took my hand from her mouth, keeping the knife in place. Helga peered around the corner of the shed.

"How was Mass, Sylvie?" I asked. "Did you go to confession? Any recent sins? Say, from this morning?"

"What do you mean?" she whispered.

"Did Carlos make it back to his post today?" I asked. "We treated him pretty roughly, but that shouldn't excuse him from working. A job's a job."

"What are you talking about?"

"About Carlos attacking me after I left here this morning." She gaped at me. "I know naught about that," she said.

"I told you that Julie's murderer still walked among us," I said.

"Carlos killed her?"

"I don't know if it was him," I said. "But someone cares enough about my questions to send him to dissuade me from pursuing them. Which means I am on the right path. I am on the right path, and you know that. Don't you, Sylvie?"

"I was going to tell you," she sobbed. "I swear that I was going to tell you. I was waiting for you to come back. But I never said anything to Carlos. I only told the priest."

"What were you going to tell me, Sylvie?"

"About Julie's father," she said. "About our former master."

"Were they one and the same?"

"Oc, they were," she said.

"Tell me everything."

"Her mother was a servant, but she did not intend to stay a servant," said Sylvie. "She was beautiful. She knew it, but she also knew that beauty loses its power in time. She set her snares for our master, who had a wife he loved but was a weak man. He succumbed, and when she was with child, she threatened to tell his wife."

"What did he do?"

"He bought her silence with a house and a garden," said Sylvie. "The child was born, pretty little Julie. But her mother died when she was two. The master took pity on her, and took her back into his household. He had me raise her."

"Did his wife know Julie was his daughter?" I asked.

"She may have," said Sylvie. "She said nothing."

"Were there other children?"

"Oc, he had a son with his wife," she said, starting to weep again. "Guerau. He was older than Julie."

"Why do you weep for him?'

"That whole house had nothing but misfortune," said Sylvie. "The wife died, and her properties and rents reverted to her family. Master had squandered much and could not keep his house. There was someone in Paris who he thought could help him. He sent Guerau to ask for help, but he never heard from him again. He never made it to Paris. He and Julie's husband—"

"Julie was married?" I interrupted.

"Oc, to another servant in the house. His name was Pelfort. They both disappeared, probably murdered on the road by bandits. The old master was frantic trying to find out what happened, but there was nothing to be found. Finally, in repentance, he went on Crusade. He left us to maintain the house, but one by one, the servants left, until there was only Julie and myself."

"I am surprised she stayed," I said.

"She was his daughter," said Sylvie.

"She knew?"

"By then, she knew," said Sylvie. "I don't know who told her, but she said that she would stand by her father and keep his house. So I stayed with her until he returned."

"And did he?"

"He came back, broken and raving," said Sylvie. "There

was little money left. He sold his possessions, closed down most of the house. There were men who came back with him. Lepers. The master thought that he could do one last good thing. He set up the leper house for them."

"The one here?"

"Oc, the one here," she said; then she laughed mirthlessly. "And to maintain it, he took the house he had bought in recompense for Julie's mother and made it a testament to his sin. The bordel paid for the leper house, at least for a while."

"Wait—the bordel was Julie's birthplace?"

"Birthplace, deathplace," said Sylvie. "She ended up here because she had nowhere else to go. And I came with her."

"Did her father know she came here?"

"She made certain that he did," said Sylvie.

"What happened to him?"

"I know not," said Sylvie. "That was ten years ago. Only the Abbess has been here longer."

"Your master," I said. "What was his name?"

"De Planes," she said. "Ferrer de Planes."

"Where is his house?"

"On the street that was named for his family," she said. "Rue de Planes. Look for the rooks flying from the ruins. They say they move in only when the master is dead. And that is all that I can tell you."

"We are leaving you, Sylvie," I said, helping her to her feet. "If you send Carlos after us again, he will be coming back a dead man."

Helga linked her hands, and I went back over the wall again. She joined me almost immediately.

"'Coming back a dead man?'" she asked. "That doesn't make any sense."

"Be charitable, I was improvising," I said. "Threatening people is not something I do regularly."

"Except to me," she said.

"You're family," I said.

"Almost family," she said.

"And you've seen how I threaten Theo."

"Usually with a crossbow."

"Are you quite certain that you want to chance being related to me?"

She nodded.

"Fine," I said. "Let's go find this ruined man in his ruined manor."

"I still don't see why all of this would get Julie killed," said Helga as we ran back to the Porte Matabiau.

"Neither do I," I said. "But she was his daughter. I wonder if an inheritance could have been at stake."

"She was a daughter, and an illegitimate one at that," said Helga. "How could she possibly inherit anything?"

"If he left a will," I said. "If he was guilt-ridden enough or mad enough, he might have left something to her."

"So, she could have been killed by whoever would inherit instead."

"If he's still alive," I said. "Or, she could have been killed by whoever becomes her heir in turn."

"Do you think that's what this is all about?" asked Helga as we turned onto the Rue de Planes.

"Now that we're here, I don't," I said. "Who would want this so badly that they would kill for it?"

We stood before the rusted gates, looking at the decaying corpse of a once-proud manor. On an impulse, I picked up a rock and threw it over the gate. It soared onto the collapsed remains of the third floor and thudded into something wooden. The resulting noise sent a swarm of black birds cackling into the sky above it.

"Rooks," I said. "Just like she said there would be."

"No one could be living there," said Helga. "No one has opened this gate in ages."

She pushed it, and it groaned loudly against the chain in protest.

"There may be another way in," I said.

I looked around, and there was my husband standing there, staring at the two of us in shock.

"How the hell did you get here before me?" he asked.

"Small world," I said, starting to smile.

"Getting smaller all the time," said a voice behind me, and I turned to see Sancho standing there, a brace of armed men at his sides.

CHAPTER 15

I dumped our child into my wife's arms and ran from the Yellow Dwarf.

"That's cheating!" I heard her yell at me.

I waved at her over my shoulder without looking back and turned the corner.

I had been participating in a lot of wagers lately. A foot-race with a fat man that I deliberately lost, a crooked toss of crooked dice with a crooked diceman, a test of Sancho's men that led us inevitably to another bout of drinking. But now I had a wager worthy of the name. I was matching wits with one of the few people in the world who could make it a fair fight.

My wife.

It was sneaky, I confess, to saddle her with Portia like that, but sneakiness was part of the game. I had no doubt that the direction my investigation was taking was the correct one, but that wasn't to say that she would not find her own way to the murderer.

For that matter, I wanted to find the murderer first because as smart as she was, and as capable as she was, I had a better chance of surviving the encounter than she had. She was good in a fight—quite deadly, in fact, as I had seen on more than one occasion, but she had been a fool for only a few years, and I had been one for—

My God, was it thirty years now?

Almost thirty-one, if I dated it from the beginning of my training with La Vache in Paris, perfecting my juggling technique instead of attending the university my father thought—

Not my father. The man I thought was my father, who instructed me through beatings and treachery because he knew that he wasn't my father.

I often wonder at God's plan for us. Why did He create a world where nobles ruled solely because of an accumulation of accidental births? Where nobles treated their families and children as commodities to be bought, sold, or traded to maintain their holds on power. No child could be born to that world and not become twisted in some way.

Unless he abandons it. Like me.

Like my wife. Only she abandoned it as an adult, choosing to leave her children behind.

Her noble children, two beautiful, intelligent, goodhearted children, whose noble father had been murdered and whose noble mother had left them.

Left them to be twisted by the other noble members of their family.

I had to get her back to them. Perhaps I could stay somewhere safely out of town while she visited. I did not think that I would receive the warmest welcome there.

The house of Llora de Bretanha was in the Comminges quarter, not far from the Porte Narbonnaise. No doubt the old count wanted to keep her nearby so that a quick walk from the château would have him in her bed in a matter of minutes. She must have been an exceptional lover to winnow a house out of him. He was a notorious consumer of flesh in his life, whose appetites demanded constant variety. And yet, there was the one woman to whom he kept returning.

The house itself was modest, fit for entertaining on an intimate scale. Na Llora was not likely to be one throwing lavish dinner parties. The nobles of Toulouse may have had no compunction about betraying their spouses, but they would not offend society by attending the old count's mistress in public.

It was nearing midday. I wondered what hours she kept at this stage of her life. The royal mistresses I have known kept pace with their patrons, rising early enough to make themselves desirable at a moment's notice. As they grew older, the amount of artifice needed to sustain their desirability required them to rise at an hour more suited to a farmer's life. However, this mistress was retired from the field of action with full honors. She could sleep all damn day if she wanted.

Then again, who is a jester to criticize someone for sleeping late?

I paused to examine the knocker on the door. It was a bronze butterfly, nearly the size of my head, with every detail exquisitely rendered down to the feelers, so thin and light that one would think they would wave in the breeze. I lifted it carefully and knocked three times.

The door was opened by a maid, who looked at me in surprise. "You are a jester?" she asked.

"I am," I said. "Come to pay my respects to Na Llora."

"She is not expecting your respects," she said.

"As the master of the unexpected, I have no respect for the expectations of my respects," I returned. "Give her my apologies for coming without warning, but tell her that I am camping on her doorstep until she grants me an audience."

"Better men than you have been turned away from this house," she informed me haughtily.

"Then there is no incentive for me to improve, is there?" I

said. "Tell her that I am getting worse, and that only she can save me. I leave it to your sense of Christian charity."

"What is your purpose is seeing her?" she asked.

I looked both ways, then beckoned for her to lean forward. I put my lips by her ear. "For the gossip," I whispered.

"Oh," she said, beginning to smile for the first time. "That might get you your audience. Wait here."

She let me into the front hall, which was a start. I swung my lute around to the front while I was waiting and started plucking at it softly, letting the music be my ambassador. I heard the murmuring of women's voices from the next room.

Then the maid returned. "She will see you," she said. "Follow me."

I bowed to her in thanks, then followed her into the front parlor, still playing.

A woman was reclining on a low couch, sipping from a goblet of wine. There was a pitcher and, to my great happiness, a second goblet. She wore a bliaut of the deepest blue, a thick leather belt with a fine silver mesh around it at her waist. She held out her hand as I came in, and I knelt before her, took it, and pressed my forehead against it.

"Is that the custom where you come from?" she asked.

"I follow no custom," I said. "That was something I did at the spur of the moment. It seemed appropriate."

"I will accept that," she said, smiling. She waved me over to a low stool by the table. "Help yourself to some wine."

"Thank you, Domina Llora," I said, filling it. I lifted it in her direction. "To your magnificent life."

She raised hers in ironic salute. "You're the new fool in town," she said. "The one with the foolish family."

"Oc, Domina. My name is Tan Pierre."

"I doubt that very much," she said, looking at me over her goblet.

Her eyes were the color of her bliaut, still clear and appraising. I could see how a man would have wanted to swim in her gaze. Even now.

"Do you like my dress, Senhor Pierre?" she asked.

"Very much."

"It's Almeria silk. Very rich, very comfortable," she said.

"It suits you," I said.

"Almeria silk is used for wrapping relics," she added, raising an eyebrow. "You are right. It suits me very well."

I grinned.

"I knew Balthazar," she said. "A funny man and a good listener. Are you a good listener?"

"I am, Domina. Most jesters are."

"Why is that, do you suppose?"

"We talk for a living, Domina. Silence for us is a vacation."

"Although there is that one fool in town who never speaks," she said. "I think that would kill me. Did you know Balthazar?"

"I met him once, years ago," I said.

"Raimon liked him," she said, a wistful smile on her face. "The old Raimon, my Raimon, of course. The current one liked him, too. He just doesn't like me."

"It is hard to imagine anyone not liking you," I said.

"Don't flatter me, Fool," she snapped. "That is not how you play this little game. I am too old to be flattered."

There was something gallant I could have said in reply, but it was flattering, so I held my tongue.

"Better," she said, her anger subsiding.

"Who was the fool when you first came to Toulouse?" I asked.

"His name was Jericho," she said. "Not his real name, either. I don't think I have ever seen a fool answer to a real name."

"Why did he call himself Jericho?" I asked.

"He played the trumpet, and he was a tumbler," she said. "He did both at the same time, which was remarkable. Not the wittiest fool, however. More of a clown, but we all drank plenty, so he was funny enough at the time. Are you a witty fool?"

"No fool should ever sing his own praises," I said. "I let others discover my worthiness for me."

"That sounds like a fancy way of saying that you are not," she said.

"Well, I confess to enough wit for me to make my living," I said. "A fool will need his wits when he becomes too old to tumble."

"Too old to tumble," she echoed. "That could be a tragic epitaph for many a life."

"I think that I understand the secret of your longevity, Domina."

"Do you now? What is it?"

"Beauty comes and goes, but wit in a woman is as valuable as wit in a fool."

"Well said, Senhor Pierre," she said, smiling again. "Your wife is a fortunate fool to be married to a man with such foolish wit. I would like to meet her."

"I shall bring her by," I said.

"Now, why have you come to see me?" she asked, her glance shrewd. "I have fallen out of fashion in Toulouse."

"I think it more likely that Toulouse has fallen out of fashion with you," I said. "Which is its loss. However, truth be told, I have come in search of gossip."

"My last stock in trade," she said. "How shall I display my wares? And what will you do for me in exchange?"

"I offer new gossip for old," I said. "I have the end of a tale, and I wonder if you possess the beginning."

"Fools' tales generally end with laughter," she said.

"It all depends on whether you find humor in a hanging," I said.

"Ah," she said. "The Parisian Prodigal. Quite a homecoming for little brother Baudoin."

"Do you think him legitimately the brother of the count?" I asked.

"I think him the brother of the count," she said. "Legitimately? Perhaps."

"But perhaps not?" I asked.

"Perhaps not," she said.

"That's a new wrinkle."

"No," she said. "It's an old one. Forty years old."

"Are you saying that Countess Constance was inconstant to the count?"

"Give me your payment first," she said. "Tell me how Baudoin came here, and how he went from a dungeon to the bed of a dead whore and back again."

I told her of Baudoin's tumultuous two days, leaving out my suspicions and subsequent discoveries.

"Poor woman," she said when I was done. "Do you know what the difference is between someone like her and someone like me?"

"Tell me, Domina."

"The luck of a noble bloodline," she said. "I came to Toulouse with my noble, wealthy parents when I was fifteen. It turned out that noble or not, the wealth had dwindled, although they kept me in the dark about it. I was presented to the court that afternoon, and to the count's bedchamber that night. My father's fortune was saved."

"Yet you stayed on."

She lifted her hand up for me to get a good look. It was heavily bejeweled, but the hand itself was lovely underneath, still supple and unlined.

"I immerse them in lotion every day for an hour while

Célie reads to me," she said. "One of my secrets. Yes, I stayed
on. I had a particular talent for being a mistress, I discovered. Much of it involved listening. So many pretty girls
prattled in and prattled back out again, still believing that
they were fascinating. They weren't. A powerful man needs
to think that he is the center of the known world, and an
eternal source of interest. I simply opened my eyes wide and
looked enthralled."

She demonstrated, and suddenly I saw the young woman
she once was, her attention solely on me.

I immediately wanted to do nothing more but to please
her.

"Very powerful," I said.

She blinked, and the young woman vanished into
memory.

"But Constance was there at the time, wasn't she?" I asked.

"Constance was rolled out for court occasions, impreg-
nated periodically, and directed to write cheerful letters to
her brother, the King of France," said Llora scornfully. "She
lacked the beauty to compete with the beautiful, and the
wit to compete with the witty. She was an ordinary woman
born into an extraordinary family. She served one purpose;
I served another."

"But she didn't stay on," I said.

"No, she didn't," said Llora. "That was the one thing she
did that actually surprised people. Hell, with all that she
had to put up with, it was a miracle she didn't kill herself. Or
him. Or me, for that matter. Raimon barely paid her any attention by that point. Barely left her any money to survive
upon while he made his rounds of the Toulousain, with me
and a dozen other women in tow. Constance was a wretched
little milksop who kept praying things would get better
while they kept getting worse, a martyr to her duty. But it

turned out that she had a plan. There was a chief servant, Simon, who had the responsibility for watching over her and making sure she behaved. Then one day in '65, he was called home on some family matter, and she slipped her last piece of jewelry to a sympathetic guard and fled the château. Only one problem—that was her last piece of jewelry, and the journey to Paris takes money."

"A month's journey, and a dangerous one for a woman alone," I said. "Not to mention with the count's men after her."

"He didn't care at that point," she said. "He was quite pleased at the turn of events. She left him, so he was in the right. It freed him up for the next marriage and whatever properties it would bring."

"You were never a candidate?"

"I had more power as his mistress than any mere wife could hope for," she said, her voice flooded with contempt. "He wanted me. As long as I had the ability to leave him, I held him."

"Fair enough," I said. "Tell me, how did Constance survive once she left?"

"She had an ally in Toulouse," said Llora. "A man. A knight, in fact, who must have read his tales of chivalry and taken the idea seriously. He gave her sanctuary at his mansion and kept it a secret."

"Yet you know about it."

"Raimon knew about it," she laughed. "From the beginning. As I said, he didn't care, but he made a good show of looking like he did. He posted rewards, threatened banishment to any who would help her, then he would come to my bedchamber and howl with laughter over her cowering in some dank cellar."

"How long did she stay with this chivalrous knight?"

"Long enough for a messenger to get to her brother, the

king, with a plea for money. When he returned with it, she left. But in the interim, I suspect the knight became less chivalrous."

"Why do you suspect that?"

"Please," she said, waving her hand dismissively. "Lovelorn woman, chivalrous man, constant threat of death—could circumstances have been any more romantic? I doubt that they lasted more than a day before falling into each other's arms. And here's another thing—Baudoin was born in '65, but what month? Constance left the château in February. If he was born in December, it wouldn't surprise me at all. After all, marital relations between Constance and my Raimon had ceased long before."

"You never know," I said. "Maybe he cheated on you with his wife."

"You are an insolent rogue," she said, purring slightly. "I like that."

"Did your Raimon know that she was with child when she left? Or that Baudoin was born after?"

"No," she said. "If he thought there was another son on the way, he would have kept her here, then kicked her out the instant they cut the cord. A child of the nobility belongs to the father, so that it may be used as bait for diplomacy. Didn't you know that?"

"I have seen it enough to be glad I am a fool."

"A smart one, from what I observe," she said. "You must definitely come back for another visit."

"I will," I promised. "With my wife. One last thing, Domina. What was the name of the knight who sheltered her?"

"De Planes," she said. "Something with an *F*—Ferrer, that's it. Ferrer de Planes. His house was on the street with the same name."

"I know the street," I said. "It's near Montardy Square.

Something about that strikes a familiar chord. Domina, my thanks. May I be so bold as to say that you are as fascinating a woman when you speak as when you listen?"

"Women become more fascinating with age," she said. "Remember that."

"I will."

"And Senhor Pierre?"

"Oc, Domina?"

"If there is still to be a hanging, do let me know," she said. "I haven't been to a good hanging in years."

I bowed and took my leave.

I felt a buzz of excitement, like I was a bee discovering a hidden field of flowers. Family, I thought. It all comes back to family in the end. If Baudoin was truly the bastard child of Constance and this Ferrer fellow, then he would have little claim to either the affections or the powers of the current Raimon. And if someone besides Llora knew or was seeking the truth about his parentage, then that someone may very well have wanted to use La Rossa to worm the information out of Baudoin. Or to kill her to keep her from revealing it.

Which actually brought Baudoin right back into the picture.

What if he was guilty? What if he was merely using me to throw everyone off the scent?

But why me? What would cause him to ask a jester for help? There were people in town who knew the territory and the players better than I did. He would have been better off if Balthazar was still alive. But maybe he didn't know about the old fool's death, so he looked to the Chief Fool of Toulouse for help, whoever it was.

Did he know about the Fools' Guild?

Possibilities. Once you start thinking about them, you

cannot stop. They were a trap as well as a tool. I needed to winnow them down.

It was time to talk to Ferrer de Planes, if he still lived. And I was going to get to him first.

Then I turned on to the Rue de Planes to see Claudia and Helga, sans Portia, staring at a ruined *maison*. I froze in astonishment. Then my wife turned and saw me.

"How the hell did you get here before me?" I demanded.

"Small world," she said, starting to smile.

Then came the second shock of the day as Sancho came up behind her with the two men I had ditched a day before.

"Getting smaller all the time," he said.

Claudia turned around at his voice, then turned back to me. She started to laugh. "This seems like a perfect time to have a drink," she said.

Sancho and I looked at each other. He shrugged.

"The nearest tavern?" I asked.

"Right over there," he said, pointing to the end of the street.

"I'm buying," said Claudia. "Let's go."

You search your entire life for a woman who will say that.

CHAPTER 16

"First order of business is to share what we each know," said Theo once we had commandeered a table.

"No, the first order of business is to order the first order of drinks," I said, summoning the barmaid. "This is my party, so I call the tunes."

"I cannot believe you didn't put drinks first," commented Sancho to Theo. "Especially with someone else buying. This business really has thrown you off your rhythm. You'll be dropping clubs next."

"By the way," I said as I filled everyone's cup, "are we trusting Sancho today?"

"Good point," said Theo, turning to the soldier. "Are we?"

"You are," said Sancho.

"He says that we are," said Theo.

"Why?" I asked, handing cups to Sancho's men, who were watching the whole interchange with bewilderment.

"You are looking for the murderer of La Rossa," he said.

"Right."

"So am I," he said. "As of today."

"What changed your mind?" asked Theo.

"Because I would like to know the truth," said Sancho. "I don't want an innocent man's death on my conscience unless I'm getting paid much more than I am right now."

"What about the man you work for?" asked Theo.

"If by that you mean the Count of Foix, then you will find that he supports your quest," said Sancho. "His best earner and possibly the only real redhead in Toulouse was murdered. He wants to see her avenged, both as a personal matter and because it's good for business. If, on the other hand, you mean the Count of Toulouse, then I have his full support as well."

"Why?" I asked.

"Because if Baudoin is his brother, he would like him ex-onerated," said Sancho. "But he couldn't do it officially for appearances' sake. So he used me to encourage you."

"Encourage me?" laughed Theo. "You've done nothing but discourage me from the first day."

"When we had that drink after you came out of the dungeon," said Sancho.

"Right."

"Which was after we both talked to the count."

"Right."

"Who told me to get you to investigate so it would be done without any connection to him."

Theo stared at him.

"But you specifically told me not to investigate it," he said. "I distinctly remember that."

"How else would I get you to do something?" asked Sancho.

"Oh, he's got you figured out," said Helga.

"You know, for a man who cannot tail someone without alerting the entire city that he's doing it, you can be pretty subtle," said Theo, knocking his cup against Sancho's in tribute.

"Thank you," said Sancho modestly.

"By the way, the last man you had following me was superb," said Theo. "You should give him a bonus come pay-day."

"What man?" asked Sancho.

"What do you mean, what man?" asked Theo.

"I haven't had anyone follow you since you lost these two tortoises," said Sancho.

"You're playing with me."

"I am not, and you are trusting me today," said Sancho. "I did not have any other man following you."

"Interesting," said Theo. "Interesting and disturbing."

"Next order of business," I said, clapping my hands for their attention. "As your hostess, and as the first to arrive at the house of Ferrer de Planes, I suggest that we share our information."

"That was my idea." Theo pouted.

"Shut up, husband. The last shall be first, the first shall be last. Sancho, what brought you here?"

"Your husband suggested that I look into who owned the bordel before Foix bought it," said Sancho.

"Ferrer de Planes," I said. "He set it up to fund the leper house."

"You already knew that?" exclaimed Sancho in a hurt tone. "You might have saved me the trouble of finding that out. It wasn't easy."

"I just learned it this past hour," I said consolingly. "And it is good to have my information confirmed, good Sancho."

"Well, all right, then," he said, mollified. "So I came to check the place out, and saw the three of you gawking at each other. I like to gawk. I thought I would join in. But there's something else about this place. You recognized it, didn't you, Pierre?"

"Baudoin asked about it when you gave us the tour of the city," said Theo.

"Oc, he did," said Sancho. "Of all the places we passed by, this was the only one that pulled a question out of him."

"What was the question?" I asked.

"Why this crumbling heap still stood in this fancy old neighborhood," said Sancho.

"He couldn't have known," said Theo.

"Known what?" I asked. "It's your turn to share what you know."

"This is where the Countess Constance came when she fled Raimon the Fifth," said Theo. "De Planes sheltered her while she awaited funds from Paris. She was here for two months, hiding in the cellar."

"Brave man to defy his count like that to help an escaped wife," I said. "He could have been hanged as a traitor."

"How romantic!" sighed Helga.

"I had the sense that Baudoin thought his mother's ally might still be here in Toulouse," continued Theo. "He said he didn't know who it was, but why else would he be so curious about the house?"

"Stands to reason," said Sancho.

"How did he know which one it was?" asked Helga.

"What?" said Theo.

"How did he know this was the house of de Planes?" asked Helga. "Baudoin's mother hadn't been here in forty years. The street isn't marked. There isn't anything to show the house belongs to de Planes. I didn't know it, and I've passed by here lots of times."

"Excellent question, daughter," I said, patting her hand. She gave me a huge smile.

"And how does this connect to La Rossa?" asked Sancho.

"Julie," I said.

"Who's she?" asked Sancho.

"La Rossa's real name," I said. "Let's see. She was in her

mid-thirties, so she was born, say, about 1170. It's been five years since Constance left and Baudoin's born. De Planes gets married sometime between 1165 and 1170, and his wife bears him a son and heir, Guerau. But de Planes has servants, including a pretty maid who leads him into temptation."

"Not Sylvie," said Sancho, shuddering visibly.

"No," I said. "Another one. He gets her with child, a girl called Julie. De Planes does the proper thing and sets them up with a house and garden outside the town walls. The maid may have continued as his mistress."

"That's why they call them extramural activities," Theo said to Helga. "They take place outside the walls."

"Humor never works in Latin," said Helga.

"I was just explaining the derivation of the word," said Theo, deflated. "It wasn't meant to be funny."

"Then you succeeded," said Helga. "No more lessons to-day. I want to hear the rest of the story."

"Me, too," said one of Sancho's men.

"The maid dies when the girl is only two," I said. "De Planes acts nobly again and brings her into his household to be raised by the cook."

"That's Sylvie," said Sancho.

"Correct," I said. "The little girl grows into a redheaded beauty. She gets married to another servant, and all is going well. But then de Planes's wife dies, and he suffers financial ruin. In desperation, he sends his only son along with the servant to Paris to seek help. I will bet that they were trying to get it from Constance."

"Makes sense," said Theo.

"Only they never made it to Paris," I said.

"What happened?" asked Theo.

"No one knows, no one ever finds out," I said. "They simply vanish."

"Constance dies in 1190," said Theo. "Baudoin is living it up in Paris. What is de Planes doing?"

"Looking fruitlessly for his son, then going off on Crusade," I said. "He comes back, say about '94, sets up the leper house and the bordel to fund it. His own house falls to ruins, and Sylvie and Julie end up in the bordel."

"Did he know that his daughter was forced to become a whore in the house he set up?" asked Theo.

"According to Sylvie, Julie made certain that he knew," I said.

"Nice," muttered one of Sancho's men.

"Plenty of reasons to kill for one family," commented Theo. "Nothing like bringing a bastard child into the household."

I squeezed his knee in sympathy. He had been such a child once, and his family ended up paying a terrible price for their parents' sins.

"I wonder if she was left anything in his will," said Theo, looking out the door at the old mansion.

"I was thinking along those lines myself," I said. "Only—"

"How could she inherit?" asked Sancho.

"I know she was illegitimate, but given de Planes's sense of honor . . ."

"You're missing the point," said Sancho impatiently. "She couldn't have inherited anything. De Planes isn't dead."

We all turned to look at him.

"You were supposed to share what you knew," I scolded him.

"I assumed you knew it already," he said. "You knew everything else I knew. You knew things I couldn't possibly know."

"He's still alive," I said, amazed. "Is he still at the house?"

"No," said Sancho. "No one's lived there for years, except for the rooks."

"Where is he?"

"You're not going to like it," said Sancho.

"Come on, out with it," said Theo.

"He caught the curse," said Sancho. "He's in the leper house."

I pulled the bell-cord for the second time that day.

"Do we have to go inside?" asked Sancho nervously.

"You could take our word about what we find out, if you like," I said.

"No, the count will want to hear it from me," sighed Sancho. "I follow the fools. I must be one by now."

"Do you have an act?" asked Theo interestedly.

The peephole opened, and Adhémar's eye caught mine.

"Domina Gile, is it not?" he asked. "I do not know that Senhor Montazin has the strength for a second visit."

"Open up, Adhémar," said Sancho. "It's not Montazin we've come to see. It's de Planes."

The door opened, and Adhémar stood there, a sword in one hand.

"I cannot permit that," he said softly. "Senhor de Planes sees no one. And you know he is under the protection of the Count of Foix."

"Do you see this?" asked Sancho, holding up a document with the seal of the Count of Toulouse. "This is better than anything you've got, whether steel or parchment. Put up your blade before I take it from you and shove it up your ass."

"You really should have said, 'Please,'" muttered Theo.

I thought that Adhémar might take them on even with numbers and armor to their advantage. Then he took a deep breath and sheathed his sword. "This way," he said, and he turned and went inside.

"You two guard the door," Sancho ordered his men. "No point in all three of us catching it."

I have never seen an order followed by two more grateful men.

"The count will hear of this," said Adhémar as he led us into the front parlor.

"We'll race you to him if you like," said Theo. "Bring down de Planes."

Adhémar moved to set up the screen.

"No," I said. "We must be certain it is him."

"Are you sure about that?" muttered Sancho.

Adhémar hesitated, then replaced the screen.

"I will bring him," he said. "It will take a while."

We could see the base of the stairs from the parlor. He disappeared up them, and the four of us sat.

"None of us knows what he looks like, anyway," said Helga. "What good is using no screen?"

"Adhémar doesn't know that we don't know him," I said. "He'll bring down the right man."

There came a careful footstep, followed by another.

Adhémar descended, tenderly carrying a shriveled old man in his arms. The man's hands were gnarled and shaking. His feet were swathed in bandages and dangled uselessly. He was clad in a quilted robe, and his face, neck, and balding head were covered with lesions, old and new. His eyes were pale blue, and looked out into nothing.

"Who is here?" he said in a croaking voice.

"Four people, senhor," said Adhémar, placing him gently on a cushioned seat. "Two fools, a soldier, and a girl."

"Which of them wants to speak with me?"

"All of us, senhor," I said.

He turned in the direction of my voice. "You do not sound like a girl, and you are not a soldier," he said. "You must be the female fool."

"You know who I am, senhor," I said. "You sent Carlos to frighten me away from you."

"I thought he could frighten a woman," he said. "But you are no ordinary woman."

"He was somewhat frightening," I said. "I had help from my daughter."

"So I heard," he said. "I had to laugh when I heard about it, and I am not a man given to laughter."

"You are Ferrer de Planes," said Sancho.

"What remains of him, I am. You must be the soldier."

"Oc, senhor. I am here on behalf of Count Raimon."

"How is he?" asked de Planes. "I remember him as a young man."

"He is well," said Sancho. "Not so young."

"I would offer my prayers to his health, but my prayers do not seem to carry much weight," said de Planes. "I prayed this week that my shame would not be revealed to the world, yet now the world sits before me in my parlor."

"Is that why you sent Carlos?" I asked. "To prevent us from finding out about you?"

"It is, Na Gile, and I ask your pardon for it."

"If you wish to make recompense, then my price is a simple one."

"Name it, lady."

"I ask that you answer our questions with the truth."

He grimaced, or smiled, I do not know which. "Your price is a steep one, and far from simple," he said. "But I shall pay it."

"You had a bastard child with a maid in your household. A daughter named Julie."

"I did."

"You took her in after her mother died."

"I gave her a roof and a way of providing for her, and when she was of age, I found her a husband. Pelfort, a servant on my staff."

"Did she know that she was your daughter?"

"I do not know when she learned it, but she did," he said. "My wife—I could not keep the truth from her. It destroyed her. She wasted away before my very eyes. I learned from Julie years later that my wife had, in a fit of rage, whipped her while calling her a bastard of a whore's child. If she hadn't known before, she certainly did then."

"Was Julie left anything in your will?" I asked.

"I had a stipend for her, enough for her to live upon had she—had she outlived me. It was not much, but it was all I could do."

"What about while she was alive?" asked Theo. "What about when she needed enough to stave off whoredom?"

"I tried," he said. "But she wanted so much, and there was little enough as there was. She had some idea that I had a fortune stashed away somewhere."

"What about the house?" asked Sancho. "That had to be worth something given the neighborhood."

"The house may never be sold while a de Planes still lives," said the old man. "There is a great-nephew waiting in Arles for me to finally leave this earth, and the house will go to him. He's more than welcome to it."

"After your wife died, you sent Guerau, your son, and Pelfort to Paris," I said. "Who were they to meet?"

He sat up, his shoulders stiffening. "I will not give you that name," he said. "It is a matter of honor."

"I would be much more impressed by that chivalry if you were not the sort of man who sends bordel ruffians to intimidate women," I said.

He slumped down in embarrassment.

"You sent him to speak to Constance, didn't you?" I asked.

"I confess it," he said, miserably. "But Guerau never went to Paris, and she never— I was a fool to try, and my son paid the price for my folly. I thought I could gain absolution by taking the Cross, but I fear that my soul will be as damned in the afterlife as my body is in life."

"How did you come to sell the bordel to Foix?" asked Theo. "Did he owe you some favor from your time together in the Holy Land?"

"I never knew him there," said de Planes. "We had no connection. He just appeared on my doorstep a few years ago and offered to buy the place, keeping the arrangement going with this house. I thought it would be a way to assure the care of my afflicted brothers after God finally took pity on me and allowed me to die."

"And you had no other connection to him?" persisted Theo.

"None," said de Planes.

We all looked each other.

Sancho shrugged. "I have nothing," he said.

"Senhor," I said gently. "You know of the death of your daughter."

"Oc, Domina," he said, tears starting to glisten in the dead eyes.

"Do you have any idea of why she was murdered?"

"The actual murder, no," he said, crying openly. "But her entire life sent her to her doom, and I am the one responsible."

"I am sorry for it, senhor," I said. "May God grant you the mercy you seek."

"Amen," said Helga.

Sancho's men hastily took a few steps back from us as Adhémar let us out.

"Well, we've exposed ourselves to contagion just to find out that there was no reason to kill La Rossa," said Sancho.

"We know more than we did, but not as much as we need to," I said.

"It's not inheritance, politics, scandal, money, or vengeance," said Theo. "What's left?"

"Hatred," I said.

"Whose hatred for whom?" asked Theo.

"Let's go to the bordel," I suggested.

"Hooray," said one of Sancho's men.

We walked down the path to the bordel.

"Oh, look who's back," I said.

Carlos was sitting at his post, his eye black, his jaw wrapped in a dirty kerchief.

"Mine," said Theo. He sauntered up to Carlos, who glared but did not rise. "Women," said Theo. "Nothing but trouble, but what are you going to do, eh? Heard mine have been causing you some inconvenience."

Carlos said nothing.

Theo squatted down, looked him in the eyes and smiled. "So far," he said, "you have been defeated in single combat by my wife and my elder daughter. Next up is Portia. She's only sixteen months old, but she is a fearsome hair-puller and bites like a wolf. My money would be on her."

Sancho and his men snickered while Carlos stayed in his seat.

Theo stopped smiling. He reached out with one finger and laid it on the kerchief binding Carlos's jaw.

"Or," he said softly, "I could be the next member of the family to take you on."

He tapped the guard's jaw with his finger. Hard. Carlos winced.

"Don't give me a reason," said Theo.

He stood, opened the door, and beckoned to us.

"What is this?" cried the Abbess as we trooped into the front parlor.

"Forgive us, Abbess, we won't be here long," I said. "Husband, if you look at her feet one more time, I will make certain that you will be of no use to any woman anywhere ever again."

"Feet? She has those, too?" exclaimed Theo innocently.

"Right," I said. "Sancho, I want you to show me where everyone was when Julie met Baudoin. Your men will be Baudoin and Huc, I will be Julie, and you, the Abbess and my husband will be yourselves."

"Who will I be?" asked Helga.

"Just stand out of the way," I said. "Position them, Sancho."

"All right," said Sancho. "I came in first, so I moved all the way to the right side, about here."

He stood at the far end of the room, in front one of the red cushioned chairs.

"Baudoin came in behind me," he continued. "With Huc behind him. They ended up side by side in the middle."

He waved the two men over, and they stood side by side, taking the time to run their eyes over the Abbess's body.

"And I was right here, just to the right of the door," said Theo, taking up his position. "The Abbess came through the door from the hall, so she was directly opposite me."

"Please make your entrance," I asked her.

"I am no puppet to be manipulated so!" she said indignantly.

"Best do it, Domina," advised Sancho, his fingers rattling the hilt of his sword.

She gave him a look filled with hate, then went out into the hallway and came back in.

"She came across to me first, then went to Baudoin," said Sancho, motioning her into the room.

"Then the Count of Foix came down," said Theo.

"Oh, I want to be him!" said Helga, and she ran out, then

came back, her cheeks puffed out and her arms making large ovals at her sides. The men chuckled in appreciation.

"He recommends La Rossa to Baudoin, then leaves," said Sancho.

"That was the signal for you to tell La Rossa to get information from Baudoin, wasn't it?" I asked the Abbess.

She nodded curtly.

"The Abbess goes to fetch Julie," I said. "Before we do that, did all of you remain where you are?"

"As far as I can remember," said Sancho.

"Oc, we did," said Theo.

"Who did Julie look at first? Who did she speak to?"

"The Abbess came in and announced her," remembered Theo. "I saw her while she was still in the hall, but she wasn't paying me any mind. I don't think the others could see her until she came into the room. Would that be right, gentlemen?"

"I can't see into the hall from this angle," said one of the soldiers.

"Me, neither," said the other.

"And Sancho is past all of you," I noted. "So, she comes in."

"She's smiling," said Sancho. "She looks at Baudoin."

"But then something went off about that smile," said Theo. "Did you mark it? It became something mocking."

"I did notice that," said Sancho. "I just thought that was her style. Something the customers like."

"Is it?" I asked the Abbess.

"Not in this establishment," she replied. "Men are respected here. At least, to their faces."

"Curious," I said. "Stay at your places. I will be Julie."

"Too short," said Sancho.

"Too much clothing," grinned Theo.

"Enough," I said.

I stepped back into the hallway.

"Announce me!" I called.

"This is ridiculous," said the Abbess.

"Do it," said Sancho.

She sighed.

"Senhors," she said. "May I present—La Rossa!"

I glided into the room, saw Theo, ignored him, and turned my attention to the soldier standing in for Baudoin. I smiled at him.

The two soldiers smiled back at me.

"I think I have discovered the problem," I announced.

"What is it?" asked Theo.

"The problem is that the two of you are idiots," I said.

"That is a problem," said Sancho to Theo.

"And the problem with the diagnosis is that there is no known cure," added Theo. "How does our being idiots help?"

"It makes me feel better about myself," I said. "Sancho, tell both of your counts to meet us in the courtyard of the château. Domina Abbess, I must ask you to join us."

"Join you?" protested the Abbess. "I've never been to the Château Narbonnais in daylight. I cannot go there dressed like this."

"Throw a cloak over that gown and have Sylvie attend you," I said. "You might pass for a lady. Sancho will guarantee your safe conduct."

"My men will escort you," he said.

The men lit up with happiness.

"Anyone else?" asked Sancho.

"Might as well get the rest of the entourage," I said. "Comminges, Sabran, the viguier. Oh, and a few more guards and the baile, in case things get out of hand. Good. Shall we be on our way?"

"Wait," said Sancho.

We turned to look at him.

"I wish to speak to La Navarra," he said to the Abbess. "Fetch her down for me."

"This is hardly the time, even if you have the money," objected Theo.

"There will be ample time for you to ridicule me later," said Sancho. "Get her right away."

The Abbess shook her head, but complied. A minute later, she returned with the Lady of the Talons.

"What's going on?" asked La Navarra, glancing across the room. "You know I will take only one at a time."

"Not anymore," said Sancho. "Hear me out. I have come to realize in the past few days that life can end abruptly, and if we wait for happiness, it may slip our grasp. I want you to pack your things and come with me. You will stay in my rooms tonight, and in the morning, we shall be married, if that is agreeable to you."

She blinked. "But I am a prostitute," she said.

"Not anymore," he replied.

"You would marry a woman who has slept with men for money?"

"I am a mercenary," said Sancho. "I have done things for money that are far worse. You have given pleasure for pay, I have taken lives for pay. I am in no position to judge you. But I want you for my own. Exclusively."

"You would marry me?"

"On the morrow, my word upon it."

"Can he be trusted?" she asked, turning to the rest of us.

"Today, I trust him on all matters," I said.

"All right," said La Navarra, suddenly radiant. "I will pack right now. It won't take long."

She skipped up the stairs.

"Great," sighed the Abbess. "That makes two girls I have to replace."

"Are you sure you know what you are doing?" asked Theo.

"Not at all," said Sancho. "That's why it will be fun. Now, I believe that we all have an appointment at the château?"

"Right," I said. "Let's go."

CHAPTER 17

"Is everybody here?" called Claudia from the center of the courtyard. "Who are we waiting for? The viguier?"

"He's coming now!" I shouted back. "Good day to you, Peire Roger!"

I was standing next to Count Raimon in the section of the courtyard between the Grand Tower and the Palace of Justice. Comminges, Foix, and Sabran were with us, along with a number of guards and attendants. The viguier emerged from the Grand Tower, looking irritated.

"Why am I being interrupted for this?" he demanded.

"Because I said so," said Count Raimon, who was standing next to me. "Now, get over here with the rest of us."

"Of course, Dominus," said the viguier, bowing immediately.

"Excellent," said Claudia, surveying the gathered group. "Normally, my husband would be leading the festivities, but he lost a wager to me today."

"Not yet, I haven't," I called.

"What is the nature of the wager?" asked Count Raimon.

"Why, as to who will be the first to find Julie's murderer," she said.

"Who is Julie?" asked the count.

"La Rossa, the prostitute found stabbed to death next to Baudoin," I said.

"Oh, was that her name?" he asked. "Never knew. Get on with it, Domina Fool."

"Very good, Dominus," she said. "Does everybody know everybody? They do? Wonderful. Now, in order to properly exonerate Baudoin, we must reveal the murderer. I think that should be done in front of the prisoner, don't you, Dominus?"

"You had better make good on all of this, Domina Fool," said the count in a low tone.

"I shall," promised Claudia. "Have your men stand ready. The murderer is dangerous. Well, all murderers are dangerous by definition, but this one . . . anyhow, alert your men."

"Baudoin will be in chains," said the count. "There will be no danger."

"Baudoin will be in chains, therefore not dangerous," said Claudia. "Yet there may be danger from the murderer. Would you be so kind as to bring him up, Dominus?"

"I am already confused," the count murmured to me.

"Try living with that all the time," I murmured back.

The count nodded at the baile, who entered the Palace of Justice. Sancho stood by with a squad, swords out.

We all stared at the entrance. Finally, the baile and two guards emerged, Baudoin in chains between them. Huc followed behind them.

The moment he was outside, Baudoin stopped and took a deep breath of fresh air. Then he looked up at the sky, searching for the sun which was emerging from behind a cloud. He nodded with satisfaction, then looked over the crowd until he saw me. He caught my eye and smiled.

"Good day to you, Senhor Baudoin," said Claudia. "We have not met. I am Domina Gile, the fool."

He turned at the sound of his name, but looked slightly blank. Huc stepped to his shoulder and translated. Baudoin's expression became one of comprehension. He whispered something to Huc, who chuckled.

"He said, he is honored to meet the wife of Tan Pierre," said Huc. "And he extends his condolences for your tragic marriage."

Claudia laughed merrily.

"He jokes while in chains," commented Count Raimon. "One must admire his style."

"Give him my thanks," said Claudia still laughing. "Few are wise enough to see the tragedy of two fools in love."

Huc translated.

"Doesn't your wife speak langue d'oïl?" asked the count.

"Fluently," I said. "I expect she's playing to the locals."

"He says that he now understands the farce inside his own tragic circumstances," said Huc.

"Well said," applauded Claudia. "And well translated. You must be Senhor Huc."

"I am, Domina," said Huc.

"Your langue d'oc is excellent," said Claudia. "Where are you from?"

"Rouen, Domina."

"Never been there," said Claudia. She turned to face me. "My lord and master, please step forward for a moment."

I immediately stepped forward. There was laughter from the crowd, which puzzled me, as I had not done anything that I considered amusing. Then I noticed that the count had kept pace with me.

"I beg your pardon, Dominus," I said. "I thought she was speaking to me."

"She was looking at me," said the count. "And she did say lord and master."

"She was looking at me," I said. "I am, as her husband, her lord and master."

"But I am lord and master over all in Toulouse," said the count.

"Whom were you addressing?" I said to Claudia.

"You, my husband," she replied.

"You see?" I said.

"My error," he said. "An easy mistake to make. You were standing right next to me. I thought she was looking at me."

"That's the problem with you important people," Claudia said.

"Is it?" replied the count in a tone that carried menace beneath its surface.

"The problem with you important people is that you think that you are important all of the time," said Claudia. "Whereas the truth is, you're important only some of the time."

"But still important more than the unimportant people are," argued the count.

"Precisely," agreed Claudia. "However, there are times when the unimportant people, who are unimportant only because they aren't as important as often as the important people, can still be more important than the important people."

"I got lost somewhere in the middle of that," I confessed.

"My husband, because he is insane, decided that Baudoin was not the murderer of Julie," said my wife. "He decided to find out who was."

This produced a number of exclamations from those present.

"He brought me into it because someone with sense should be involved," continued Claudia. "But the flaw in his investigation was that he assumed that Baudoin was an important man."

She turned to the prisoner.

"Senhor Baudoin, are you an important man?"

Huc whispered. Baudoin smiled and whispered back.

"He used to think so," said Huc. "But he was recently dis-abused of the notion."

"It's all relative," said Claudia. "Speaking of which, being a relative is what makes you important, isn't it?"

"He says he had hoped that it would," said Huc.

"Dominus," said Claudia, turning back to the count. "I come before you to speak for the unimportant. The women. The servants. The whores. The dead. I beseech you, will you hear my petition on their behalf?"

"At this moment, Domina, you are the most important person in this courtyard," said the count.

"Very gallant, but hardly true," she said. "Will you admit two more unimportant people to this courtyard? I will vouch for them."

"Very well," said the count.

Claudia turned with a dancer's flourish and clapped her hands twice, the sounds echoing about the walls.

"Any idea where this is going?" muttered the count.

"None whatsoever," I said admiringly. "But I have a feeling that I lost this wager when I first set eyes upon her."

"Lucky man," said the count. "Domina Fool, who are those women?"

"Ah, you could not be expected to know them," said Claudia as Sancho's men led the Abbess and Sylvie through the gates. "I will ask the Count of Foix to make the intro-ductions."

The Count of Foix turned dark red with anger. "You go too far, woman!" he said.

"Manners, manners, senhor," she admonished him. "You should not be condescending merely because they are your employees. However, since it falls to the fool to maintain courtesy in this court, allow me to present the Abbess and her servant, Sylvie."

The two women bowed low.

I had the distinct impression that the Count of Toulouse and the Abbess were already acquainted, but neither let on.

"Greetings, ladies," said the count. "You may rise."

They straightened, the Abbess looking steadily at the men, many of whom shifted uncomfortably. Sylvie looked around in wonderment. She had probably never been here before.

"Now, Dominus," said Claudia. "Here is where things should—"

"Pelfort!" screamed Sylvie in shock. "Pelfort! How can you be alive?"

She was staring at Huc. He looked back at her in horror.

"No," he whispered.

"Pelfort, where is your master?" she screamed, tottering toward him. "Where is Guerau de Planes?"

"Silence, you old witch!" he screamed, drawing his sword.

He ran at the old woman, who stood frozen in fear. I was too far away. The two nearest guards were too slow.

But Claudia wasn't. She went in low, crashing into the side of his knee. He swung, and my heart stopped, but the sword passed harmlessly over her head as the two of them tumbled to the ground. He screamed in agony, and she rolled away and sprang to her feet, a bloodied dagger in her hand. He lay bleeding onto the flat stones of the courtyard, the back of his left thigh sliced open.

"I suggest, senhor," said Claudia to Huc, "that when pretending to be from the north, you do not speak langue d'oc like a native Toulousan. Sancho, he'll need a surgeon if you want him to talk."

"Come on, you sluggards," said Sancho to the two guards. "You just let a woman show you up in front of the count. Get this bastard patched up and brought to the Grande Chambre."

"Oh, and would you be a dear and wash this off for me?" added Claudia, tossing her dagger to one of them.

She walked up to me smugly, held up one finger, then turned to the count.

"I will explain everything inside," she said. "I would be grateful if someone could get Sylvie a cup of wine. She's had quite a shock. And unchain Baudoin. He's no murderer."

"But is he my brother?" asked the count.

"Maybe, maybe not," said Claudia. "That puzzle is not mine to solve. By your leave, Dominus, I will attend you in the Grande Chambre."

She went inside. He looked at me quizzically and held up one finger.

"The wager was for one month of getting up with the baby," I said.

"Steep," he said, wincing. "All right, everyone inside. Let the prisoner free, and bring him in with us."

Baudoin looked at the baile without comprehension as the latter unlocked his fetters.

"Will someone explain to me what just happened?" he cried.

"Come on in," I said to him in langue d'oïl. "It's going to be a long story. I will take over Huc's duties as your translator."

"Have I been freed?"

"Freed and exonerated," I said. "It appears that your man Huc killed La Rossa."

"Huc? But why?"

"The long story is this way," I said, taking his arm. "By the way, just out of curiosity, in what month were you born?"

"November. Why?"

It still didn't settle the issue of the issue. Could have been a last attempt at reconciliation between Constance and her husband. Could have been a premature birth of an adulterous liaison.

Could have been none of my business.

"Now that you are free, you must have us as the entertainment for your first birthday in Toulouse," I said smoothly. "But remember to pay us in advance. Shall we join the others?"

When we entered the Grande Chambre, the servants were scurrying about, setting up chairs in a semicircle around my wife. Helga waved to us from a seat near the back. We went to sit with her.

"These are the best seats you could get?" I asked.

"We're fools, not nobles," she said. "Except for Baudoin. Nobody knows what he is."

Baudoin laughed. She had been speaking in langue d'oïl so that he was made aware of the gibe.

"I will be honored to sit with fools, young lady," he said.

"I'm Helga," she said.

"I am Baudoin, and I am at your service," he said, bowing and kissing her hand.

"I like Parisians," she said, batting her eyelashes.

I sat between them. I am not sure which one I was protecting.

"Domina Fool, you have the floor," announced Count Raimon.

"Thank you, Dominus," she said. "In your courtyard a few minutes ago, I demonstrated to you how two men standing next to each other might each think a woman standing some distance away is looking solely at him. Earlier today, my husband, my daughter, three of your soldiers and I re-created the events of the night Baudoin went to the bordel. I stood where Julie stood, and two of your soldiers stood where Baudoin and Huc stood. I smiled at one, and both smiled back, each thinking he was the one upon whose face my favor fell. Both Sancho and my husband, who were present at the bordel that night, thought that La Rossa was looking at Baudoin with a smile that turned to one of mockery. But the smirk was not for Baudoin. It was for Huc. Or, as he was once known, Pelfort."

"But who is this Pelfort?" asked the count. "You say he spoke like a Toulousan."

"He was a servant here," said Claudia. "He served the family of de Planes. Julie, another servant of that household, was his wife."

"Ferrer de Planes," said the count. "I vaguely remember him. He lost his son, and went on Crusade, didn't he?"

"Oc, Dominus. His son and Pelfort went on a journey to Paris, but disappeared along the way and were never seen again. Julie ended up in the bordel.

"The night Baudoin came there, Pelfort was at his side. She looked at one of them, and was killed that night. My husband and I looked for every possible reason why Baudoin would kill her, and found none. Clearly, Baudoin was not the reason. But if she was killed because of some secret she knew, and it wasn't Baudoin, then it had to have been Huc. The servant. The unimportant man.

"So, I decided to go back into Julie's past. There I found a husband, a servant who disappeared with his master's son. I thought, if he came back, he may very well have something to hide. I thought, if she recognized him, he might have a reason to kill her. And I thought, if she recognized him, maybe Sylvie could as well."

She paused to take a goblet of wine handed to her by a servant.

"My thanks, all this talking is thirsty work," she said. "So, I arranged for them to be in the same place to see what would happen."

"What if he kept his composure?" asked the count.

"I didn't think that he would," said Claudia. "He had seen his wife reduced to whoredom because he had failed in whatever mission de Planes had sent him on. He had seen her take his new master to bed with a taunt on her face. He had killed her. And then he was so stricken that he still came to her funeral, under the pretext that he was investigating on behalf of his master. But Huc was supposedly in Toulouse for the first time. How could he expect to know anyone at a local funeral? No, Dominus, he was under tremendous strain. I did not think his protective shell could withstand another assault."

"It didn't withstand her dagger, either," I whispered to Helga.

A soldier entered and whispered something to the baile. The baile immediately came to the count and whispered in his ear.

"Bring him," ordered the count.

The baile signaled to the soldier, who left immediately.

"I am told that the surgeons have stanched the bleeding," said the count. "They have saved him for the hangman. Shall we hear what he has to say?"

"Oc, Dominus," said Claudia.

"For this, you should sit by me, Domina Fool," he said, and a chair was immediately placed by his.

She looked up at him with a mixture of expressions I could not read from where I sat.

"I am not used to sitting so high, Dominus," she said slowly. "I might become dizzy."

"You get used to it," said the count, patting the seat. "Come. You have earned it."

She walked toward him, uncertain at first, but with confidence increasing in every step. By the time she settled gracefully into the chair, it was as though she had been born to be there.

Which she had been, once upon a time.

They brought Huc—no, they brought Pelfort in on a litter, his wrists bound to the poles, his leg wrapped in bloody bandages. The soldiers propped him up so that he would face the count and the lady fool by him.

"You tried to kill an old woman in my courtyard today," said the count. "That alone would be enough for me to have you hanged. But there is the matter of the young lady you stabbed to death while she slept by your master."

"She was no lady," spat Pelfort. "And she was awake. She never thought I would do it. She never thought I would do anything."

"What happened to young de Planes?" asked the count.

"I killed him," said Pelfort. "I killed him, and I am sorry for it, but I was young and foolish. The plan was to make it look like we were attacked by bandits on the road—"

"The plan?" interrupted Claudia. "Whose plan?"

"Julie's plan," said Pelfort. "When she learned we were to travel to Paris to get help. She said it was the perfect opportunity. I would kill Guerau de Planes, and she would be the only descendant of Ferrer. She would get him to leave everything to her. Then we would be—"

He shook his head in disgust.

"I could not deny her anything," he said. "She was everything to me. A gift from God, rewarding my loyal service. I waited until we were a week's journey north, then I attacked him. But he sensed it, somehow, and we struggled. I was able to kill him, but not before he had dealt me a grievous wound. I managed to drag him off the road and tumble him into a ravine, but I could not make it back. I lay there for God knows how long before some pilgrims found me and brought me to a town.

"I lay in the hospice for what they told me was months,

drifting in and out of fever and nightmare. When the fits and fevers finally passed, I couldn't go back. I couldn't face what I had done to my master. I, who had been his loyal servant."

"Where did you go?" asked the count.

"Anywhere I could find work," he said. "But I could not stop thinking of how I had betrayed my old master. Finally, I resolved to make it up to him. I decided to complete my original task and go to Paris to appeal to Domina Constance."

"Constance?" cried the count. "What Constance?"

"The old count's wife," said Pelfort. "Your mother."

"But what had de Planes to do with her?"

"I know not," said Pelfort. "He had said that he had done her service once, and that he hoped that she could return the same."

"What service could he have done?" wondered Raimon.

I did not know if anyone present knew the answer to that besides Claudia, Helga, Sancho, and me, but it did not seem the proper moment to volunteer the answer.

"I knew not," said Pelfort. "But I went to Paris, only to find that she was dead. So I sought out her son, hoping to appeal to his sense of duty. I changed my name, thinking I would give him the information and move on. But he could not help. He was dependent on the good graces of the king, and he had little to spare. He expressed his sympathy, then asked if at the very least, he could take me on as a servant. I was penniless and desperate. I became his man."

"And you had the audacity to return to Toulouse," said the count.

"I had inquired of merchants from there as to my master's old house," said Pelfort. "I learned that it was in ruins, that the master had disappeared, and that the household was scattered. It had been eighteen years, and I thought no one would recognize me. But I was wrong."

"Why did you kill her?" asked Claudia.

"Because she said she would expose me," said Pelfort. "She put on a display of her whorish ways and took Baudoin to bed, and I knew she was twisting the knife with every sinful word she whispered in his ear. I sat in that parlor, hearing her cries of false passion from above. I could not sleep. I kept seeing Guerau's bloody face staring up at me.

"In the morning, when I went up to summon him, she was awake. She looked at me and said, 'You put me here. We could have been masters of a great house, but you failed, as you always do.' 'But I didn't fail,' I said. 'I killed him.' She ignored me. 'I will see that you pay for what you did to me,' she said. 'I will see that you hang for Guerau's death.' And she smiled at the thought, and I picked up Baudoin's dagger and stabbed her before I could even think."

He stopped, the sweat running off of his brow.

"Do you wish to be brought to Assizes?" asked the count.

"It would be a waste of time," said Pelfort. "I have not long, I think."

The Abbess rose, strode angrily to the center, and knelt before the count.

"Give him to us, Dominus," she said. "Let us have our revenge."

"No," said the count. "You will have justice, not revenge. Your hands will not be bloodied."

"She was killed in our house," said the Abbess.

"You are the mistress of that house," said the count. "But I am the master of this one. My house is Toulouse, and I shall see that the law is carried out. Hang him at noon tomorrow."

The soldiers picked up the litter and carried him away.

The Abbess stood, looked scornfully about the room, then turned and left. Sylvie hurried after her.

"Where is Baudoin?" asked the count.

"Here, Dominus," said Baudoin, approaching him.

"This man's story might be said to bear out yours," said the count.

"I will not have my identity vouchsafed by a murderer," said Baudoin. "I will await the proofs from Paris, by your leave."

"Nobly spoken, no matter what your history," said Raimon, smiling. "You don't mind moving into a room here at the château until then, do you?"

"I have had a room here at the château for several days," said Baudoin. "If you mean one in a different building, then by all means, Dominus."

"Done," said the count.

"Domina Fool, what may I do to repay you for my life?" asked Baudoin.

Claudia sat for a moment, then leaned over to the count and whispered in his ear. He thought for a second, then nodded.

She got up from her seat, approached Baudoin, and slapped him as hard as she could. He fell to the floor, then sat up, rubbing his cheek in astonishment.

"Live your life without humiliating another woman, and you will have repaid me," said Claudia. "But someone should have done that to you years ago."

She looked over at Helga and me.

"There's a baby waiting for us," she said.

"Right," I said. "Dominus, by your leave."

"You have it," said the count. "Thank you, Fools, as always, for the entertainment."

"It's what we do," said Claudia.

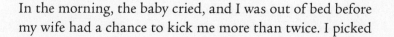

In the morning, the baby cried, and I was out of bed before my wife had a chance to kick me more than twice. I picked

Portia up, changed her linens, then took her down to the lower room and fed her. Then I wrote a letter.

We were playing happily together when Claudia and Helga came down, fully dressed.

"Where are you two off to so early?" I asked.

"We cannot tell you," said Claudia.

"Are you going to the hanging later?" I asked.

"Yes," said Claudia. "Are you?"

"I think that I will," I said. "I like seeing justice done. By the way, I don't know if I have told you this lately, but you are the most extraordinary woman I have ever known."

"Thank you," she said, kissing me.

"Before you go, I want you to see this," I said, handing her the letter I had written.

She glanced at it quickly, then more carefully. When she was done, she looked up at me, her eyes glistening.

"Careful," I said, dabbing at them with my napkin. "You'll ruin your makeup."

"Thank you," she said. "For everything."

"It is up to Father Gerald to decide whether or not he will permit us to travel," I said. "And it won't be until we see Folc actually installed as the Bishop, but I think we should be able to leave come October. You should be able to see your children for Christmas if all goes well."

"Always a fearsome holiday for us, isn't it?" she said, smiling through the tears.

"We'll have to find some way to keep them from locking you in a tower and me in a dungeon," I said.

"We'll figure out something," she said. "We're smarter than everyone else, remember?"

"And there's me," added Helga. "I'll break you out. I'm the best lock-picker in the house."

"I would say the best in the family," I said.

"The family?" she repeated, her eyes wide.

"Claudia and I spoke about your situation last night," I said. "We're going to adopt you."

"Theo!" she squealed, jumping on me and hugging me hard.

"How soon can we marry her off?" I asked Claudia.

"A few more years," she said, as Helga transferred the hug to her.

"Going to need another dowry now," I sighed. "Get out, the two of you. All of this emotion is making me nervous."

"See you at the hanging!" Helga called as they left.

The gallows was set up outside the Palace of Justice. Vendors ringed the courtyard, selling roasted chestnuts, apples, and sweetmeats. I looked around for my wife and newest daughter, but I didn't see them in the crowd. I did see Llora de Bretanha, resplendent in a sea-green gown, her figure still capable of attracting a few glances from men who did double-takes when they saw her white hair.

Being a tall man, I felt no need to maneuver my way to the front. I bought some apples and sliced a few pieces off for my daughter. I made sure that the sling prevented her from seeing what was going on.

There was a roar from the crowd, then Pelfort was carried out, still unable to walk thanks to my wife's skill with a dagger. They hauled him up the steps, and the noose was settled around his neck, then tightened.

The baile stepped forward to read the sentence, but there was a commotion by the gates before he could start.

"Let us through!" cried a woman's voice. "We are here to see justice in Toulouse!"

Red.

The color red overwhelmed us.

One by one, they came in. Woman after woman, each with her hair dyed red, wearing a red gown, her lips a wet scarlet, her nails gleaming like fresh blood. They were all the same, and they were all different. I could see for a moment their faces: The Abbess, magisterial in her scorn; Marquesia, her lips petulant; La Navarra, sporting a gold band now, but standing with her sisters, and the others from the house in which La Rossa had lived and died. But there were more women. Others, from the houses that officially didn't exist in the Comminges quarter, from the one no one knew about near the Abbey of Saint Sernin, from the houses across the bridge in Saint Cyprien. All the prostitutes of Toulouse, banded together, marching in a red phalanx through the retreating crowds of churchgoing hypocrites.

And in the middle of this red brigade marched my wife, her hair subtly altered from its normal auburn to the same lurid shade as the others.

They filled the space before the gallows, and Pelfort looked at them in dumb terror.

"We are here to see Toulousan justice done!" shouted the Abbess. "But if God is in His heaven, then your Hell will look like this for eternity. You, Senhor Baile. Pronounce the sentence."

The baile, hesitantly, pronounced Pelfort's doom. The hangman stepped forward.

"Wait one moment," commanded the Abbess.

A small version of the red women stepped to the front. Helga.

She sang in a pure voice that filled the entire château.

Igne divini radians amoris
corporis sexum superavit Agnes,

et super carnem potuere carnis
claustra pudicæ.

The Hymn of Saint Agnes, I thought.

Spiritum celsæ capiunt cohortes
candidum, cæli super astra tollunt;
iungitur Sponsi thalamis pudica
sponsa beatis.

And then, every woman in the courtyard joined her.

Virgo, nunc nostræ miserere sortis
et, tuum quisquis celebrat tropæum,
impetret sibi veniam reatus
atque salutem.

O Virgin, I thought. Now have pity on our lot, and who-ever celebrates your victory day, let him earnestly pray for forgiveness of guilt.

And salvation for himself.

"Now!" shouted the Abbess.

The hangman shoved Pelfort off the platform, and he plummeted toward the sea of red until the rope caught him and snapped his neck.

CHAPTER 18

On a hot, sunny Wednesday toward the end of June, I was juggling in Montardy Square when I heard someone walk by, whistling a familiar melody. I picked up where it left off, and someone tossed something into the tambourine I had set out for contributions.

"Yellow Dwarf," I muttered. "Dinner's on us."

I concluded my routine, made one last appeal for coins, then collected what I had earned for the morning. Nestling with the money was a small piece of parchment, folded the proper way with a seal depicting an ass's head in red wax.

I ambled to a street where I knew I was safe from observation, slid my dagger under the seal, and read the letter. Then I took off at a run toward the Château Narbonnais.

I sought out Sancho when I got there.

"Did you hear?" he asked as soon as he saw me. "The viguier's man is back from Paris. You should come along."

"Take a look at this," I said, showing him the letter.

He read it twice, then looked up at me in concern.

"It may be nothing," I said.

"Or a very large something," he replied. "Should be interesting, given what we know."

"Let's find out," I said.

We hurried to the Grande Chambre, where the count and his coterie had already gathered.

"Ah, Tan Pierre, good," said Count Raimon. "You have saved me the trouble of sending for you."

"Are you in need of entertainment, Dominus?" I asked, reaching for my lute.

"Today, I hope to entertain you," he said. "Was Baudoin sent for?"

"Oc, Dominus," said a servant. "He was with his language tutor. He will be here shortly."

Baudoin came in. "Greetings, my noble lord," he said in langue d'oc. "I trust that you are well."

"I am, senhor, and thank you," replied Raimon. "Our messenger has returned from Paris."

"Ah," said Baudoin, taking a deep breath. "Good."

"Arval Marti, step forward," said the count.

Marti came before him and knelt.

"We give thanks to God Almighty for your safe journey," said Raimon. "Were you successful in your mission?"

"I was, Dominus," said Marti.

"And what did you learn about this man Baudoin's claims?" asked Raimon.

"That they are fraudulent, Dominus," said Marti.

"No!" shouted Baudoin. "He lies."

"Bind him," ordered the count.

Two soldiers stepped forward immediately to comply.

"Here we go again," muttered Sancho.

He walked over to Baudoin and stopped the soldiers.

"Begging your pardon, Dominus," he said. "I don't think you should do that yet."

"I'm sorry, I'm not sure I heard you correctly," said the count. "Did you just countermand my direct order?"

"One moment, Dominus," said Sancho. "Senhor Fool?"

"Oc, Sancho?" I answered.

"What does 'countermand' mean again?"

"One of those military terms you soldier types love to throw around," I said. "It means that you gave an order reversing another one, I think."

"Oh. I always wondered," said Sancho. He turned back to the count. "No, Dominus, I did not countermand your direct order. I'm simply offering an opinion on the matter."

"Did I ask for your opinion?" asked the count.

"That you did not, Dominus," conceded Sancho. "But I am of the opinion that you need my opinion, so I offered it to you without your asking. Taking the initiative, as it were."

"Bind Sancho, too," commanded the count.

"No, no, no, can't let that happen," I said, going to Sancho's side. "Not until Senhor Marti answers a very important question for me."

"What farce are you playing now, Fool?" asked the count.

"One you asked me to play, Dominus," I replied. "Or have you forgotten?"

The count stepped down from his throne and looked at Sancho, who stood there calmly despite the shackles being attached to his wrists. He then looked at me. I returned his gaze evenly.

"Very well, Fool," he said. "Before I have you thrown in the dungeon with these two, ask Senhor Marti your very important question."

"Thank you, Dominus," I said. "Senhor Marti, here it is. Did you deliver my letter as well?"

"Oc, Fool," he said. "And was treated most disrespectfully by the recipient."

"Sounds like Horace," I chuckled. "Did he send you a reply?"

"He did, Fool," he said, pulling a folded piece of parchment from his pouch.

I stepped forward, took it, and opened it.

"What does it say?" asked Raimon.

"It confirms Marti's information," I said, reading it.

"Very well," said Raimon, turning to Baudoin. "I am sorry for it, Senhor Baudoin, or whatever your name is. I was enjoying your company."

"There's one problem, Dominus," I said.

"Oh?"

"This letter is a forgery," I said.

The count stared at me.

"How do you know?" he asked.

"My colleague Horace and I have a special way of corresponding," I said. "My letter was folded a particular way, then closed without the use of a seal. That was a signal to let him know that it was being delivered by a messenger I did not necessarily trust."

"Dominus, I protest!" cried Marti.

"This reply came back the same way," I said. "But I received this letter this same day from a different messenger, one who is known to me personally."

I held up the one that came by the Guild route.

"Note how it's folded, note the seal," I said, bringing it up to him.

"And the contents, Fool?" asked Raimon.

"Read them for yourself," I said.

The count read it, then looked at Baudoin.

"This Parisian jester, Horace, vouches for you," said the count. "And he describes you to the life."

He handed the letter back to me.

"So, Senhor Marti," he said. "The question is, do I place my faith in you, or in this fool and his colleague?"

"Your faith would have to extend further than Marti, Dominus," said Sancho.

"How so?"

"Marti was handpicked for this mission by your viguier, Peire Roger," said Sancho.

"So he was," said the count thoughtfully.

"There are some things you should know about the viguier, Dominus, before you make your decision," said Sancho.

"What are they?"

"Following your directions, Dominus, I allowed myself to become indebted to a local gambler earlier this year," said Sancho. "I did so to find out to whom he might sell my debt, so that I could learn who is behind some of the corruption going on in this city. The debt was purchased by the Count of Foix."

"Go on," commanded Raimon.

"I started doing Foix's dirty work, and discovered, as you know, that he also owned the bordel where La Rossa was killed, having purchased it from Ferrer de Planes. I had thought there might be some connection between the two from their time in the Holy Land, but de Planes denied it."

"Dominus," said the Count of Foix. "This is outrageous."

"Quiet," said Raimon. "Continue, Sancho."

"The Count of Foix purchased the bordel shortly after his release from captivity in Aragon," said Sancho. "I knew that the Countess of Foix and the Count of Comminges had been instrumental in securing that release, but I recently learned that the viguier had been the man most responsible for rescuing him, working behind the scenes."

A morsel of information from my wife's conversation with Foix's wife, I thought.

"Following that avenue, I looked to see if there had been any connection between Ferrer de Planes and the viguier," said Sancho.

"Had there been?" asked Raimon.

"There had, Dominus," said Sancho.

"Ferrer saved my life," said the viguier, stepping forward. "Under circumstances that imperiled his own. When he was reduced to living in the leper house with that bordel supporting him, I helped as much as I could, but I lacked the funds to sustain it. That is why I prevailed upon the Count of Foix to take over the operation to repay me for aiding him. We kept this quiet so as to avoid any shame to the de Planes name."

"So, Baudoin was directed to that bordel at your behest?" asked the count.

"Oc, Dominus," said the viguier. "We were using La Rossa to glean what information she could from him. But she was killed before she could pass on what she found out."

"Well, that's all very well," said the count. "The problem remains, my old friend, as to who Baudoin is? Must I send a different messenger? A team of them, with the majority vote to render the decision? Whom do I believe, a jester who has been here six months, or an advisor who has been with me for my entire tenure as count, and with my father before me?"

"You should believe the man who has your best interests at heart," said Peire Roger.

"Fool, your response," said Raimon, turning to me.

"Your best interests are for you to decide, Dominus, not me," I said. "I am here only to bring you the truth, as all good jesters do."

"Peire Roger, I ask you directly," said the count. "Did you send this man Marti on a mission to discredit Baudoin, no matter what the truth was?"

The viguier hesitated, then started to speak.

The count held up his hand. "That is all I need to know," said Raimon. "You are relieved of your duties."

"Dominus, forgive me," said Peire Roger, bowing his head. "But one last word. Brother though he may be, he is not a friend to Toulouse. He is a Parisian, a member of the court of France. A true brother would have returned to you long before now."

"A true friend would have told me the truth," said Raimon. "For your years of service, I pardon you for this transgression. Sancho, escort him to his office, and see that nothing of value leaves."

"Oc, Dominus," said Sancho, bowing as the soldiers removed the shackles. "This way, senhor."

Peire Roger followed him.

"Excuse me for one moment, Dominus," I said.

I chased them into the hallway.

"A word with you, senhor," I said, stopping Sancho and Peire Roger.

"What, Fool?" said Peire Roger.

"The day I spoke with you in your office. Did you follow me afterwards?"

"I did," he said.

"Why?"

"You were asking about my time on Crusade with Foix, and about Baudoin. I had been unaware that you were pursuing any investigation until then. I wanted to see what you were doing, so I followed you."

"You could teach Sancho's men a trick or two," I said. "You were very good."

"So were you, Fool," he said. "You have won, today. But I am not convinced that you did Toulouse any favors in doing so."

"I have saved an innocent man from hanging," I said. "Twice, now."

He looked out the window at the courtyard where the gallows sat silently in anticipation.

"I suspect that you merely delayed the inevitable," he said. "Good day, Fool."

I returned to the Grande Chambre. Baudoin was seated next to his brother, the two of them conversing easily.

"Well, I must go see my wife," Raimon was saying. "We will have to find someone suitable for you, now that you have been established."

"I've never had a wife before," said Baudoin.

"I've had too many," sighed Raimon. "But you'll get used to it. Tell me one last thing. Was our mother happy during her time in Paris?"

"She seemed to be," said Baudoin.

"I am glad for it," said Raimon. "Good day, Baudoin."

The Count of Toulouse stood and embraced his brother. As the latter left, he looked at me and nodded. I waved.

The count and I were alone in the Grande Chambre, as we had been so many times now.

"Fool, I cannot express my thanks enough," said the count.

"Sancho did most of the legwork on this matter," I said.

"He will be amply rewarded," said the count. "The position of viguier is available. Do you want it?"

"Hell no."

"I knew that would be your answer," he said. "But I thought I should do you the courtesy of offering."

"Most generous of you, Dominus," I said. "But I think you would trust me less if I actually was in a position of power."

"Keep telling me the truth, no matter what happens," he said.

"I will, Dominus. How do you feel right now?"

"Happy," he said. "Actually happy. I had forgotten what that is like. I have gained a brother today. And things are going well with my wife."

"You have discovered the secret, Dominus."

"What secret, Fool?"

"The key to living life is not to stave off death," I said. "It is simply to live your life."

"Is that all?" he asked.

"Well, keep on dyeing your hair," I said.

He laughed, a deep, satisfying belly laugh. Then he turned somber. "I could have had him executed," he said, looking at the door Baudoin had just exited. "My own brother. Tell me, Fool. How did you know?"

I thought back over everything I had learned and done in the last two months. It is true that Sancho had toppled me off the precipice into this investigation, but I had already begun leaning over the edge, staring straight down into the abyss, steeling myself to leap.

"It was when I talked to him," I said. "Sometimes you just believe a man."

"As simple as that?"

"As simple as that."

He closed his eyes. "I knew he was my brother," he said. "From the moment I saw him. He has my mother's face. You never forget your mother's face."

And the Count of Toulouse sat on his throne and wept.

HISTORICAL NOTE

I inform Your Nobility, as the one in whom alone
after God I place all my hope, that on the day on
which our servant Simon departed from me I left my
house and took refuge in the house of a knight of the
town [Toulouse]. I am left without the wherewithal
to find food or to give anything to my servants. The
Count has no care for me, nor does he help me or give
me anything from his lands for my needs. For this
reason I ask you, imploring Your Highness, that if
the messengers who are on the way to your court tell
you that I am well do not believe them. Had I dared
to write to you then, I would have told you at greater
length of my distress. Farewell.

> —*Letter from Constance, Countess of Toulouse, to her brother, the King
> of France, 1165.* Recueil des historiens des Gaules et de la France,
> 16:126 *(English translation by Fredric L. Cheyette from* Ermengard
> of Narbonne and the World of the Troubadours, *Cornell Univer-
> sity Press, 2001).*

There are dates attributed to events and people in histories
that may or may not be accurate. This letter, duly copied
into the sixteenth volume of a collection of letters to three
French kings, is dated 1165, so we may assume that that is
the year Constance left Toulouse and returned to Paris. But

the date given for the birth of her third son and last child, Baudoin, is also 1165. Where was he born? What month? The texts are silent.

The historian Laurent Macé states that Baudoin came to Toulouse for the first time in 1205. Given Raimon V's penchant for trading his children's marriageability like baseball cards, it seems unlikely that Baudoin had spent any time there previously, or he would have had the same marital adventures as had his siblings before him. The question remains, where was Baudoin for the first forty years of his life? This translation of the chronicles of the Fools' Guild suggests that he was in Paris, but I have found no references either to him or his mother after their arrival. Given the disappointment and the shame of the failure of the marriage, it is not surprising that Constance was banished from the pages of contemporaneous accounts. She was adamant in her refusal to return, standing firm even in the face of the pressure brought by Pope Alexander III in 1174.

One account of the Albigensian Crusades states that Baudoin returned to Toulouse in 1194 after the death of his father, but that Raimon VI refused to recognize him, forcing him to return to Paris. Again, the accuracy of this account cannot be verified. One Internet genealogy posits the marriage of Baudoin to a noblewoman of the house of Lautrec, a town not far from Toulouse. This Toulouse-Lautrec lineage supposedly continued unabated until the nineteenth-century production of Henri Toulouse-Lautrec, the famous painter. However, a close examination of the Web site reveals the candid acknowledgment that there are no records supporting this claim prior to the fourteenth century.

Baudoin's inability to communicate would have been likely. The linguistic differences between langue d'oc, spoken in the south of what is now France and langue d'oïl, spoken in the north, were significant. Langue d'oc was much more closely related to the Catalan of that time, to the point that native speakers of the two languages would have had a much easier time understanding each other than a Toulousan would a Parisian.

Peire Roger, the viguier at the time of this account, did step down from the post in 1205, according to known accounts. The reasons for his resignation had been unknown until this translation. One thing may be said for him: His predictions of the falling out of the two brothers and Baudoin's eventual fate proved to be accurate. The histories of the Albigensian Crusades agree that Baudoin abandoned his brother to join the crusading forces led by Simon de Montfort in 1211. After years of battle, Baudoin was betrayed and taken captive while sleeping. Raimon, when presented with the brother who had betrayed him, ordered that he be executed. The order was carried out by, among others, the Count of Foix. Baudoin, cousin to the King of France, brother to the Count of Toulouse, was hanged in 1214.

ACKNOWLEDGMENTS

The English translation of the *Hymn of Saint Agnes* is by Friar J. T. Zuhlsdorf, and is used with his permission, for which I give him my profound thanks.

Having my jesters stay in the same place for two consecutive books allows me to thank once again all those scholars acknowledged in the previous book. In addition, I owe a great debt to Fredric L. Cheyette's *Ermengard of Narbonne and the World of the Troubadours* and Leah L. Otis's *Prostitution in Medieval Society*. The ever-growing list should also include Malcolm Lambert, Arnaud Esquessier, Gabriel de Llobet, and Claudie Pailles. I take full responsibility for any errors made.